P9-DMK-033

PRAISE FOR

ROBERT B. PARKER'S THE BRIDGE

"Knott brings some serious literary chops to *The Bridge*, creating an atmospheric tale with an intriguing mystery at its heart. Fans of Parker, westerns, and mysteries should be reading these books religiously, as they comprise one of the better series in any genre currently being published." —Bookreporter.com

"An extraordinarily entertaining novel." —*Booklist*

"*The Bridge* gives us everything we love about the Hitch & Cole series . . . The two gunmen are in good hands." —MysteryPeople.com

"A must read." —*The Historical Novels Review*

AND FOR THE COLE AND HITCH NOVELS

"Hits with the intensity of an eight-gauge shotgun blast . . . Virgil and Everett's fates are in excellent hands." —*Tulsa World*

"Robert Knott . . . has penned the next great saga . . . Parker fans are going to love it!" —Ed Harris, Academy Award–nominated actor

"As fresh as anything out there." —*The Boston Globe*

NOVELS BY ROBERT B. PARKER

THE SPENSER NOVELS

Robert B. Parker's Cheap Shot
(by Ace Atkins)

Silent Night
(with Helen Brann)

Robert B. Parker's Wonderland
(by Ace Atkins)

Robert B. Parker's Lullaby
(by Ace Atkins)

Sixkill	*Double Deuce*
Painted Ladies	*Pastime*
The Professional	*Stardust*
Rough Weather	*Playmates*
Now & Then	*Crimson Joy*
Hundred-Dollar Baby	*Pale Kings and Princes*
School Days	*Taming a Sea-Horse*
Cold Service	*A Catskill Eagle*
Bad Business	*Valediction*
Back Story	*The Widening Gyre*
Widow's Walk	*Ceremony*
Potshot	*A Savage Place*
Hugger Mugger	*Early Autumn*
Hush Money	*Looking for Rachel Wallace*
Sudden Mischief	*The Judas Goat*
Small Vices	*Promised Land*
Chance	*Mortal Stakes*
Thin Air	*God Save the Child*
Walking Shadow	*The Godwulf Manuscript*
Paper Doll	

COLE/HITCH WESTERNS

Robert B. Parker's The Bridge
(by Robert Knott)

Robert B. Parker's Bull River
(by Robert Knott)

Robert B. Parker's Ironhorse
(by Robert Knott)

Blue-Eyed Devil	*Resolution*
Brimstone	*Appaloosa*

THE JESSE STONE NOVELS

Robert B. Parker's Blind Spot
(by Reed Farrel Coleman)
Robert B. Parker's Damned If You Do
(by Michael Brandman)
Robert B. Parker's Fool Me Twice
(by Michael Brandman)
Robert B. Parker's Killing the Blues
(by Michael Brandman)

Split Image   *Stone Cold*
Night and Day   *Death in Paradise*
Stranger in Paradise   *Trouble in Paradise*
High Profile   *Night Passage*
Sea Change

THE SUNNY RANDALL NOVELS

Spare Change   *Shrink Rap*
Blue Screen   *Perish Twice*
Melancholy Baby   *Family Honor*

ALSO BY ROBERT B. PARKER

A Triple Shot of Spenser   *Love and Glory*
Double Play   *Wilderness*
Gunman's Rhapsody   *Three Weeks in Spring*
All Our Yesterdays   (with Joan H. Parker)
A Year at the Races   *Training with Weights*
(with Joan H. Parker)   (with John R. Marsh)
Perchance to Dream
Poodle Springs
(with Raymond Chandler)

ROBERT B. PARKER'S

THE
BRIDGE

Robert Knott

B

BERKLEY BOOKS
New York

BERKLEY

An imprint of Penguin Random House LLC
375 Hudson Street, New York, New York 10014

ROBERT B. PARKER'S THE BRIDGE

A Berkley Book / published by arrangement with The Estate of Robert B. Parker

Copyright © 2014 by The Estate of Robert B. Parker.
Penguin supports copyright. Copyright fuels creativity, encourages diverse voices,
promotes free speech, and creates a vibrant culture. Thank you for buying an authorized
edition of this book and for complying with copyright laws by not reproducing, scanning, or
distributing any part of it in any form without permission. You are supporting writers and
allowing Penguin to continue to publish books for every reader.

BERKLEY® and the "B" design are registered trademarks of Penguin Random House LLC.
For more information, visit penguin.com.

ISBN: 978-0-425-27808-6

PUBLISHING HISTORY
G. P. Putnam's Sons hardcover edition / December 2014
Berkley premium edition / December 2015

PRINTED IN THE UNITED STATES OF AMERICA

10 9 8 7 6 5 4 3 2 1

Cover photograph: *Steel Bridge* © Getty Images / Jim Steinfeldt.
Cover design by Andrea Ho.

This is a work of fiction. Names, characters, places, and incidents either are the product
of the author's imagination or are used fictitiously, and any resemblance to actual persons,
living or dead, business establishments, events, or locales is entirely coincidental.

If you purchased this book without a cover, you should be aware that this book is
stolen property. It was reported as "unsold and destroyed" to the publisher, and neither
the author nor the publisher has received any payment for this "stripped book."

Penguin
Random
House

For Julie

ROBERT B. PARKER'S

— THE —

BRIDGE

Prologue

The dense muss of stars was unusually ominous and threatening, as if the whole tangle of constellations was up to no damn good. The wide night sky pushed down hard on the four weary horsemen, appraising them, like a powerful and intolerant observer.

With their tilted brims and slouching shoulders, the mounted men rode single file and without words, as their horses carried them toward their destination. They were all fairly young. One was a hefty fellow with a large gut; the second was gangly with a narrow face and shoulders; the third was also skinny but was dark-skinned, maybe a half-breed; and the fourth was small and wiry.

Hard to know what the hell these night riders were thinking. What was going on in their heads? They would have had to feel the overhead pressure, the challenging and unforgiving weight. The stars loomed close enough to reach out and touch; a twisted twinkling expanse. The four horsemen rode slowly, deliberately, up the eastern rim of the Rio Blanco River.

The only sound was the occasional clink of a bit, the footfalls of their horses, and the soft rumble of the white-water river in the canyon far below.

The dropping moon provided enough light for them to see their dogged and hell-bent way, and just ahead, where he was supposed to be, they saw the big man waiting for them.

They had met him only once before. They knew from the brief encounter he was not someone to cross. Not ever. He was different, above average in every respect. He could smile and show his nice white teeth, but he was menacing and ill-tempered to his very core. There was something even more dangerous about him: it was as if he were from another place in time. One of the riders told the others that the big sonofabitch reminded him of what the warrior Achilles might have been like. He was handsome and raw-boned. He had a warrior swagger to him as if he'd single-handedly just wiped out an army and was looking forward to his next victim. His movements were swift and specific. He had thick, broad shoulders and his hands and forearms were sinewy with muscle. His neck was wide and corded. He had a full head of shiny, coarse hair and his eyes were deep-set and dark blue.

The night riders were also fearful of the two brothers who would accompany them later, but they were in this, all of them. They would not turn back and they could not turn back, not now, not tonight. They were all committed to what they rode out on this night to do.

The big Achilles man got to his feet in the buckboard. He stood looking at them as they neared and then jumped down from the wagon as they came to a stop.

"You're late," he said.

He threw back a canvas uncovering the wagon's freight.

"What about the telegraph lines," he asked, before they could defend their belated arrival.

"They're cut," the dark-skinned man said, as he dismounted.

"You see anybody?"

"We did not," the hefty man said.

"Anybody see you?"

"No, nobody."

"You sure?"

"We are," the hefty man replied.

"All right," he said. "Let's get a move on it."

"How far from here?" the small, wiry man said.

"Quarter-mile," he said. "From here we go in on foot. Each one hauls a load."

"Where we gonna meet 'em?" the hefty man said.

"Just carry your load and follow me," he said. "Got one hour before sunup."

The riders didn't waste any time. They tied their horses under a stand of small sycamores and went about the task at hand.

One by one, each of the men removed the supplies from the buckboard and followed the big warrior man, the Achilles man.

They walked along a narrow deer path through thickets,

high above the river. As they neared their destination, they could hear someone up ahead of them.

"Far enough," a man's voice said.

The voice was raspy, with a distinct southern drawl.

They knew it was one of the brothers, and then they saw them both. The two men stepped out from a cluster of briars near a tree-covered wash that folded off down toward the river some two hundred feet below.

The brothers were stout men, with full, bristly beards and tangled, unruly hair. Two of the riders had known the brothers in earlier days and were not any more comfortable with them than they were with the warrior man.

Both brothers were intelligent men, but they were mercurial and quick-tempered. They presented themselves as polite and forthright, but a strange, disconnected quality lurked within. They both were quiet and though their eyes were kind, there was a constant callous and mistrusting element about their demeanor.

"Don't ever turn your back on them," the dark-skinned man said to the others.

This night, however, what these men were focused on was the brothers' shrewd scheme. They recruited the warrior man and the four riders, and if everything went as planned, they all would make a lot of money. More money than any of them would have made in a lifetime.

Before tonight, they had done a mock run of the plan. Each man knew his job. When the taller brother said, "Let's go," they moved out.

It did not take long for them to plant the dynamite.

One of the men, the heavyset man, knew everything

about how and where it should be placed. He had been the one who showed the others what to do. His extensive knowledge of explosives was the very reason for his recruitment in the first place.

Daybreak was upon them and the first rays of sun began to appear as the heavyset man instructed the younger brother how to terminate the last connection.

"I remember," the younger brother said.

The heavyset man nodded. He started off walking toward the trail that led back to the buckboard. The others were ahead of him and he followed them as he unspooled the wire.

After the younger brother made the final connection and was headed back toward the deer path he came face-to-face with Percy O'Malley.

"Hey," Percy said. "Good morning."

The brother was startled to see the old man.

"Morning, Percy," the brother said.

"What are you doing out here so early?" Percy said.

The brother looked around the old man to see if there was anyone behind him.

"I'll show you," the brother said, as he walked to the edge.

The old man followed him.

The brother pointed to the river, two hundred feet below.

"Look," the brother said.

When Percy leaned over to look, the brother pulled his long knife from its sheath, cupped his hand around the old man's mouth, and slit his throat. He shoved the man off the side and watched as his body tumbled into the river.

If he had stopped to look, he would have seen the body swept up by the current, leaving a murky red trail dispatched behind it.

By the time he made it back to where the other men were, the heavyset man had the wires connected on the terminals of the detonator.

They had a good vantage point from their location.

"Who wants to do the honors?" the heavyset man said.

"Me," the warrior man said without hesitation.

He got down on his knees and the others closed in behind him.

"On three," the warrior man said.

"One . . . two . . ."

He lowered the plunger handle on the detonator and the men watched the three-hundred-foot iron bridge that crossed over the Rio Blanco River explode in a monstrous blast, earth-quaking and sulfurous as if it came from deep down in hell, delivered by the Evil Red Devil himself.

— 1 —

Weather."

"Is," Virgil said.

"Don't look good," I said.

"No," Virgil said. "It don't."

Virgil and I were watching a faraway line of darkness coming toward us from the north.

"Got this place shingled just in time," I said.

Virgil glanced up, looking at the underside of the porch overhang we were sitting under.

"Know soon enough if we got any leaks," I said.

"'Spect we will."

"This'll be the first sign of weather since we've been back here in Appaloosa," I said.

"It is," Virgil said, looking back to the clouds. "Ain't it?"

"Been warm and dry," I said. "Hot, even."

"Has," Virgil said.

Virgil put the heels of his boots on the porch rail and

tipped his chair back a little. We sat quiet for a long moment as we watched the dark weather moving slowly in our direction.

"What is it," Virgil said, tilting his head a little. "Where are we, Everett?"

"November, Virgil. Second day of."

Virgil shook his head a little.

"What the hell happened to October?"

"You had those two German carpenters you hired working my backside off on this place, that's what happened," I said. "Good goings for you things have been quiet in the outlaw racket."

"Temperate times," he said.

Virgil rocked his chair a little as he looked at the clouds.

"Hope it's not the calm before the storm," I said.

"Never know," Virgil said.

"No reason to think about outlawing that's not yet happened," I said. "Or be downright superstitious."

"No," Virgil said. "No reason."

We sat quiet a moment, watching the faraway storm.

"Bad weather does make folks desperate," I said. "People get out of sorts."

"Been our experience," Virgil said, "people get cold, desperate, and hungry."

I leaned back in my chair and looked through the open doorway into the house.

"Speaking of it," I said. "What do you think she's cooking up in there?"

"Don't know," Virgil said. "Allie said she was making something special."

"That don't sound good."

Virgil smiled a little.

"She's trying," he said.

"Maybe you ought to get her a cookbook," I said. "With recipes. Where she learns how to measure stuff out and how long to cook it and what goes with what and so on."

"I offered," Virgil said. "She told me all good chefs cook by the seat of their pants."

We both thought about that for a moment.

"You got some of that Kentucky?"

"I do," Virgil said.

"Might as well have ourselves a nudge or two," I said.

"No reason not to," Virgil said.

Virgil removed his boots from the porch railing and lowered the front legs of the chair he'd been tilting back in. He got to his feet just as three men on horseback wearing oilcloth slickers rounded Second Street, riding directly toward us at a steady pace. It was Sheriff Sledge Driskill with two of his deputies, Chip Childers and Karl Worley.

"Got some intention," I said.

"They do," Virgil said.

— 2 —

ight be the end of those temperate times we were talking about."

"Might," Virgil said.

Sledge and his deputies slowed as they neared and came to a stop just in front of the porch.

"Virgil," Sledge said. "Everett."

"Afternoon," I said.

Virgil eased up to the porch steps.

"Sledge," Virgil said with a nod. "Boys."

Sledge was a big man with thick black eyebrows and a full dark beard streaked with silver. Karl was a skinny Canadian fella, an ex-cowhand who was never without sheep chaps. Chip was a chubby overgrown kid with a large wad of tobacco crammed in his cheek.

"What brings you here?" Virgil said.

"Wanted to let y'all know," Sledge said, "got some business away. And the town will be scarce of us for a bit. Only deputies left on duty will be Skinny Jack and Book. Chastain is sick in bed with a stomach bug."

"Where you headed," Virgil said.

"We're headed up to the bridge camp."

"Now?" I said.

"Yep," Sledge said, tipping his head to the dark clouds on the northern horizon. "Storm's a comin'."

"That it is," I said.

"Need to beat it best we can," Sledge said.

"Why the bridge camp?" Virgil said.

"Know Lonnie Carman?"

Virgil shook his head, then looked at me.

"Know who he is," I said. "Little fella with the tattoos, did some time, works at the Boston House?"

"That's him," Sledge said. "He don't work there anymore. He's been working on the bridge crew."

"What about him?" Virgil said.

"Well," Sledge said. "His new wife, Winifred, believes something has happened to him."

"What?" Virgil said.

"He didn't return from his bridge shift when he was supposed to," Sledge said.

Bridge camp was a construction site a day's ride south of Appaloosa. The bridge had been a major undertaking for the territory. It spanned a wide chasm across the Rio Blanco, where rotating crews of workers had been constructing the massive timber-and-steel truss crossing for the better part of two years.

"Why does she think something has happened to him?" I said.

Sledge shrugged a bit.

"Says it's unlike him. Says he's punctual. She came to see me yesterday. Said Lonnie was supposed to be back home by now. Said she sent two wires to the way station near the bridge where they correspond bridge business, materials and what have you, but got no response back. I told her, give it a little time, maybe he was just busy bridge building."

"She's been back three times since," Karl said.

Sledge nodded.

"Each time she's been more riled. She put her nose in my face," Sledge said, shaking his head a little, "said if I didn't go and find her husband she was gonna come roust the two marshals in town to do the lookin' and, well, I don't want that. Having her coming over here pestering y'all."

"She hollered in his face last time," Chip said, then spit a stream of tobacco juice in the dirt. "Eyes damn near popped out of her skull."

"Hollered, hell," Karl said. "She screamed like a cut calf."

"I didn't have the heart to tell her maybe he run off," Sledge said.

"I know I damn sure would," Chip said. "Can't imagine marrying a lady like that."

"Hell, no," Karl said with a nod in agreement. "Me for sure, neither."

"No matter," Sledge said. "Wanted to spare you two of the misery of her coming over here. We're gonna ride up, see if we can find the poor sonofabitch."

Virgil nodded some.

"We'll be here," he said.

Sledge gave a sharp nod, then backed up his big bay a bit.

The lawmen turned their horses and rode off south. We watched them as they galloped off and disappeared behind the mercantile at the end of the street.

"Winifred?" Virgil said. "That the fearsome lady churns butter at the grocer?"

"It is," I said.

Virgil nodded a bit, then walked into the house to get the Kentucky whiskey.

— 3 —

Virgil and I had been working our job as territorial marshals for close to a year before we returned to Appaloosa. We spent the last part of the summer and near the whole of the fall helping the two German carpenters Virgil hired to rebuild Virgil and Allie's house.

It was a bigger house than the one Allie had burned to the ground during a cooking mishap while Virgil and I were over in the Indian territories. The new house was a two-story with a three-sided porch. I told Virgil, and Allie, I was happy to help build it but had no interest in painting it. So, with the exception of the place being unpainted, the house was complete.

"She's barefoot, covered in flour from head to toe," Virgil said when he came back out with the Kentucky and two glasses.

Virgil poured us a nudge, put the bottle between us, and sat back in the chair.

"To the house," I said, raising my glass.

"By God," Virgil said, raising his.

"And to not being bossed around by those goddamn German boys no more," I said.

Virgil offered a sharp nod.

"They're particular," Virgil said.

"You could call 'em that."

We started to tip the whiskey back when Virgil stopped and looked toward the darkness in the far distance.

"You hear that?" Virgil said.

"Thunder?"

Virgil shook his head.

"No," he said.

I listened.

"Hell," I said. "Music."

Virgil nodded and then we saw coming over the rise in front of the darkness to the north a tall, colorfully painted wagon with musicians sitting on top, playing a lively tune.

Virgil shook his head a little.

"Don't that beat hell?" I said.

"Does," Virgil said.

Leading the wagon was a single rider on a tall horse. Behind the wagon with the musicians playing music on top were other wagons trailing behind, six wagons in all.

"That's that troupe was up in Yaqui, no doubt."

"What troupe?" Virgil said.

"Beauchamp Brothers Theatrical Extravaganza, they

call it. A traveling group from New Orleans," I said. "They go town to town doing dramatic shows, dancing, magic, got 'em a sharpshooter and clairvoyant fortune-teller, that sort of thing. Allie's been talking about it for weeks. Said it's been all the talk at the ladies' social."

"She never said nothing to me," Virgil said. "First I heard of it."

"She talks to me, Virgil."

"Talks to me, *too*."

"I listen to her."

"Well, hell, Everett, I *listen* to her."

"Not when she's just going on you don't."

"Well, sometimes she talks just to listen to herself speak, Everett," Virgil said. "More than sometimes. You know that."

"I do."

I got out of my chair and called into the house, "Allie."

"What?"

"That Beauchamp Brothers bunch is coming into Appaloosa."

"*What!*" Allie exclaimed. "*Really? My goodness.*"

She came running out of the front door, taking off her apron. She rolled it up and threw it in Virgil's lap. A puff of flour dust exploded up in Virgil's face as Allie leaned over the porch rail and looked in the direction of the music.

"They weren't supposed to be here until next week," Allie said. "Oh my goodness, my goodness, my goodness. Isn't this exciting, Everett?"

"Is, Allie."

"Help me up, Everett?"

I held on to Allie's hand so she could step up on the rail for a better view. Even though Allie was no longer a spring chicken, she still had a youthful beauty about her. Her agile body was firm, her eyes sparkled, and her skin glowed like that of someone half her age.

"Careful there, Allie, you don't slip and hurt yourself," Virgil said, as he bullwhipped the apron, freeing it of flour.

"Oh, Virgil."

Folks started to gather in the street, looking in the direction of the Beauchamp Brothers Theatrical Extravaganza as they entered town. Now that they were closer, we could clearly see musicians playing banjo, trumpet, trombone, and tuba as a set of cymbals clanged together.

The single horseman leading the way held up his hand like he was a chief quartermaster halting his cavalry.

The musicians climbed down from the painted wagon and formed a line behind the horseman, never missing a beat.

"That must be him," Allie said. "That must be Beauregard Beauchamp leading the way."

"Everett said this extravaganza is the Beauchamp Brothers," Virgil said. "Might well be the other brother."

"Oh, *no*," Allie said. "Boudreaux was killed a few years ago by a tiger."

— 4 —

B oudreaux?" Virgil said, looking at me.

"A tiger?" I said.

"Yes," Allie said. "Isn't that the awfulest thing? He was the tamer, and the tiger got mad or hungry or something and attacked him, chewed him up."

Allie focused on the lead horseman and smiled.

"That must be Beauregard," Allie said, as she worked pieces of her hair back into place.

At that moment somebody scurried from one of the wagons and handed the rider a long megaphone.

He moved his horse on into town. The band followed, playing as they marched behind him. He called out into the megaphone.

"Hello, Appaloosa. My name is Beauregard Beauchamp."

"You were right, Allie," Virgil said.

"We are the Beauchamp Brothers Theatrical Extravaganza and we will be in your fair city of Appaloosa for a full week. Offering you nightly entertainment. A new and exciting show every night. The whole family is invited, young and old alike will find something that will make them laugh, warm their hearts, and tickle their innards."

Beauregard's mount was a spirited white horse with black socks, mane, and tail. Beauregard himself was handsome. He sat upright in his shiny black saddle, wearing a sharp blue striped suit, gray shirt, red tie, and a wide-brim white hat that turned skyward at its edges. He sported a full black mustache and long, shiny hair.

More people came out to see the theatrical parade as it made its way into town.

"Oh, my," Allie said. "Oh, my, oh, my."

A few young children scurried out to walk along with the members of the troupe as Beauregard carried on with his ballyhoo.

"Aaaappaloosa," he shouted, as the group continued into town. "We are pleased to announce we will be bringing you the *finest* entertainment this side of the Mississippi to your splendid township. We have a large tent we will pitch, and starting tomorrow evening, there will be a seat inside that tent for everyone to enjoy the Beauchamp Brothers Theatrical Extravaganza. So come one, come all. We have special prices for our opening night tomorrow night, so don't miss out."

He rode directly by our front porch and smiled at us, tipping his hat. Allie turned, looking to Virgil and me, and beamed like a little girl.

"Isn't he just the most glorious?" Allie said, as she looked back to Beauregard riding by. "Just glorious."

Virgil looked at me and nodded a little.

"He sure is, Allie," Virgil said.

"Glorious," I said.

The band members followed Beauregard as they moved through town. We watched as each of the brightly colored wood-topped wagon trailers passed by. Painted across the side of each trailer, colorful lettering boasted the variety of acts: *Exciting Dramatic Plays!—The Darndest Dancing!—Heavenly Singing!—Sharpshooting!—Majestic Music!—Dr. Longfellow's Magic Show! (The doctor will gladly cut you in half!)*

A few of the show's players waved from the wagon windows as they passed by.

"Only thing missing in this outfit is one of those Indian flute-blowing snake charmers," Virgil said.

Last in line came a red-painted trailer with fancy gold lettering: *Peek-a-Boo Madame Leroux ~ Fortune-Teller. (Futures Told & Your Legendary Afterlife Adventures Revealed!)*

I noticed a very attractive lady with ivory skin and black hair looking out from a window. Her gaze was off in the distance, but suddenly her focus shifted directly toward me. She didn't smile or wave, but I was certain she was looking at me.

There was something mysterious and haunting about her gaze.

Must be Madame Leroux, I thought. She remained looking at me and I looked at her until her trailer passed.

"Beauregard ought to put his brother to rest," Virgil said. "Change the troupe's name."

"Change the troupe's name?" Allie said.

Virgil nodded.

"Beauchamp's Theatrical Extravaganza," Virgil said. "Less of a mouthful."

"Oh, Virgil, don't be silly," Allie said. "Clearly you don't know the first thing about showmanship and advertising. You don't go and spoil a name brand just because a brother got gobbled up by a tiger, for land's sake. There's a business to advertising. Mrs. Winslow's Soothing Syrup, for instance . . . Ol' Mrs. Winslow's been dead and gone forever and a day, and it's a good thing they haven't changed the name to . . . to Deceased and Six-Feet-Under Mrs. Winslow's Syrup. They wouldn't sell nothing."

Allie uncocked her scorn as quickly as she'd cocked it, then turned her attention back on the passing troupe as if Virgil had said nothing.

Virgil looked at me and smiled a little, then glanced up to the dark clouds in the far distance that were slowly rolling in behind the Beauchamp Brothers Theatrical Extravaganza, headed for Appaloosa.

"Regardless of what it's called," Virgil said, "I don't suspect the weather's gonna be too favorable for opening night."

— 5 —

Allie said the dinner we ate was just like the food they make overseas in Europe. Virgil told her it tasted more like the food they make south of the border in Mexico. That incited a minor disagreement between the two of them that was working its way toward an argument when I interrupted.

"Something burning?" I said.

"Oh," Allie said. "My pie."

Allie got up from the dinner table and hurried into the kitchen. She opened the oven and waved at the escaping heat with a towel.

"Thank goodness, it's fine," Allie said. "Perfectly fine. The filling under the pecans just oozed out is all. It'll be delicious."

"Oh, hell, Allie," Virgil said. "I don't think I could eat another bite."

"Me, neither," I said.

"Oh, nonsense," Allie said, as she placed the pie on the trivet between Virgil and me. "Doesn't that look good and crispy?"

Allie fanned it a little with her towel.

"It does, Allie," I said.

"You got a good scald on it," Virgil said. "I'll give you that."

"Oh," Allie said, returning to the kitchen. "I churned up some cream to go with it."

She returned with the bowl of cream. She whipped the substance with a wooden spoon before putting the bowl on the table.

"I'm sorry, it was fluffier before," Allie said. "It'll be good, though, just spoon a little across the top."

"Smells good," I said.

Allie left the dining room and walked off down the hall.

I cut a piece of pie, put some cream on top, and slid the bowl over to Virgil.

Virgil cut a piece and put it on his plate when Allie returned to the dining room, putting on a silk bonnet.

"Would you be so kind as to clean up for me, Virgil?" Allie said, as she tied the bonnet under her chin.

"Where you going?" Virgil said.

"Well, I'm off to gather the ladies of our social and pay Mr. Beauchamp and company a proper welcoming visit."

Virgil looked to me, then to Allie.

"You think that's necessary?"

"I do," Allie said. "It's not every day Appaloosa has

someone as renowned as Beauregard Beauchamp visit us. And, as the new spokesperson of the ladies' social, I thought it would be kind to make certain we do not let this occasion of ceremony slip by like it's just any ol' day like yesterday or the day before. Everett can help you with the dishes. Can't you, Everett?"

"Sure," I said.

"Wonderful, thank you," Allie said, and then leaned down, kissing Virgil on top of his head. "Maybe we can play some cards when I get back."

"Sure," I said.

"Might want to take your umbrella," Virgil said.

After Allie left, Virgil pulled a cigar from his pocket and I took a bite of the pecan pie.

"Tell you what," I said. "That's good."

Virgil looked me, then looked to the pie.

"Is," I said.

Virgil slid the cigar back in his pocket and took a bite. He nodded and took another bite.

"Damn sure is."

After we finished a second piece of pie, Virgil and I cleaned up the kitchen and went back out on the front porch with the bottle of Kentucky.

It was almost dark out now when we settled in with the whiskey. The storm clouds we had been watching previously were close to being upon us and a light cool breeze preceded the looming darkness. It was quiet out and not many people were about. We could hear the evening train on the other side of town. It let out one long blast of its whistle as it neared the station.

"Beauregard Beauchamp," Virgil said, as he pulled the cigar from his pocket.

I looked to Virgil but didn't say anything.

"He look familiar to you?" Virgil said.

"No," I said. "Look familiar to you?"

"Something about him seemed kind of familiar."

"Always something about everybody, isn't there?"

"'Spect there is, Everett," Virgil said, then bit the cigar tip and spit it over the porch rail. "'Spect there is."

He fished a match from his pocket, dragged the tip across the grain on the porch post, and lit the cigar. He puffed on the cigar and got it going good.

"Allie sure seems to think he's special," Virgil said.

"Does."

"Thinks he's talented," Virgil said.

"And renowned," I said.

Virgil looked at me and discharged a sliver of tobacco from his lips with a spit.

"And glorious," he said.

"That, too," I said.

— 6 —

I played some lengthy games of Dark Lady with Allie and Virgil, and the three of us drank more of the Kentucky than we should have. Allie went on and on about Beauregard and how special he was. She said he held court in the town hall that night and how wonderful it was for her and the ladies' social to welcome him and the troupe to Appaloosa.

Allie told us Beauregard introduced some of the Beauchamp players and his wife of three years. She was a blond actress, the leading lady, named Nell from San Francisco. Allie went on and on about how smart and beautiful she was and how in love they were and what a splendid couple they made.

I left Virgil and Allie's place at about half past midnight. There was a light rain falling over Appaloosa and the temperature had dropped significantly.

I crossed Main Street by the Boston House Hotel

saloon and saw Fat Wallis McDonough through the
open saloon doors. He was closing up, putting chairs
on the tables. When I stepped onto the boardwalk, Wallis looked up and saw me. He stood upright and put his
large hands out wide like a welcoming kinfolk.

"Well, Everett Hitch," he said warmly.

"Evening, Wallis."

"How goes it?" Wallis said.

"Goes and goes."

"Whiskey?" he said.

"Looks like you're closing up."

"Always open for you, Everett," Wallis said. "Always
open for you."

He removed two upside-down chairs from a table and
set them upright on the floor.

"Sit yourself down," Wallis said.

"All right," I said. "Just a smidgen, though."

Wallis moved his big body behind the bar. He didn't
glide as swift and easy as he used to when Virgil and I
first met him.

"I got some special stuff," Wallis said.

Wallis was the time-honored chief barman at the
Boston House Hotel saloon. Virgil and I had plenty of
history with the Boston House, some good and some
not so good.

I looked about the room. It hadn't changed too
much. I walked between the tables. I looked through
the doors into the lobby and thought about the day
Virgil and I first arrived in Appaloosa and signed up as
peacekeepers on the landing by the front windows. I

turned back, remembering how within minutes of assuming our roles we had walked into this room and Virgil shot two of Randall Bragg's hands right where I was standing.

Bragg, I thought. *That sonofabitch.* I hadn't thought about Randall Bragg in a long while. I turned and looked to the piano in the corner. I walked over to it and pressed a key.

Bragg. I slapped him down right here, called him out after the no-good sonofabitch lured Allie and had his way with her. *Good riddance.* I gave the sonofabitch a chance. I gave him a gun, told him to come out and face me or I'd come back in there and kill him. I gave the sonofabitch an opening. At least that's how I summed it up, anyway, how I tallied it, how I put it together.

For whatever reason the Boston House Hotel saloon seemed to have a dark cloud hanging over it.

"Not seen much of you since you and Virgil have been back in town," Wallis said, carrying a tray with two glasses and a bottle of whiskey with a fancy label. "Where you been keeping yourself?"

"Virgil's had me busy working on his new house."

"I've not seen him in here since you been back this time."

"He's had his hands full."

"I'll leave it at that," Wallis said. "I saw the house. It's looking good."

"It is," I said.

I took a seat. Wallis set the two glasses on the table

and poured us each a few fingers and took a seat next to me.

"Lot of building going on everywhere these days," Wallis said. "That train keeps a'comin' and more people keep getting off of it, and as far as I can tell nobody's getting on. Town's getting bigger every goddamn day."

"Damn sure is," I said.

"Hell, in the last few years you and Virgil have been away doing your territory marshaling, this place has grown from a small chickenshit town to a burgeoning goddamn city."

"Little too big for my liking, Wallis," I said. "I kind of liked it the way it was."

Wallis nodded.

"Business is good, though," he said. "Hell, it's tripled with all the mining expansion north of town and the upstart of cow-calf outfits. Place is six square blocks now, can you believe that?"

"I don't have a choice," I said.

"Streetlamps, boardinghouses, support businesses on every damn street," Wallis said. "Mining, construction, cattle. Means employment, though. City's now chock-full of goddamn cowboys, miners, and migrants from every damn where seeking goddamn promise. Damn near two thousand people now, two thousand. Can you believe that?"

Silently, almost ghostlike, a lovely woman appeared in the doorway.

"Excuse me," she said.

Her accent was foreign. French, maybe.

Wallis looked at me, then back to the woman.

"Yes?" Wallis said.

She was strikingly beautiful. I knew this must be Madame Leroux, the woman with the ivory complexion I saw looking out the window of the fortune-teller's trailer when the troupe rode into town.

She stood still with her shoulders relaxed and her chin held high. She glanced around, looking at the room some. She took a sure step forward. Her movement was graceful and self-assured, like that of a poised dancer.

She was willowy and her eyes were bright blue. Her dark hair was wavy, parted in the middle and so long it likely had never been cut. She wore bohemian jewelry and clothing. Long strands of colorful beads and shells draped around her slender neck, and large gold hoops dangled from her ears. Her dress was black velvet with lace, and hanging on the edge of her sharp bare shoulders was a long tasseled shawl that glimmered in the dim saloon light.

"I need something strong," she said.

— 7 —

Wallis looked to me, then back to her.

"I'm sorry?" Wallis said.

"Something intoxicating?" she said.

Wallis glanced at me with a slight frown, then got his heavy body up from the chair and moved to her. He looked out the door past her to the boardwalk as if he were looking for someone else.

"Are you by yourself, ma'am?" Wallis said.

She followed his look behind her.

"As is everyone."

I don't think Wallis understood her philosophy, and if he did he didn't particularly appreciate it.

"Well, it's late and women moving around this time of night by themselves ain't normal."

"Well, I don't suppose I am particularly normal," she said coyly as she took a step forward past Wallis and looked about the saloon. "At least as is what has been divulged to me on occasion."

She had not looked at me, not directly. I watched her and she knew I watched her. She was an assured performer, doing what she did best, and she was good. Aside from the fact she was eccentric and beautiful there was something else arresting about her presence. She possessed a strong self-sureness unseen in most women.

"History," she said, glancing back to Wallis.

"What?" Wallis said.

"Your saloon," she said, "has history."

"Yes, well," Wallis said, "the saloon is kind of closed up here at the moment."

"I see. Am I interrupting?"

"Just having a nightcap with my old pal," Wallis said, nodding to me.

She turned her head slowly and leveled her dancing blue eyes on me for the first time. Her look was penetrating. She was looking into me as if she was seeing inside me three long blocks and to the left.

"Bon ami du soir," she said.

"Give the lady a drink, Wallis," I said.

"Oh," Wallis said. "Certainly. What can I get for you?"

"Would you have anything perhaps curative or therapeutic?"

Wallis put his big fists on his hips.

"Therapeutic?" Wallis said. "Well, I don't have anything to cure what ails ya and I got no absinthe, if that's what you're looking for. I've got rum, rye, whiskey, beer, brandy, and—"

"Brandy," she said.

Wallis looked at me. He nodded and moved off to the bar.

I removed a chair from atop the table and placed it upright.

"Here ya go."

"*Merci*," she said.

I caught a drift of her sweet scent as I held out her chair.

She sat and I sat next to her.

She remained looking in my eyes. Her dark eyelashes were thick and long and her eyes were penetrating. They were lively, mysterious, haunting, and extremely curious.

"You're with the troupe," I said.

"No."

"I saw you."

"I saw you, too," she said.

Her eyes stayed aimed directly at me like she was trying to shoot her thoughts through me. She placed her hands shoulder length apart on the table.

"I'm not with them," she said.

"You're new?"

She nodded, smiling wryly.

"I'm temporary," she said.

"Seems like the wrong time of year to be traipsing around putting on a show."

She didn't say anything.

I just looked at her.

She was staring at me.

I stared back at her and I think she smiled.

"Deputy Marshal Everett Hitch," I said.

"Oui," she said. "I know who you are, Deputy Marshal."

"You do?"

"We've met."

I shook my head.

"We've not met," I said.

"On the contrary," she said.

"Don't believe so."

"Now that I'm seeing you close and clearly, I'm certain," she said. "It was a long time ago."

"Where, a long time ago?"

"Bien," she said with a shrug. "Perhaps I am mistaken."

"Madame Leroux?" I said.

"You must have read that somewhere," she said with a smile.

"Hard to miss," I said.

She smiled, nodding slightly.

"Futures told," I said. "Legendary afterlife adventures revealed."

"Not all are so lucky," she said. "I'm afraid."

"Hocus-pocus," I said.

"Ah," she said. "A naysayer?"

"Just my perspective," I said.

"Oui," she said. "Something everyone is entitled to."

Wallis came back from the bar with the brandy.

"On the house," he said.

She tossed one side of her long hair behind her shoulder.

"Merci," she said to Wallis, but remained looking directly at me.

Wallis looked back and forth between us, and like the amenable barkeep he was, he excused himself.

"I'm going to just finish up with a few things," Wallis said.

He rapped his knuckles on the table.

"Enjoy," he said.

She watched Wallis as he walked off into the back room, then looked at me.

"I needed to speak to you, Deputy."

"Everett," I said.

"Oui, Everett."

"Why didn't you say so?" I said.

"I needed to be sure," she said.

"About what?"

"About . . . something I saw."

"And now you're sure?"

"Oui."

"What?"

"It's rather private."

I looked to the back room. Wallis was nowhere in sight.

"Just you, me, and the narrow space between us."

"You are in danger," she said.

— 8 —

I smiled. I don't think she was accepting or appreciative of my smile, but I couldn't help it. Maybe it was the whiskey I drank while playing cards with Virgil and Allie. Maybe it was her strange beauty. Regardless, the thought of her telling me I was in danger made me smile.

"Well, no offense," I said. "But in my line of work, danger is always present."

"No offense taken," she said. "I understand your skepticism, but in my line of work danger never lies."

I smiled.

"What kind of danger are we talking about here?"

"I'm not sure," she said.

"You're not sure?"

She shook her head.

"Not completely, and what I see, what I know, can only provide you awareness, I'm afraid . . . Fait accompli."

"So, what did you see? What do you know?"

"No need to be patronizing," she said.

"I'm not. I'm listening."

She looked around the room for a moment.

"Can we walk?"

"Don't you want to finish that brandy?"

"Not much of a drinker, I'm afraid," she said. "Perhaps you could walk me."

"Sure," I said.

"*Merci,*" she said.

I let Wallis know we were leaving. He stepped out from the back room, drying his big hands with a small towel.

"Good night," he said.

"*Au revoir,*" Madame Leroux said, and I escorted her out of the Boston House saloon.

The rain seemed to be coming down harder now. They weren't big drops, but the rain was massive and solid, like it was falling from thick, dense clouds.

We walked for a ways under the awnings of the boardwalk before she spoke.

"When I saw you, I saw something," she said. "Something not good."

"What's that?" I said.

"Normally, I keep others' *événements,* um . . . visions of misfortune to myself," she said. "I remove myself. It is a code of ethics in my line of business."

"But you feel an ethical need to share something not good with me?"

"*Oui,*" she said. "You see, you being an officer of the

law as you are, I felt it was my obligation, my *respon-sabilité*, to share this information with you."

"By all means," I said. "Go right ahead."

"I saw men," she said. "Young men, running."

I laughed.

She stopped.

I stopped and looked back to her.

"You must believe me," she said.

"Men?" I said. "Running?"

She nodded and we continued walking.

"What men?"

"I don't know," she said. "They were scared . . . I saw them again, tonight. That's why I needed to see you. They've returned."

"Where did you see these men?"

"I do not know exactly who they were or where they are," she said. "That is why I needed to see you. To see if I might have something clearer, stronger."

I began to feel unusually comfortable with this odd woman I'd just met and this strange unfolding she was sharing with me. Not for a minute did I take to heart her nonsensical bullshit or her vocation, for that matter, but I obliged.

"What makes you think I'm in danger?"

"I understand your doubt," she said, picking up on my skepticism. "But I know what I see, what I feel."

She pulled her shawl up to cover her head and we walked past a storefront without an overhang. We felt the steady rain until we were back under an awning over the boardwalk.

"How did you know where to find me?" I said.

"Hocus-pocus, Everett."

"Because you've seen these men and how they felt to you," I said. "You feel I'm in danger?"

"Yes," she said.

She lowered her shawl.

"What do your friends call you?" I said.

"What do you mean?"

"Don't tell me," I said. "You have none?"

"Oh," she said, "on the contrary, I most certainly do."

She tapped her temple and said, "I have plenty of friends with me, at all times."

"What do they call you?" I said. "What is your given name?"

"Séraphine," she said. "My name is Séraphine."

We stayed under the awnings as we walked and were exposed to the rain only when there was a break overhead between structures. We turned and walked past a few boardinghouses.

Beneath a canvas cover on the opposite side of the street, three skinny young fellas sat under a lamp, playing cards on a whiskey barrel. They watched us as we passed.

We walked on for a ways, then Séraphine stopped.

"There it is," she said.

I stopped and turned back to her.

"What?"

She was looking down like she was looking for something on the ground. She turned and looked back to the men playing cards.

"Something has happened," she said.

I looked back to the men. They weren't looking in our direction. They were doing just what they were doing, playing cards. One of them laughed. I looked back to her. She looked at me with a troubled look on her face.

"What?" I said.

She looked downward again.

"You okay?"

She shook her head.

"What is it?" I said.

"It's not good," she said.

"Your friends talking to you?"

"No," she said. "Your friends."

We were standing partially in the rain. I took her by her arm and led her under an overhang of the last structure by the pole lamp at the end of the street.

"My friends?"

"Yes," she said. "Your guides."

She sat on a bench in front of the building.

"What about them?"

"Codder," she said.

"Codder?" I said.

"Yes," she said. "Do you know of something or someone named Codder or perhaps Cotter?"

"No."

She shook her head violently, as if she were trying to get the vision to formulate clearly.

"I don't know," she said. "I wish I could tell you what

to look out for, but I don't know. Not now, anyway, but you must believe me."

"Well," I said. "It's kind of like Mother Nature. Not much can be done about the forces of nature."

"I'm trying to help you," she said.

"You've readily allowed there are men running, scared. Something or someone named Codder or Cotter, but it doesn't mean anything to me."

"Just be aware," she said. "Keep those thoughts with you."

She stood and took a step closer to me.

"Now I must go. I'm just here," she said, pointing toward the vacant lot where the troupe was camped. "I will scurry through this rain to the dryness. I will see you again."

She moved a little closer. She leaned in and kissed me, but as I worked to kiss her back she pulled away.

"Be careful, Everett."

With that she took off running in the rain toward the troupe's encampment.

I watched her until she faded away into the dark of the rainy night.

"Hocus-pocus," I said.

— 9 —

The following morning I woke up to the sound of thunder. I looked out the window and it was still raining. It was colder than it had been when I had finally drifted off to sleep in the early morning hours.

Since Virgil and I had been back in Appaloosa I'd been sleeping in a small alley room I'd rented above a survey company on the south side of town. The room consisted of a small bed, a chair, a washbasin, a dresser, a small Pettit and Smith heater, a window, and a door.

I laid in bed looking out the window and watched the rain falling for some time. My head was throbbing a little. I thought about the card game with Virgil and Allie and my strange encounter with Madame Séraphine Leroux. *Codder, Cotter*, I thought, *and men running. What the hell am I supposed to make of that?*

I spent the first half of the day in the Appaloosa Livery, the main livery stable in town, drinking coffee with Salt, an old Teton Sioux blacksmith, while I shinbone-oiled my saddle and tack.

I liked old Salt. I'd known him for years. He was a small, easy-moving man with dark, intelligent eyes. What I liked most about Salt was he didn't say much and when he did he was always worth listening to.

When I left the livery, Salt told me the weather was going to get much worse before it got better.

I walked across town and stopped in for some fried chicken at Hal's. I sat by the window with two elderly ranchers. They talked about how we needed this water, their fields, their livestock, the price of grain, and life on the farm. I shared with them what Salt had said about the forecast. Most everyone in Appaloosa, including the two ranchers, knew Salt and revered him as a man of wisdom and understanding. Upon hearing Salt's weather predictions, the old ranchers didn't waste any time to leave. Saying though they were appreciative of the water, they needed to get back to their spreads and prepare for worsening conditions.

I smiled, thinking about Séraphine. I thought she should throw in with Salt. *Hell, between the two of them, they could strike gold.*

Séraphine. The name suited her. I kept imagining I would turn around and she'd be behind me.

Hal brought me a plate of fried chicken from the kitchen. He set it in front of me and poured me some more coffee.

"There ya go, Hitch," Hal said.

Hal was a six-foot-six mountain of a man, an ex-slave

from Alabama with a shock of white hair and an infectious wide grin.

"Looks good, Hal," I said.

"Enjoy," Hal said, then looked out the window.

I followed Hal's glance.

Seven men on horseback were riding slowly up the street. Three had on kepi hats; the four others were wearing Union slouch-brims.

"Soldiers," Hal said.

"Is," I said.

"Looks like them boys been in it for a while," I said.

"It sure do," Hal said.

"Must be up from Fort Union," I said.

Hal nodded.

When they rode by the window, the bearded lead rider turned his head slowly and looked at me. He looked haggard. He raised his hand up from his saddle and gave a limp wave as they moved past the window.

"Don't seem all together," I said, "do they?"

"No, Hitch," Hal said. "They don't."

When I left Hal's, a dandy moving quick on the boardwalk damn near collided with me. Another man was coming quickly right behind him and then I heard a gunshot.

I turned, seeing a big man in a slicker holding a pistol. He fired a second shot. He was shooting at the men I'd just encountered.

I pulled my Colt and stepped back in the doorway of Hal's as two more shots rang out. The big man came running by the door of Hal's.

"Drop your pistol," I shouted.

He turned, raising his pistol at me.

I moved quickly behind the doorjamb and he fired on me.

I stuck my pistol around the jamb and returned fire in his direction; two shots, and I heard him groan loudly, "Aw, damn . . . Lordy hell."

I stepped back and peeked out the window. He staggered in the street, holding his side, and then dropped in the mud on his ass.

"I'm Deputy Marshal Hitch," I said. "Throw that pistol away from you or I'll kill you."

He looked around some, then tossed the pistol in the street.

I stepped into the doorway with my Colt trained at his head.

He looked up at me, shaking his head some, then leaned over slowly on his side.

I looked to my left. The two men he'd been firing on stepped out from an opening between two buildings down the way and looked in my direction.

"Stay where you are," I said.

They stopped.

"Hands away from your body."

They did as I told them.

The big man in the street rolled onto his back, looking up at the rain falling in his face as he clutched his side.

"What's happened here?" I said to the two men standing on the boardwalk thirty feet away.

"He tried to kill us," one of the men shouted, like he was about to burst into tears.

"Both of you. Walk over here. Now."

The two men followed my orders.

"Either of you heeled?"

"No," the taller of the two said.

They walked shoulder to shoulder up the boardwalk and stopped when they got close to me. One of the men was stocky, with a trimmed red beard and a high top hat. The other, the taller man, was slim, clean shaven, and wearing a high ribbon bowler. They both wore suits with fancy silk ties.

"Who are you?"

"I'm Grant Minot," the bearded man said.

Grant's voice was soft with a Yankee lilt. He nodded to the taller man next to him.

"This is my partner, Elliott Warshaw," Grant said.

"Why was he trying to kill you?" I said.

"He came into our office," Grant said, "claiming we owed him and his brother, Ballard, and . . ."

"You goddamn sure do, you silly shit," the man lying on his back in the street interrupted. "You goddamn sure do."

"And who is this man?"

"I'm the man who tried to kill those two fucking crooks is who I am," the man said. "Just wait and see what happens when Ballard gets wind of this."

"He's Bolger Orsley," Grant said. "Bolger and his brother, Ballard, worked for us."

"And wasn't paid," Bolger said with a groan.

"Just keep your mouth shut," I said to Bolger.

Bolger lifted his head.

"You just wait," Bolger said. "When Ballard finds out what you did to me . . ."

"Not another word," I said.

Bolger sneered at me, then lowered his head back in the mud.

I called back into the café. "Hal?"

"Yessir," Hal replied.

"Do me a favor," I said.

Hal came to the door. He ducked under the door and stepped out.

"Wha'cha need, Hitch?"

"Go and get Doc Crumley, will ya, Hal?"

He looked at Bolger lying in the street.

"On my way," Hal said.

"And stop by Virgil and Allie's place," I said. "Let Virgil know what happened here. Find any deputies along the way, tell them, too."

— 10 —

Grant and Elliott were sitting side by side on a sofa in Doc Crumley's front office when Virgil entered with Lewis "Book" Page, one of the deputies Sheriff Driskill left on duty. Book carried a short-barrel twenty-gauge. He was a hefty overgrown kid with rosy red cheeks and thick spectacles.

Virgil scanned the room, then met my eyes.

"You good?" he said.

"I am."

Virgil nodded. He didn't smile, but I could tell—inside—he was smiling a little.

"Hal fill you in?" I said.

"He did," Virgil said.

Virgil looked to Grant and Elliott sitting next to each other.

"This them?" Virgil said.

"They are," I said.

"You boys okay?"

"We are," Grant said. "This just shook us up, as I'm sure you can imagine."

Virgil looked at me.

"The fella doing the shooting?" Virgil said.

I nodded to the back room of the office.

"Doc's working on him now," I said. "Skinny Jack's in there making sure he don't try nothing more."

Virgil walked to the back-room door. I opened it.

Skinny Jack, a deputy with a scruffy goatee, was seated in the corner with a Winchester across his lap.

He stood up when he saw it was Virgil.

"Oh, Marshal Cole, sir," Skinny Jack said.

Bolger was lying facedown on the table as round-faced Doc Crumley stitched his exit wound. He looked up over his spectacles at Virgil as he pulled the thread tight.

"Hey, Virgil," Doc said.

"He gonna live?" Virgil said.

Crumley straightened up, stretching the ache out of his back some.

"Oh, yes," Doc said. "'Fraid so. He's drunk as a skunk at the moment."

"Regardless," Skinny Jack said, "I got my eye on him, Marshal, in case he wakes and tries to get shitty."

Virgil nodded.

"You seen him around before, Skinny Jack?"

"We have," Skinny Jack said. "He's been picked up

a few times drunk. Heard bad things about him, but we've not experienced nothing serious, not until now, anyway."

Virgil nodded and looked back to the partners sitting on the sofa. I closed the door to the back room and Virgil faced the men.

"This is Grant Minot and Elliott Warshaw," I said.

"I'm Territorial Marshal Virgil Cole."

"We've heard all about you, Marshal," Grant said. "Your reputation precedes you."

Elliott nodded.

"What happened here?" Virgil said.

"That beast of a man in there tried to kill us, for God sake," Grant said.

"I've been apprised of what went down," Virgil said. "Why don't you tell me why he tried to kill you?"

"Bolger, um, Mr. Orsley," Grant said, "came into our office with a gun, demanding pay."

"Pay he's owed?" Virgil said.

"Well, yes," Grant said. "But, well, it's complicated."

"Why don't you uncomplicate it for me?"

"It's a commerce issue, really," Grant said.

Elliott put his hand on Grant's hand.

"Let me explain," said Elliott.

Grant nodded, smiling pleasantly at Elliott.

"Bolger and his brother, Ballard, worked for us," Elliott said. "They delivered goods for us."

"Goods?"

"Yes," Elliott said. "We supply the Rio Blanco crews with food, and Bolger is, well, *was* our driver."

"The bridge?" Virgil said.

"That's right," Elliott said.

"Where's the rub?" Virgil said.

Elliott turned his head to the side and looked to Grant.

"The problem," Grant said, providing the meaning of *rub* to Elliott.

"Oh. Well, Bolger and Ballard had been making delivery runs to the camp twice a week," Elliott said, "and for two weeks consecutive we've not been paid and therefore we were unable to pay Bolger and Ballard."

Elliott glanced to Grant. Grant bobbed his head a little.

"Where's Ballard?" Virgil said.

"We don't know," Elliott said. "He's a mean man, and when he hears about this, he will become even meaner, I'm sure of that."

Grant nodded.

"With him loose we will need protection," Grant said, "I can tell you that."

"I assure you we did everything in our power to pay what we owed. This is a new business for us," Elliott said. "We were both employed as tailors previously. We wanted to start our own business and heaven knows cash flow is a necessity for a new enterprise. We certainly don't blame Bolger or Ballard for being upset, but, well, there was simply nothing we could do."

"You can imagine how we felt," Grant said. "I think perhaps Bolger was drinking."

"Inebriated is more like it," Elliott said with a huff. "Both of them are drunks. We didn't know that when we got into business with them."

"One thing you should know about Ballard," Grant said.

"What's that?" I said.

"Well, I know Bolger talks about him like they are close but Ballard was very mean to him," Grant said.

Elliott nodded.

O ne day, the last delivery, actually," Elliott said, "they got into a bad fight and Ballard hit Bolger, told Bolger he was no longer part of the business."

"We haven't seen Ballard after that," Grant said.

"Or the buckboard," Elliott said.

"Ballard took the buckboard?" I said.

They nodded.

"He did," Elliott said.

"Bolger, however," Grant said, "kept coming around, asking us for money."

"Then he came with the gun," Elliott said.

"We tried to reason with Bolger," Grant said. "Thank God Elliott pushed him when he was standing over me with the gun in my face."

"He stumbled and we took off running," Elliott said.

"Who's supposed to be paying you that ain't paying you?" Virgil said.

"We're the middlemen, so to speak. Our deal is with

a grocer in town," Elliott said. "The contractor pays them and they pay us."

"Grocer claims it's the contractor," Grant said. "That is why I stated it was a commerce issue."

"Why'd he try and shoot you, Everett?" Virgil said.

"Bad weather, I reckon."

— 11 —

Before we left Doc Crumley's office Virgil opened the door and looked into the back room again. He instructed Skinny Jack and Book to take turns keeping an eye on Bolger.

"Get him locked up as soon as the doc says he's okay to be moved," Virgil said.

"He's not hurt. He'll be walking easily on his own accord by morning," Doc said.

"Keep the door locked and be ready if this brother of his wants to show up and lend a hand."

"Will do," Skinny Jack said.

Virgil nodded and moved to Grant and Elliott. They were watching him like trained lapdogs awaiting instruction.

"You boys want to press charges, I imagine?" Virgil said.

Grant looked to Elliott and Elliott looked to Grant. They looked back to Virgil and nodded in unison.

"We do," Elliott said.

"Most certainly," Grant said. "We need him to be unable to get to us."

"Yes," Elliott said. "He should be locked up."

"Indeed," Grant said. "But what about Ballard?"

"You got no idea where he is?" Virgil said.

They shook their heads.

"Know where he lives?" Virgil said.

"No," Elliott said. "We have no idea."

"When we first hired them they were so nice, polite, and clean actually," Grant said. "But then, after a few runs up to the river bridge, they were always dirty and smelled of liquor. All the time. Elliott said something to them about drinking on the job and oh, my. That's when we knew we had hired degenerate dregs."

"They turned on me," Elliott said. "And I thought they were going to kill me right then and there."

Virgil looked to deputy Book.

"Get these fellas to fill out a full report, Book," Virgil said. "Get it to the office and we'll get it processed in the morning."

"Yes, sir," Book said.

Virgil looked back to Grant and Elliott.

"We'll get this report filed with the DA's office first thing," Virgil said. "In the meantime, you boys find someplace to stay where you won't be expected to stay. Don't want this brother of his showing up to fuck with you."

Grant looked to Elliott. His face twisted up. He started to cry. Virgil glanced to me and I followed him out the door.

The rain was still coming down and it seemed that it was getting a little colder. We stood under the overhang for a bit, watching the rain.

"Allie heard when Hal came and told me what went down in front of his café," Virgil said. "She damn near bawled just thinking about the notion of something happening to you. Said she wouldn't know what to do without you."

I nodded but didn't say anything.

"She gets scared," Virgil said, "thinking about what we do."

"You and me been at this line of work for a long time, Virgil," I said. "It's what we do."

"Is," Virgil said.

"She's just never got used to it," I said.

"No," Virgil said. "She ain't."

"It's not just gun work," I said. "Lots of circumstances and incidents can be attributed to not being here on this earth anymore."

"The unexpected is always more expectant with gun work, though, Everett, you know that."

"Is," I said. "Of course it is."

We watched the rain for a bit.

"Old Salt was right," I said.

"'Bout?"

"Weather getting worse before it gets better."

Virgil nodded and pulled his watch. He flipped open the lid and checked the time.

"Allie was thrilled to know you was okay," Virgil said. "She was appreciative as well she wouldn't have to cancel her ladies' social shindig on account of something bad happening."

"Appreciative?" I said.

Virgil nodded.

"What shindig?"

"For the traveling troupe," he said, as he shut the lid on his timepiece and put it back in his pocket. "The mayor's gonna formally welcome them."

"Now?"

"'Bout an hour from," Virgil said.

I thought about that for a moment as I watched the rain pour off the porch roof, making a trench line in the street between the boardwalk and hitch.

"You expected at this shindig?" I said.

"Seeing how you are upright and alive," Virgil said. "We are."

"How about we get a beer first?" I said.

"How 'bout it," Virgil said with a nod.

We walked a bit, listening to the rain on the metal roof covering the boardwalk. We came to Grove's Place, a lively saloon where cattlemen from the stockyards gathered.

— 12 —

We entered Grove's and the saloon was more spirited than usual with stockyard hands and cowboys off work because of the nasty conditions.

Virgil and I got us a beer and stood next to a tall table by the window and watched it rain.

"Calm's over," I said.

Virgil nodded.

"Outlaw racket come back in business today," I said.

"Did," Virgil said.

"Weather comes woes," I said.

We sipped our beer and didn't say anything for a while.

"This Ballard fella," I said. "Sounds like he might have a bone or two to pick."

"Does," Virgil said. "Don't seem like he's going to appreciate you shooting his brother, Bolger, none."

"No," I said. "I don't, either."

"Might be a good idea if we locate him before he locates you," Virgil said.

I nodded and we watched the rain for a bit as we sipped our beers.

"Damn monsoon," I said.

"Happens once and a while," Virgil said.

A group of young cowhands across the room burst into laughter after one of them told the punch line to a joke.

Virgil looked over to them and smiled a little.

"You notice when the Beauchamp group come into town," I said, "the good-looking woman sitting in one of the trailers?"

Virgil shook his head.

"No," he said. "Didn't."

"I met her," I said. "She's the fortune-teller."

Virgil looked at me.

I sipped my beer for a moment before I said anything else.

"After I left your place last night, I stopped in and drank some whiskey with Wallis at the Boston House and in she walked."

Virgil turned his head slightly and looked at me out of the corner of his eye.

"Goddamn good-looking lady," I said.

"Good," Virgil said.

"She told me my life was in danger."

Virgil leaned his elbow on the tall table and smiled a bit.

"She know you're a lawman?"

"Does," I said.

Virgil nodded.

"That'd be like telling a farrier he'd get kicked," Virgil said. "Or a banker would be receiving a large sum of money."

"True," I said.

"Same concerns Allie's got for us," Virgil said. "More bullets move around us than move around most people."

"She calls herself Madame Leroux," I said. "Funny thing was, some of Madame Leroux's hocus-pocus foretold what I encountered today."

Virgil looked at me out of the corner of his eye.

"She didn't get all of it just right," I said.

Virgil grinned.

"What'd she allow?" he said.

"Said she saw men running, scared," I said. "That's what happened when I left Hal's, those two dandies, Grant and Elliott, came running right by me. Damn near run over me."

Virgil grinned, wider this time.

"Hell," Virgil said. "Most men are scared of their own shadow and they run all the time."

"Something about her," I said.

"Always something about a woman, Everett," Virgil said. "Fortune-teller or not."

"There is," I said.

"What'd she not get right?" he said.

"She asked me if I knew someone or something of some such named Codder or Cotter."

"Codder or Cotter?"

"None of those boys involved in the scuffle in front of Hal's was named Codder or Cotter," I said.

"Well," Virgil said with a chuckle. "That's a goddamn good thing, Everett."

"It is," I said. "Be a bit unsettling to think she really knew what she was talking about."

"Reckon she can't be right all the time," Virgil said.

"No," I said. "Reckon not."

Virgil smiled again.

"Figure she weren't completely shy on the hocus-pocus fiddle-faddle, neither," Virgil said with a smile, "what with them two running an' all?"

"No," I said. "Not completely."

— 13 —

By the time we got over to the town hall in the newly constructed Rains Civic Building on Main Street, the shindig was under way. Virgil and I stood at the back of the large room that served as a courtroom when the judge was in town and a town hall meeting room when community business needed to be discussed.

Appaloosa's mayor, Ashley Epps, was standing behind the small lectern, speaking to the good-sized crowd that Allie and the ladies' social had rallied up.

"Considering the weather," I said, "they got a good turnout, it appears."

"They do," Virgil said.

Ashley was a young family man who was fairly new to Appaloosa. Besides being the mayor, he was also the minister of the Baptist church, with ambitions of becoming the territorial governor.

He was small but mighty, a well-spoken man with a genuine Baptist conviction he wore on his shirt cuff. He had a flashy smile, golden skin, and wheat-colored hair.

Behind Ashley was the majority of the Extravaganza troupe. There were about thirty people in all. Most were outfitted in some kind of colorful costume, including the band members with their instruments, and a pair of jugglers dressed like jokers on a deck of cards.

"Colorful lot," Virgil said.

"They are," I said.

Virgil leaned over to me a little closer.

"Which one's the fortune-teller lady?" Virgil said.

I shook my head.

"Don't see her."

Beauregard was wearing a fancy embroidered suit. He had on an expensive-looking hat, different from the one he was wearing when he rode into town. A fan of turkey feathers rose from one side. Next to Beauregard sat a beautiful young woman.

"Must be the wife Allie was talking about," I said. "Nell."

Virgil nodded slightly, looking at her.

Allie was right, Nell was real pretty; she was small, with delicate features, large brown eyes, and wispy blond hair that curled around her face like a delicately carved frame.

"Tender kindle," he said.

"For ol' Beauregard," I said, "she damn sure is."

"Pretty," Virgil said.

"I'll give you that," I said.

After Ashley took advantage of sharing his political aspirations and views of the territory's future to the captive audience of Appaloosa citizens, he turned his attention to the troupe gathered around him.

"Appaloosa is thrilled to have Beauchamp Brothers Theatrical Extravaganza here in the great growing city of Appaloosa. So without further ado."

Ashley looked to Beauregard.

"That's a word you show folks use, is it not?" Ashley said with a wiggle of his head. "*Ado?*"

Beauregard smiled a crooked smile under his big mustache and nodded a little.

"So without further ado," Ashley said with a big grin, "please welcome the one and only Mr. Beauregard Beauchamp."

Ashley stepped away and the crowd applauded as Beauregard took a few unsteady steps on his way to the lectern.

"Thank you, Appaloosa," he said without a slur. "Thank you."

Beauregard's voice was huge and was taller than both Virgil and me. He was older than he appeared when we saw him riding into town on his horse. His long, dark hair and full mustache were dyed and it was apparent to both Virgil and me he was liquored up.

"Got a few posts missing," Virgil said.

"He does," I said.

"And thank you, Mayor, for welcoming us, we appreciate your kindness," Beauregard said. "First, I'd like to say a big thank-you to the App . . . Appaloosa ladies' social for helping us, as we get ready to bring Appaloosa some fun and excitement to your fantastic community, especially you, Miss French."

"He's seasoned," I said.

"Yep," Virgil said.

The crowd applauded again.

Allie was sitting in the front row, enamored with the happenings.

"With a little assistance from God above," Beauregard said, "helping us clear out some of this intemperate, this inclement weather, the Extravaganza will be set up soon and under way."

Beauregard looked to Ashley.

"If you, Reverend Epps, and your congregation would be so kind to help us out with some good old-fashion prayers. We . . ."

Beauregard gestured to his troupe.

"All of us," he said, "would be most grateful."

Ashley nodded and grinned.

"We'll see what we can muster," Ashley said.

Beauregard bowed a little, then turned back to the crowd.

"But we thought here tonight," Beauregard said. "Prayers or no prayers, we tonight thought . . ."

Beauregard paused dramatically and then repeated.

"We tonight thought we'd take this opportunity to give you a little peek of what to expect."

Beauregard looked to the musicians and nodded.

"Here's a favorite tune of ours," he said. "'My Grand-father's Cock' . . . *CLOCK*, I mean *clock*. 'My Grandfa-ther's *Clock*.'"

The crowd clapped as the band members got to their feet and started playing the upbeat song.

"I know that face," Virgil said.

"Beauregard?"

Virgil nodded as he looked at him intently.

The musicians were a lively group and they danced a little jig as they played. Beauregard held out his hand for Nell to come up. She stepped up and after the band got a few progressions out of the way she sang along. She was animated and expressive as she sang, and in no time at all she had the whole crowd singing along with the popular tune.

Beauregard stepped off to the side. He misstepped a little but caught his balance. He stood back and watched Nell proudly. He folded his arms across his ribs and smiled.

Virgil and I watched for a moment, then Virgil said, "I'll be damned."

"Remember?" I said.

"I do."

"Where?"

"I'll be damned," Virgil said again.

"Gun hand?" I said.

Virgil shook his head.

"Snake-oil salesman."

"That fits," I said.

"Does," he said, shaking his head a little.

"Where?"

"A time ago. Way before you and me started working together, before town work, even. I was working the big gambling room at the Menger Hotel in San Antone. He come around there, selling his remedies. Thought he was the cock of the walk. A young buck then, full of himself."

Virgil stopped talking for a moment and just watched for a bit.

"One evening," Virgil said, "he sat at the wrong gambling table. They caught him cheating. Rough bunch, they was gonna string him up . . ."

Beauregard took Nell by the hand between the verses of "My Grandfather's Clock" and the two of them danced along with the music.

"Looks like he still thinks of himself as the cock of the walk," I said.

Virgil nodded a little.

"Drinking his remedies, too," I said.

"I'll be damned," Virgil said. "That's sure enough him. He was flashy back then, younger, but flashy. I locked him in a closet till the ruckus settled and the gamblers cleared."

Virgil just shook his head from side to side a little.

"When I let him out he wanted to fight me," Virgil said. "Best I remember, I slapped him a few times and kicked him out the back door and into the trash like the spindly miscreant he was."

"Likely still is," I said.

"Seems," Virgil said.

— 14 —

The band played some more festive tunes with Nell singing along. Then the magician, Dr. Longfellow, performed a few disappearing-handkerchief tricks followed by the jester clown jugglers, who made the crowd roar with laughter. As soon as the little show finished up, Allie hurried up behind the lectern.

"Hello, everyone," she said. "We, the ladies' social of Appaloosa, want to let y'all know we have provided some refreshments, cookies and cakes and some lemon punch, so everybody stay, mingle with our special guests, and enjoy."

The crowd did just that and the flock of folks gathered around the troupe as they worked their way to the table like cattle headed to feed.

Allie looked up, seeing Virgil and me standing at the back of the room, and scurried through the throng of people over to us.

"Oh, Everett," Allie said, as she clamped her arms around me. "Thank God you are okay."

"It's okay, Allie," I said.

Allie didn't move; she just squeezed me harder, keeping her face nestled in my chest.

I looked to Virgil.

"I'm right here, Allie," I said.

Allie just squeezed me tighter.

"Hell, Allie," Virgil said. "Let him breathe some."

Allie removed her head from my chest. She cut her eyes at Virgil a bit, then looked up to me but remained clutching me tight.

"Oh, Everett," Allie said. "Thank God in Heaven you are okay. I was so worried about you."

"Thank Samuel Colt," Virgil said.

"Virgil Cole," Allie snapped, as she looked to him. "I swear, you can be so callous."

"Nothing callous about being a good gun hand and returning fire," Virgil said.

"Oh," Allie said. "You're impossible."

Virgil smiled.

"I guess that's good," Virgil said.

Allie looked back up to me.

"I'm just grateful you're here and alive," Allie said.

I smiled at her.

"Well, Allie," I said. "You're entirely welcome . . . You put together a good gathering here."

"Thank you," she said. "I'm happy about the turnout."

"Might have myself a piece of cake," I said. "Maybe some of that lemon punch."

"Oh, yes," Allie said. "Come and see what we got."

Allie pulled me away from Virgil and over to the desserts spread out across the table.

Virgil followed us through the crowd of folks over to the table, and as we neared I noticed Beauregard look over at Virgil. He was standing with Nell as he talked with Ashley, but he was focused on Virgil. I could tell he recognized Virgil. He leaned close to Ashley and it was obvious he asked Ashley about Virgil. Ashley looked over to us, he said something to Beauregard and then escorted Beauregard and Nell our way.

"Virgil, Everett," Ashley said. "Let me introduce you to Beauregard Beauchamp and his lovely wife, Nell."

"Oh, yes," Allie interjected with enthusiasm as she took over the introductions. "Virgil, Everett, this is Beauregard and Nell. Beauregard, Nell, this is Virgil and Everett. Virgil is my, my . . ."

"Marshal Cole," Virgil said.

Allie blushed a little.

"And this is Everett," Allie said. "Virgil's deputy marshal."

"I was just letting Mr. and Mrs. Beauchamp here know you are our celebrated territory law officials and what a wonderful privilege it was for the growing community of Appaloosa that the two of you resided here."

Beauregard held out his hand to Virgil, but I shook his hand instead.

"Virgil's not much on shaking hands," I said. "Pleasure to meet you both."

Nell looked at me and smiled. Beauregard remained focused on Virgil.

"We've had the pleasure of meeting before," Beauregard said to Virgil. "Have we not?"

"Believe we have," Virgil said.

Beauregard squinted a little.

"Card game," Virgil said. "San Antone."

Beauregard chewed a few hairs of his mustache.

"Menger's," Beauregard said. "The hotel?"

Virgil nodded.

"Well, isn't that just the best," Allie said. "Old friends."

"Yes," Beauregard said. "Old friends."

Virgil smiled pleasantly but didn't say anything.

"Long time ago," Beauregard said.

Virgil nodded a little.

"Was," he said.

"Well, maybe you two can just pick up where you left off?" Allie said.

"Maybe," Virgil said.

— 15 —

Ashley cornered me before I left the town hall only to let me know he was planning on being the new territory governor and he hoped to have Virgil and my endorsement come Election Day.

Goddamn rain, I thought, as I crossed the street and headed back to my alley room above the survey office. The streets were now mud and the ruts were beginning to get deep. *Got to let up sometime soon.*

When I left the boardwalk I walked across a single plank over the soggy narrow passage to the stairs. I took the first step leading up to my room and noticed lamplight in my window. I stopped before taking another step and drew my Colt.

I took one slow step at a time. The stairs were solid. They didn't creak as I ascended, and I made my footfalls cautious and quiet as I moved up. I stayed low, not showing myself as I passed under the window overlooking the rungs, then eased to the side of the opening and peeked in.

Sitting on the bed was Séraphine. She was looking directly at me through the window as if she knew I would be peeking in.

I was glad it wasn't Bolger's bad brother I'd heard about waiting on me.

I opened the door.

"Hello, Everett," she said.

I stayed standing in the doorway.

She watched as I slowly slid my Colt back in its holster.

I smiled at her. She smiled at me.

"Hey," I said.

Her blue eyes were catching the light just right from the lamp fire. It was nice to see her looking at me, and it felt good to look at her back.

"You didn't show for the theatrical town hall presentation?" I said.

"I'm here," she said.

"Yes, you are."

She was sitting on the bed with her back propped up on the headboard, looking casually at yesterday's newspaper. She folded the paper simply and put it to her side. She was relaxed and calm. Her long legs were extended on the bed and crossed at her ankles. She was wearing a pair of Mexican cowboy boots with riding heels that were unusually clean, considering the weather.

She was dressed different from when I saw her the night before. She was wearing a simple cream-colored muslin dress, like a long, thin sleeping gown. The flimsy fabric allowed the valleys, hills, and curves of her slender body to be revealed fully, and I appreciated the contours.

"You look good," I said.

"Do I?"

"You do."

"That's good?" she said.

"It is."

"Merci," she said.

"Merci back," I said.

The mysterious fortune-teller, I thought. I entered and closed the door behind me.

I'd been all over. Met a lot of women in my time, some with taste and some without a lick of it. Some, through the many years, have been refined and some downright uncouth. Some smart and some not so smart, but I'd never run across anyone like this woman, Séraphine.

She had a sense of herself. She was self-assured unlike any woman I'd ever met. Her strange and suspect profession was fitting for her in some ways. Might be the only way this sultry, unusual, almost otherworldly creature could exist.

She had a horsehair belt around her narrow waist. Her long, dark hair was pulled up and concealed under a black bowler hat that was a few sizes too large for her. She was wearing her large gold hoop earrings but was without her long strings of beads and shells.

"I hope you don't mind," she said.

"That you look goddamn good?"

"That I am here in your room."

"I'd mind if you weren't."

"Good."

I took off my hat and slicker and hung them on some long nails next to her slicker.

"I know what happened with you today," she said.

"Don't talk," I said.

I walked over to her and stood, looking down on her. Her eyes looked slowly up my body and met mine.

I reached for her just as she reached for me. I pulled her up to me, and our lips met but I did not kiss her. I just looked in her eyes and she looked in my eyes as I held her in my arms. She removed her bowler and tossed it. Her long, dark hair tumbled across my arms.

I kissed her and she kissed me back like she was hungry and had not eaten for some time.

I felt as though I was dreaming for an instant.

I held her back away from me and looked in her eyes again. I wanted to see her. I wanted to make sure it was really her I was kissing. Her eyes were moist, almost as if she were crying.

She was looking at me with a calm-but-desiring expression. I reached down and she helped me remove her belt. I slung it to the floor.

She started unbuttoning my shirt and kissing my chest.

I took her by her shoulders and pushed her back on the bed.

I let her lie there for a moment as she looked up at me. Her chest was moving. She was breathing heavy.

She reached up for me.

Then I moved down on her. I put my hand behind her neck and pulled her lips to mine.

— 16 —

In the morning, we laid in bed listening to it rain.

"This storm's put a damper on the Beauchamp outfit getting the show under way," I said.

She nodded a little.

"Such is the Moon of Mother Nature," she said. "Not too much can be assured when it comes to the forces of Mother Nature's Moon."

I was on my back. Her head was on my shoulder and her leg was draped over me. She was touching my chest with the tips of her fingers.

Sonofabitch, I thought, as I looked at her. *Séraphine.* She was unlike anything I'd ever experienced before. It felt like time had goddamn stopped or something. *Who was this woman, where the hell did she come from?*

Nothing had been said for a long while.

Then she said quietly, "You know, I'm much older than you."

I smiled to myself.

"No," I said. "You're a good twenty years younger."

She continued to caress my chest delicately but didn't say anything for a long moment . . . then: "I'm certain why I am here, Everett."

"Why?"

"For you."

"I'm right here," I said.

"*Oui,*" she said. "You are."

"*Oui,*" I said.

She looked up into my eyes and smiled.

"*Oui,*" she said softly again.

"In my time," I said. "I've avoided asking women about most everything."

"You are smart," she said.

"I always figured it best to let sleeping dogs lie," I said. "But I'm compelled."

"About?"

"You," I said. "Where do you come from?"

She leaned up on her elbow and looked at me.

"As you say, it's best for sleeping dogs to lay."

"Looks like we're beyond that," I said.

"It's just better," she said. "Just know I am here for you."

She sat up and turned to face me.

"I know what you went through," she said.

"Somebody tell you, word on the street? Or did you see it in your mind's eye, the friends, guides, and such?"

"I wanted to warn you," she said.

"You already did that, remember?"

She shook her head.

"You did," I said.

"What happened was not what I saw before."

"There's more to it?"

"There is," she said.

"What?"

"What happened was something altogether different," she said. "That I'm clear on."

"That so?"

"*Oui,*" she said.

I smiled at her.

"You don't believe me?" she said.

I didn't, but I allowed.

"You said you saw men running, scared," I said.

"*Oui.*"

"Well, there you go, that is what happened, two men came running by me, scared for their life; another man was shooting at them."

She shook her head.

"What I saw was different," she said.

"I'm listening," I said.

"What I saw, with the men, was in water," she said.

"Water?"

She nodded.

"Well, it was raining and wet. I don't know if we can stand much more water than what we have coming down."

She shook her head.

"It was not here," she said.

"Not here in Appaloosa?"

"Oui," she said.

"So," I said. "How is it, if what you saw was not here in Appaloosa, but I'm here in Appaloosa, my life is in danger?"

"I don't have all the answers," she said.

"Well, I can't do anything other than what I do," I said.

"Just watch out," she said.

"It's what I do," I said. "Watch out. I'm always aware, rest assured."

She nodded.

"Can't live in fear of the unexpected," I said.

"No," she said sadly. "I know. I wish I could tell you more."

"Well, I appreciate the advice," I said.

I looked at my watch on the chair next to the bed.

"I'll be going," she said.

Séraphine removed her leg that was draped across me and sat up on the edge of the bed.

"I'll walk you."

"No," she said, and then gave me a peck on the cheek. "Not necessary."

I stayed there on the bed and watched her dress.

Her sharp-angled figure was strong and without blemish. She held her shoulders back and her chin high and all of her moves were elegant and languid. Something about her *did* make her seem as if she were older than me.

Within a matter of minutes, Séraphine together and dressed, she leaned over, twisting her long hair into a tidy bale atop her head and crowning it with her bowler. She leaned down and kissed me again, sweet-like on the lips, then slipped on her slicker and walked out the door.

I moved to the window and watched her descend the stairs. She walked across a single board leading to the boardwalk. She stepped up on the boardwalk, stopped and turned. She looked back up seeing me looking at her. She snugged her derby, continued on, and was gone from sight.

Good Goddamn.

— 17 —

I dragged my straight razor across the concave belly of my seasoned whetstone and got the blade good and sharp. I heated up some water in a tin cup over the lamp, whipped up some pumice and goat-milk shaving lather with my boar-bristle brush, and then gave myself a proper slow shave. I thought about her as I worked the sharp steel across my face. I thought about how she smelled, how she felt, and the words she had spoken to me.

Goddamn lovely she is, really nice, smooth and lovely. Hocus-goddamn-pocus.

"Aha . . ."

The straight razor I was working up my neck toward the corner of my jaw took a nick of skin and blood instantly showed through the lather and snaked down my neck.

That's what cogitating about a woman will get you, I thought. *Hocus-goddamn-pocus.*

I finished up my shave, and after I stopped the bleeding I scrubbed my teeth good, dressed, and left the room.

The rain had subsided for the moment, but it was dark out and for sure it was getting colder. As we had arranged, I met Virgil at the sheriff's office at nine o'clock to collect the report for the DA that Book took from Grant and Elliott.

Book was drinking coffee when we entered.

"I sat with Bolger through the night," Book said. "All he did was sleep. Skinny Jack's there with him now."

"No sign of his brother?" Virgil said.

"No, sir, no sign. Doc said we can get him over here and lock him up in a short-short."

Virgil nodded.

"Any word from Sheriff Driskill from the bridge camp?" Virgil said.

"Nope," Book said. "Not a word."

Virgil looked at me.

"That's peculiar. They should have made it to the bridge by dark yesterday," Virgil said.

I nodded.

"What about Deputy Chastain," I said. "He still sick?"

"Far as I know," Book said. "I haven't seen him."

Virgil nodded.

"You boys keep alert," Virgil said.

"Yes, sir," Book said. "We will, sir."

Virgil and I drank some coffee with Book for a bit, then we walked Grant and Elliott's report over to the district attorney.

We were waiting in the front room of the DA's office when Carveth Huckabee, Appaloosa's DA, walked in.

He was a squat-figured man with a wide chest and a big voice. Carveth had a ruddy complexion, a bushy head of strawlike hair, and an easygoing attitude.

"Nice weather for a duck," Carveth said.

"Is," Virgil said.

"Glad to see you're still with us, Everett," Carveth said.

"Me, too, Carveth."

"I was abstracting money at five-card from pesky mining esquires last night and I heard about the whole thing," he said. "The heralded subject of the said shoot-out was on the table."

"Figures," I said.

Carveth nodded.

"It will most certainly make tomorrow's untrustworthy newspaper," he said. "Come on in."

Virgil and I followed Carveth into his office. He sat behind his big oak desk and Virgil and I sat across from him.

"Haven't seen hide nor hair of you fellas," Carveth said. "Things have sure enough been good and peaceful here in Appaloosa. Think Sheriff Driskill puts the fear of God in most folks."

I handed Carveth the report and he looked it over.

"Both the men Bolger Orsley shot at want to make sure he gets his due," I said. "Gets locked up, stays locked up. They're scared of him."

"He shot at you, too," Carveth said.

"Yes," I said. "He did, but I'm not scared of him if he's out or not."

"No, I wouldn't think there's much that would scare you, Everett, and you, Virgil, but make no mistake about Bolger," Carveth said. "Him and that brother of his are both bad apples."

"So it seems," I said.

"I'm surprised these two men, Grant and Elliott, hired them in the first place," Carveth said.

"They don't know much about the likes of Bolger and his kind," I said.

Carveth nodded.

"I heard about those two, Grant and Elliott," Carveth said. "They're different."

"In some ways," Virgil said, "I suspect they are, but it don't give Bolger the right to pull on 'em."

"No, of course not," Carveth said. "Bolger and Ballard both have been arrested on numerous occasions all over the territories. His brother, Ballard, is the one to worry about."

"We've heard," Virgil said.

"Any idea where he is?" Carveth said.

"Don't," I said.

"He's a hard case," Carveth said. "I know he spent some time locked up down in Huntsville."

"What for?" Virgil said.

"Don't know," Carveth said. "As far as whether Bolger stays locked up, that'll be of course for Judge Callison to decide. Bolger will be held till his arraignment, and that'll be a while."

"Why a while?" Virgil said.

"Judge won't be through here till the end of the month," Carveth said. "Most likely, considering the nature of Bolger's charges and firing on an officer of the law, well, he'll likely stay locked up without bail till his trial."

Virgil nodded.

Carveth looked at the report for a moment, then set it on his desk and leaned back in his chair.

"I heard there are some Union men in town," Carveth said. "Know anything about that?"

"I saw 'em," I said. "Yesterday."

"Word is they're on the hunt for a raiding party," Carveth said.

"What raiding party?" Virgil said.

"I don't know," Carveth said.

"Indians?" I said.

Carveth shrugged.

"Don't know," Carveth said.

"How do you know what you know?" Virgil said.

"More card talk," Carveth said.

"What, exactly?" Virgil said.

"Not much gets by the esquires. A few of them were having some whiskey at Clancy's Saloon, said one of the soldiers came in, bought some whiskey. They said he talked some, that's all I know."

I looked to Virgil.

"After the shooting with Bolger, I didn't think too much about 'em," I said. "I figured they were just passing through, maybe up from Fort Union."

"Know where they are now, Carveth?" Virgil said.

"No," Carveth said. "But I can tell you, the esquires told me all they know, that much I am sure of. They said the soldier told them they were on the hunt and would continue to hunt until they found the raiders."

— 18 —

When we left Carveth's office the rain had started up again. The wind had picked up some, too, and the day was dark.

We buttoned up our slickers under the porch over-hang as we watched some traffic moving slowly in both directions on the muddy street.

"What do you think about the unit?" I said.

"Don't make good sense," Virgil said.

"Us not knowing about no raiding party?"

Virgil nodded.

"No," I said. "It don't."

"We got no wire."

"We didn't."

"If something has happened in these whereabouts," Virgil said, "it's our jurisdiction."

"We should know," I said.

"Should," Virgil said.

"Whether the military is on the hunt or not," I said.

"Yep," Virgil said. "We goddamn sure should have been notified."

We watched a team of mules pulling a buckboard. They passed us carrying a heavy load covered with a tarp. The skinner hawed the team around the corner in front of us and moved on up Third Street.

"Might be a good idea we find the soldiers," I said. "Figure out what's what."

"If they're still here," Virgil said.

We crossed the street and stopped back by the sheriff's office. Book was standing in the open doorway. He was leaning on the doorjamb with his twenty-gauge tucked under his arm and a cup of coffee in his hand when we walked up.

"Book," Virgil said. "Know anything about some soldiers coming into town?"

"Soldiers?"

"Yep," I said. "Soldiers. Seven of them came into town yesterday, claiming to be looking for raiders that attacked some settlers. They rode in midday, right before Bolger started up."

"No," Book said. "I don't. Should I?"

"Not necessarily," Virgil said. "Not necessarily."

Virgil turned and looked down the street. He thought for a minute and looked the other way. He started walking and I followed.

"Keep sharp, Book," Virgil said, without looking back to him. "Keep sharp."

"Yes, sir," Book called back, as we walked away up the boardwalk.

Appaloosa had enough hotels and boardinghouses now that it provided us the need to do some looking.

The first place we checked was the Appaloosa Livery. There were other liveries in town and many lodging stables, but we started with Salt at the main livery.

Salt was coming through the rear door, leading a skinny dun, when we entered.

"Salt," I said.

Salt said nothing. He just lifted his chin, which was his way of saying, What can I do for you, what do you want, and why are you here? as he continued walking with the dun toward a stall.

"Looking for some soldiers that came into town," I said.

Salt opened a stall and led the dun inside. He circled the horse inside the stall, leaving the dun facing the gate.

"Figured we'd see if you got their horses," I said. "Might know where they're staying?"

Salt removed the dun's lead and closed the gate.

He shook his head.

"No soldiers," Salt said, as he grabbed a pitchfork.

Virgil was looking out the rear door, watching the rain. He nodded a little, then looked to Salt.

"Good enough," Virgil said. "'Preciate it, Salt."

Salt nodded a little as he forked some hay over the gate into the dun's stall.

"Like you said, Salt," I said. "Weather's damn sure got worse."

Salt didn't say anything as he forked more hay over the gate and into the stall.

Virgil and I turned and started back toward the front door.

"It will turn," Salt said.

We looked back to Salt as he forked more hay.

"It has only just begun," Salt said, without looking at us.

— 19 —

We stopped under the large barn's overhang before we stepped back out into the weather.

"Save some walking around in the rain," I said. "Best place to figure out who's doing what would be the Boston House."

"Wallis?" Virgil said.

"Not much gets by him," I said.

Virgil nodded.

We left the barn and crossed over some long boards lying in the mud to the opposite side of Main Street and we walked up to the boardwalk to the Boston House Hotel.

The Boston House had experienced many changes through the years, but it was still the finest hotel in town. With business flourishing in Appaloosa, the hotel was more often than not sold out.

When we arrived at the hotel the streetside saloon

doors were closed, so we entered through the main entrance.

Tilda, the long-standing waitress of the establishment, was busy serving breakfast to a dining room full of hotel guests.

"Look who's here," I said.

I didn't need to say it. Virgil saw everything, always.

"Yep," Virgil said, without looking directly at Beauregard, sitting at a corner table with young Nell.

"Your old friend," I said.

Virgil smiled a little.

"And his tender kindle," I said.

Virgil nodded without looking at them.

Beauregard followed Nell's look in our direction just as Tilda greeted us.

I tipped my hat toward them, but Virgil's attention was elsewhere.

Nell smiled. Beauregard looked to her.

"Hello, Marshal Cole," Tilda said. "Deputy Marshal Hitch."

"How do, Tilda," Virgil said.

"Tilda," I said, as I removed my hat.

"Breakfast?" she said.

"Not at the moment," Virgil said.

He looked toward the saloon doors.

"Wallis in?" Virgil said.

"I believe he just got here."

Tilda set her tray down and pulled open the tall sliding pocket doors that separated the dining area from the saloon.

"Wallis?" she called.

"What?" Wallis said from the back room.

"Marshal Cole and Deputy Marshal Hitch are here."

"Thank you, Tilda," Virgil said.

"You want some coffee?" Tilda said, as Virgil and I entered the saloon.

"No," Virgil said. "Thank you, Tilda."

Wallis walked out of the back room.

"Well, hellfire," Wallis said. "If it's not the both of you."

"Morning, Wallis," Virgil said.

"Seen Hitch here the other night, but you've neglected to so much as stop by here and say hello."

"Gone sensitive, Wallis?" Virgil said.

"I have indeed," Wallis said. "Nightly I've been crying myself to sleep like a baby."

Wallis smiled big.

"Early for the two of you," he said, as he glided his big body around the copper-topped mahogany counter. "What can I get ya?"

Virgil shook his head.

"Just want to ask you," Virgil said. "Know anything about a soldiering outfit in town?"

"Some," Wallis said. "Just heard some about that last night."

"What some?" Virgil said.

"My understanding," Wallis said. "Some settlers were killed on the rut and they're looking for who did it."

"Know where the soldiers are?" Virgil said.

"Dag's Hotel, I think. Were, anyway."

Virgil nodded. He looked around the barroom a little before he looked to me.

I nodded.

"Thank you, Wallis," I said.

"You came back in," Wallis said. "Let's do some reminiscing."

"'Bout what?" Virgil said.

"'Bout the price of rice in China, Virgil," Wallis said. "What else?"

Virgil smiled.

We turned and walked back to the exit. When we got to the doors separating the bar from the dining area, Beauregard and Nell were on their way out. Beauregard halted, looking at us, and smiled.

— 20 —

Hello, gentlemen," Beauregard said. "I would attempt to shake your hand again, Marshal Cole, but I understand your reasons for not putting yourself at risk of something sudden and unwarranted."

"No reason," Virgil said.

"Not that I'm a risk," he said with a big grin.

"Good to know," Virgil said.

Beauregard looked to Nell.

"I'm a lamb, aren't I, dear?"

She smiled. It was a nervous smile.

Beauregard placed his fists on both sides of his hips, pulling back his frock coat, then nodded to Nell.

"Nell, here, noticed the two of you right away when you walked in. Fact, you got her attention real good at the town hall, too. She told me after we met you that you both seemed to be men of substance. Instantly, didn't you, dear?"

Virgil didn't say anything.

I nodded to her and smiled.

She smiled, then glanced to Beauregard with ill-disguised irritation.

"Isn't that right, dear?" he said.

She smiled weakly.

"Isn't it?" he said.

"Yes," she said, as she lifted her chin and pulled her shoulders back.

"My wife has an eye for men of substance," he said. "Don't you, dear?"

She didn't say anything.

"Don't you?"

She looked down, then to the door and back to Beauregard.

"Yes," she said.

"Yes," Beauregard said, as if he were a slave trader talking to his stock. "She has an eye."

Nell just looked away.

"Marshal Cole," Beauregard said. "I must say your lady friend, your significant other, is just lovely beyond lovely. Don't you think, dear?"

"She is," Nell said. ". . . Allison."

Virgil nodded a little.

"Yes, Allison," Beauregard said. "Just beautiful."

Virgil nodded. He didn't want to nod but he did and he also didn't want to say anything but he did that, too.

"She is."

"Lovely lady," Beauregard said. "Right, dear?"

"Yes," Nell said.

"She was so welcoming," he said. "The whole ladies' social, too. Allison told me if we needed anything, anything at all, don't hesitate to ask."

Virgil didn't say anything.

"Appaloosa's a friendly place," I said.

"Not completely," Beauregard said, leaning in like he had a secret to tell. "I understand there was a skirmish on the street. An altercation that left a man shot."

"We don't tolerate no-goods," Virgil said.

"Indeed, Marshal, indeed," he said, then looked to Nell. "Men of substance and quick resolve, my dear. You do have a good eye."

Beauregard was a first-class shit, and I could tell Virgil had had his fill.

"You folks have a good day," I said.

"We will," he said, "and rest assured just as soon as this darn weather clears we'll be bringing your fine friendly city some delightful friendly entertainment."

"No doubt," I said.

Virgil tipped his hat.

"Ma'am."

I followed him out the door. We turned to the west and walked up the boardwalk toward Dag's Hotel.

"Early to be hitting the bottle," I said.

"Not for the by-God glorious Beauregard Beauchamp," Virgil said.

— 21 —

Dag's Hotel was on the west side of Appaloosa, across the tracks. It was a dingy place where mining crews stayed. Two big miner boys walked out as Virgil and I entered.

The lobby smelled of tobacco and whiskey. The room was cluttered with café tables and twenty-gallon barrels for chairs. Spittoons were scattered about under the tables, and the walls were devoid of any kind of hanging decoration with the exception of a stuffed buffalo sporting a lady's pink bonnet.

A counter lined the back of the lobby, with a set of stairs behind it leading up to the rooms. A potbellied stove sat in the corner with pots of coffee sitting on top.

Sitting at a table by the window was a bearded old-timer, wearing overalls and a train engineer's cap. He was sipping coffee from a tin cup and scribbling intently in a notebook.

Virgil and I made our way through the tables to the counter, where a tough-looking heavyset woman was perched on a stool. She looked a little more like a man than a woman, and when she spoke her voice was raspy.

"How do," she said. "You fellas looking for a room?"

She was missing a few teeth, both top and bottom, and it gave her raspy voice a slight whistle when she spoke.

"No," I said.

I pulled back my slicker and coat lapel and showed her my badge.

"We're marshals," I said.

She looked back and forth between Virgil and me.

"Oh," she said. "I've heard about you two. Name's Sandy. How can I help you?"

"We're looking for some soldiers," I said.

Sandy shook her head.

"Had some soldiers here, but they done left."

"When did they leave?" I said.

"This morning."

"Time?" Virgil said.

"Early, just after daylight."

"Say where they were headed?" Virgil said.

"No," she said.

"Say anything?" I said.

"They didn't say much of anything. They got here, 'bout, oh, noon yesterday, were wet as rats. They dried out, came and went a little bit in the afternoon and evening for food and whiskey and such, but they're gone now."

"You saw them this morning?" Virgil said.

"I did," she said. "They sat in here, had some coffee but stayed to themselves. Weren't the friendliest soldiers I ever met."

"Don't think they're soldiers," the old man in the engineer's cap said.

We turned, looking at the old-timer.

"What's that?" I said.

"Before I took on with the Santa Fe," he said. "I spent most my born days with the blue."

"That's Jasper," Sandy said. "Don't listen to him. He don't got both oars in the water."

"Said the barn hog to the wild piglet," Jasper said.

"Don't you go on with your storytelling and name-calling, you old fool, or I'll throw you out on your ass," Sandy said, and then leaned across the desk on her elbow. "He don't work for the railroad no more, they cut him loose 'cause he's nuttier than a pecan pie."

"Don't listen to her," Jasper said. "I got my suspicions about those soldiers, or one of them, anyway. Which makes me think the lot of them was nothing but gray-back rebel blue dressers."

"Jasper," Sandy said. "Hush."

Virgil moved toward the old man a step.

"What makes you say that?" Virgil said. "They were dressers."

"'Cause I know soldiers."

"Go on," Virgil said, taking another step toward the old man.

"I was sitting right here. One of 'em walked in last night. I talked to him," Jasper said.

"What'd he say?" Virgil said.

"He was full of shit," Jasper said.

"He say anything about them being after a raiding party?" Virgil said.

"He did," Jasper said.

"What'd he say?"

"They'd been dispatched to look for a party that robbed and murdered some settlers on the trail."

I moved away from the counter and Virgil and I walked a little closer to Jasper.

"He offer up any details about that?" I said.

Jasper shook his head.

"No."

"Why do you think he's full of shit?" I said.

"I asked him a few questions about his outfit, where all he'd been stationed. He was plum full of shit."

"What did he tell you?"

"Said he was from Colorado," Jasper said. "From Fort Lewis. I told him, well, hell, I knew Big Bill of Fort Lewis."

"Bill?" Virgil said.

"Lieutenant Colonel William Lewis was a friend of mine," Jasper said. "Fort Lewis was named after him."

Virgil looked to me.

"So what gave you suspicion?" I said.

"He told me he didn't know Bill, but that he'd met him at the fort in the past. *Ha.*"

"And you didn't believe him?" Virgil said.

"Nope."

Virgil looked at me.

"Why?" I asked.

"Bill never set foot in Fort Lewis. He was dead. He got killed before the goddamn fort was even built," Jasper said. "They just constructed the fort and put his damn name on top the gate."

"This soldier fella," Virgil said. "He the only one you talked to?"

"Yep," Jasper said. "And like I tell ya. He was no soldier, he was a dumb shit. Dressers, I figure, the lot of 'em."

— 22 —

Virgil and I left Dag's Hotel and walked in the rain toward the tracks.

"By God," Virgil said.

"What do you allow?" I said.

"Think the old man might not be nuttier than a pecan pie," Virgil said.

"Me, too."

"There was something about them boys," I said. "Something about them didn't seem right when I saw them riding into town."

"Like what?"

"Don't know," I said. "I didn't really think about it then. They were rough-looking. Didn't give it much thought, but in hindsight and with Old Man Jasper's summation I suspect they are no-goods that are up to no good."

"'Spect you're right," Virgil said.

"What kind of no-good is the question," I said.

"Is," Virgil said.

"So these boys come into town, haggard like they were, and tell people they're on a searching party?"

Virgil nodded.

"What do they gain by that?" I said.

"Validatin' their existence," Virgil said.

Virgil and I made our way to the sheriff's office. When we arrived, Book was sitting behind the desk and Clay Chastain, Sheriff Driskill's senior deputy that had been laid up with a stomach bug, was sitting across from him.

We could see Bolger through the door separating the office from the cells. He was lying on the bunk, facing the wall.

"Howdy, Virgil, Everett," Chastain said with his extra-long drawl. "Sorry as all hell I been under the damn weather, but I'm back. Back in the damn weather now."

Chastain was a tough, rawboned man from Dallas, Texas. He had a scar across his face that traveled from above his eyebrow to the top of his jawbone. Chastain had an edge of intimidation to his demeanor that worked in his favor as an officer.

"Is some weather," Virgil said. "Ain't it?"

Chastain nodded.

"Damn sure is," Chastain said.

"Good you're back," Virgil said.

"Book said you were looking for some soldiers?" Chastain said.

"We were," Virgil said.

"Find 'em?"

"Didn't," Virgil said.

"Think they pulled out," I said.

Chastain looked to Book.

"Book said something about settlers being attacked and the soldiers were on the hunt."

"That's the word they shared with a few people around town," Virgil said.

Chastain looked back and forth between Virgil and me.

"You mean you two weren't notified?" Chastain said. "No telegraph?"

"Weren't," I said.

"That don't make sense," Chastain said.

"That's how we see it, too," I said.

Chastain nodded a little and sat back in his chair. He looked over to Bolger on the bunk in his cell.

"Know all about the scuffle," Chastain said, tilting his head to Bolger. "Good you got him."

I nodded.

"Glad to know this sonofabitch is locked up," Chastain said.

"Fuck you," Bolger said, turning from facing the wall to look at Chastain.

"I don't care you been wounded," Chastain said slowly and calmly. "I'll come in there and bust your ass up so bad you'd wish you been shot dead by Hitch. Keep yer ass quiet and don't test me."

"Wait till my brother gets wind of this," Bolger said.

Chastain rose out of his chair with ease and walked slowly to the door between the cell and office.

"Where is this brother of yours you keep going on about?" Chastain said kindly.

"Ha," Bolger said. "Fixin' to come down on all of you like a Gila monster on sun frogs."

Chastain hooked his thumbs just on both sides of his belt buckle.

"Shut yer ass up," Chastain said smoothly. "Not one more word."

Bolger snarled a little and rolled back over on his side facing the wall and Chastain closed the thick wooden door between them. The wall separating the cells from the main office was thick stucco and the door was three inches of oak. When it was closed the prisoners couldn't hear any office business and the officers didn't have to listen to the prisoners snore or bellyache.

Virgil looked to Book.

"Any news from Driskill, from the bridge?"

Book shook his head.

"Nope," Book said. "Nothing, Marshal."

"Peculiar. Awful peculiar," I said.

— 23 —

The dark clouds Virgil and I had watched coming in behind the Beauchamp Brothers Theatrical Extravaganza had settled in over Appaloosa to stay.

It had been rainy and dark for three solid days and each day grew darker, colder, and wetter than the previous. The streets were muddy from boardwalk to boardwalk and in some places they were completely covered up with water.

I stood under the awning of a drilling office near the park where the troupe was camped. I mulled over the idea of moseying over and knocking on the trailer door of Madame Séraphine Leroux's trailer, but I talked myself out of the notion.

The troupe hadn't had a chance to set up their tent, and if they had it was doubtful there'd be much of an audience for the show with the weather like it was. It was cold out now, and with the temperature continuing to drop, it seemed certain the rain would be turning to snow soon.

I walked back to a billiard place I like to visit now and again called The Racket on Fifth Street.

I played a few games of straight with some Irish fella that had stopped over in Appaloosa hoping the weather would clear before he continued his travels south. After I took him of a few dollars he left and I started up a series of yellow ball, red ball with the skinny old talkative court clerk named Curtis Whittlesey. The Racket was normally a quiet establishment, but because Curtis liked to talk and then talk some more, it wasn't as pleasantly peaceful as I liked.

It was hard for Curtis to let silence linger too long, but he was a fair player, so I put up with him.

"Millicent is from Milwaukee," Curtis said. "You ever met anyone from Milwaukee, Everett?"

Curtis didn't give me time to answer. In fact, I don't think he gave a shit whether I'd ever met anyone from Milwaukee or not.

"Folks from Milwaukee are different," Curtis said. "Take Millicent, for example. You know what she does every Tuesday, Thursday, and Saturday?"

Curtis answered for me.

"Daybreak, she walks around this town three times. All the way around Appaloosa, three times, every Tuesday, Thursday, and Saturday. Says it helps her connection joints and constitution. Ha. Constitution, hell. Helps me that she's out of the damn house and I have some morning peace and quiet. I'll tell you something, Everett, peace and quiet is damn sure a hard commodity to come by these days. 'Course, Millicent hasn't been out of the house since this weather set in, so it just been . . . well, it's been downright suffocating."

"Your shot," I said.

"Oh," Curtis said.

Curtis chalked his stick, leaned over the table, and lined up a shot.

"You're yellow."

"Oh," Curtis said. "Yes."

Curtis surveyed his options and lined up his shot on a yellow ball. He planted his tongue firmly between his teeth, stroked his pool cue a few strokes, took his shot and missed.

"Shit," Curtis said. "Weather's fault, Everett. Bad goddamn weather."

"No doubt," I said, as I walked around the table.

"I tell you, it is just plain goddamn bad," Curtis said. "Millicent hasn't been to the coops because of the damn puddle behind the house in two days. I told her when we built we should have put the foundation on higher ground but she wouldn't listen to me. I told her all them chickens would most likely drown before this was all over."

Curtis kept talking as I lined up a shot in the corner pocket, and made it. I put good inside low English on it and brought the cue ball back just exactly where I wanted it and lined up my next red ball.

My time at West Point was not entirely wasted on learning soldiering. I spent many of my off days shooting call shot and carom, and made myself into a pretty fair hand around the felt.

"Good shot," Curtis said, and then went directly back into his ramble about the rain, his house, and his wife.

The door opened and deputy Skinny Jack entered, wearing his wet oilskin slicker. He removed his rain-soaked derby.

"Excuse me, Mr. Whittlesey . . . um, Deputy Marshal Hitch?" Skinny Jack said, looking to me as he pulled water from his scruffy goatee. "Western Union operator Charlie Hill brought over a wire just now for Marshal Cole."

"'Spect he's at the house, Skinny Jack."

"I figured I'd find you first."

"What is it?"

"From the way station, near the bridge camp," Skinny Jack said, as he turned his hat nervously.

"Sheriff Driskill find Lonnie?"

Skinny Jack shook his head.

"Something bad has happened," Skinny Jack said.

"What?" I said.

"Some people have been killed."

Skinny Jack looked to Curtis, then back to me.

"Go on," I said.

"There was an attack at the Rio Blanco Bridge."

"What kind of attack?"

"The bridge . . . has been . . . blown up."

"Good God," Curtis said.

"What?"

Skinny Jack nodded.

"Why on earth?" Curtis said.

Skinny Jack shook his head.

"Don't know. That's what the telegram said. Somebody blew up the bridge. I left the wire in the office on account I didn't want to get it all wet and smudge out what was on it, but the bridge was blown up and some people were killed."

"When?"

"Two days back," Skinny Jack said.

"And this telegram was just received?" I said.

Skinny Jack nodded.

"Note said the wire had been cut," Skinny Jack said. "I suspect it took that long to find the break, fix it. I don't know. All I know is what was on the wire."

"Good God," Curtis said again.

"Wire from Sheriff Driskill?" I said.

"No," Skinny Jack said. "It was from the way station operator."

"Where are Sheriff Driskill and the other deputies, Karl and Chip?" I said.

"No word," Skinny Jack said with a gulp.

— 24 —

This news of the bridge disaster temporarily shut Curtis up. Silence swelled in the billiard room for a moment as the thought of what Skinny Jack said lingered.

"My God," Curtis said. "That bridge was a massive construction. Tons of wood and iron well over two hundred feet long . . . my God."

Skinny Jack nodded.

"Who was killed?" I said.

Skinny Jack just shook his head.

"Goodness," Curtis said. "Was G. W. Cox one of them?"

Skinny Jack shook his head.

"I don't know, the telegram didn't say."

"What do you know about G. W. Cox?" I said.

"He's the Rio Blanco contractor, wealthiest man in Appaloosa these days. Was an attorney from Philadelphia, a damn fine one, but he's in the contracting business now," Curtis said. "His company was the one that won the territory bid to build the bridge."

"Any back and forth with telegrams?" I said to Skinny Jack.

"No," Skinny Jack said. "Just the one, then I came to find you. It's just plumb awful. Two of my good friends was working there."

"Curtis?"

Curtis looked at me, raising his nose up a bit.

"This G. W. Cox," I said. "He live here, in Appaloosa?"

"He does," Curtis said. "Unless he's on the road. He travels a lot, back east."

"He spend time at the bridge?"

"He's the contractor, like I said, so he's there some," Curtis said. "At least I would imagine so."

"You know where he is now?"

"I think he's here," Curtis said, "in Appaloosa, but I don't know for certain."

"You know where he lives?"

"Why, yes," Curtis said. "He lives in the big house at the top of Fourth Street."

I nodded and set my cue down flat on the table.

"I know you have a gift of gab, Curtis," I said. "And under most circumstances it don't bother me none too much, but under this particular circumstance I need you to keep your mouth shut about this."

Curtis looked at me like I'd hurt his feelings as I put on my slicker.

"Understand?" I said.

"Oh, why, yes," Curtis said. "Goddamn, sure, Everett, sure. Not to be shared. That I understand. Completely. I won't say a thing to anybody, Everett, I promise."

"Good," I said.

"This is just awful, though, just awful," Curtis said. "Millicent and I were by there on our way back from visiting her sister. We watched them work on the bridge for a while . . . it's massive . . . my God . . . was massive . . ."

Curtis kept talking as I snugged on my hat. He followed Skinny Jack and me to the door. I opened the door and stepped out into the worsening weather. Skinny Jack followed, closing the door behind us, silencing Curtis.

We crossed the muddy street in the sleeting rain to the opposite boardwalk and walked south toward the sheriff's office.

When we got in the office the door to the cells was open and Bolger was on his bunk, snoring away with his mouth open. I closed the door separating us from Bolger, and Book got up from the desk and handed me the telegram. Book and Skinny Jack looked over my shoulder as I read.

"This is heinous, is it not, Deputy Marshal Hitch?" Book said.

"What's that mean?" Skinny Jack said.

"Um . . . wicked," Book said.

"It most certainly is, Book," I said, then folded the

telegram and put it in the dryness of my shirt pocket. "It most certainly is."

I retrieved my eight-gauge from the gun rack. I'd been keeping the double barrel in the office for safekeeping since our return to Appaloosa.

"Where's Chastain?"

"Walking the town," Book said.

"He know about this?" I said.

Skinny Jack shook his head.

"Not yet," Skinny Jack said. "I came looking for you right away, didn't see him 'fore I found you."

Book moved his big body to the window with his hands shoved in the front pockets of his baggy trousers.

"Who could have done this?" Book said.

"Hard to say," I said.

"You think the attackers might come here to Appaloosa?" Book said.

Book remained looking out the window.

"Come here and try and do something heinous?" Book said.

"Naw," Skinny Jack said. "That ain't gonna happen, be foolish to try that. We got too many people."

"They could actually be here," Book said, wide-eyed. "A lot of people come and go in and out of Appaloosa, Skinny Jack. They could be here now, right amongst us, and we'd never know it."

Skinny Jack looked at Book for a moment and his Adam's apple moved up then down in his throat as he considered Book's assessment.

"Maybe Sheriff Driskill, Karl, and Chip caught who-ever did this?" Skinny Jack said hopefully.

I grabbed my shell belt and strapped it on.

"Maybe," I said.

Book and Skinny Jack followed me as I moved to the door.

"What will you do?" Book said.

"Get Virgil. Figure, sort things out," I said, as I opened the door, meeting the cold air.

"What should we do?" Book said.

"Find Chastain, let him know," I said. "Get my horse and Virgil's horse saddled and ready. Get panniers on one of the mules, too. Pack some feed, kindling, coffee, grub, medicines, hand tools, and get us some blankets, cold-weather coats and gloves from the locker."

Book nodded and looked out the door past me.

"Snowing," Book said.

"Is," I said.

— 25 —

I walked the wet streets in the falling snow to Virgil and Allie's place. I could see embers rising from the chimney and could smell the wood burning in their fireplace as I neared. I walked up the steps and knocked on the door. After a moment Allie looked out the window. I waved to her and she opened the door, holding a glass of whiskey.

"Everett, how about this? Snow."

"Yes, it is."

"What a pleasant surprise," she said with a little slur. "Come on in."

She leaned close and kissed me on the cheek next to my lips. I could smell the whiskey on her breath.

"Where's Virgil?"

"He's out back getting some wood for the fire."

She held up her glass.

"Having a nightcap, would you care for one?"

I shut the door and leaned my eight-gauge on the wall next to the jamb.

"Sure."

"Make yourself comfortable," Allie said.

I took off my slicker and hat and hung them on the coat rack. Allie retrieved a glass from the breakfront in the dining room and poured me some whiskey.

"What brings you to see us?" she said.

Thankfully, Virgil entered from the back door carrying a bundle of scrap lumber in his arms and diverted the necessity of me needing to answer Allie's question.

"Everett," Virgil said.

"Virgil. Got it going, I see?"

"Did."

"Drawing okay?"

"It is," Virgil said.

"Guess those German boys knew what they were doing," I said.

Virgil crossed the room and set the wood down near the hearth.

"Gotcha a nudge?" he said.

"Do," I said, holding up the glass.

Virgil looked over, noticing my eight-gauge near the door. He stood up straight with his shoulders back, looking at me.

"Something up?" he said.

"Bad doings, Virgil," I said.

I removed the telegram from my shirt pocket and handed it to Virgil.

"From the way station near the bridge," I said.

"Driskill find that Lonnie fella?"

"Read," I said.

Virgil unfolded the telegram and leaned close to the fireplace for better light.

"What is it, Everett?" Allie said.

Virgil read the telegram, then looked to me, shaking his head.

"Goddamn," Virgil said.

"What is it, Virgil?" Allie said.

"Two days ago," Virgil said.

I nodded.

"What is it, Virgil?" Allie said again.

"It appears there's been some people killed, Allie," Virgil said.

"Oh," Allie said. "My goodness."

Allie looked back and forth between Virgil and me.

"Who? What people?"

"At the bridge," Virgil said. "On the Rio Blanco."

"Who, at the bridge?"

"Don't say," Virgil said. "Says the bridge has been destroyed."

"*What?*"

"What it says," Virgil said.

"May I," Allie said, holding out her hand for the telegram. "No reason to keep me in the dark."

Virgil looked at me, then handed the telegram to Allie.

Allie read the note.

"Lord," Allie said. "The bridge has been blown up, payroll robbed, and some folks have been killed. Oh my God, Virgil."

She walked quickly to the front door and looked outside, craning her neck. Then she turned back, looking at us. She reread the telegram and shook her head.

"This is awful."

Virgil got the telegram from Allie. He walked back near the fireplace and read it again.

"Had to be Indians," Allie said. "Savages. My God. Those poor, poor people."

"Not, Allie," Virgil said.

"Well," Allie said. "Surely you don't think white men did this, do you?"

"I do," Virgil said.

"Indians are not too inclined to go about blowing things up, Allie," I said.

Virgil looked at the telegram, then looked up to me. He walked back and forth in front of the fireplace for a moment.

"When was this?" Virgil said, holding up the telegram.

"Tonight."

Virgil looked at the telegram and shook his head a little.

"Any other correspondence with the operator?"

"No."

Virgil nodded a little.

"Let's get geared up, Everett," Virgil said, "get over there."

"I got Skinny Jack and Book outfitting us now," I said.

"Tonight?" Allie said with alarm.

Virgil was already walking off down the hall, heading for the back room, when he answered.

"Yes, Allie," he said. "Tonight."

"What about me?" Allie called out to Virgil down the hall. "You can't just leave me here with dynamiting murderers on the loose."

"This happened a long ways away, Allie," I said. "Bridge is a day's ride from here."

"No matter," Allie said.

"Can't take you with us, Allie," Virgil called from the back room.

"There's always something taking you away from me. Sometimes I wonder if you want bad things to happen so you and Everett can go off and be heroes."

"Oh, hell, Allie," I said. "You know better than that."

"Well," Allie said, "it's just that I've gotten used to you being here. Having y'all here makes this lonely place a home."

"It's what we do, Allie," Virgil replied, walking back up the hall and into the room with his gun belt.

"Oh, for God sake, Virgil. You always say that."

Virgil didn't say anything as he strapped on his holster.

"Well, Allie, this is an obvious inextricable circum-stance," I said.

"Whatever that means, Everett," Allie said with a huff. "Don't mean you need to speak for Virgil."

"He's not speaking for me, Allie," Virgil said.

"Is too," Allie said.

— 26 —

Virgil and I left Allie standing behind the front door.

"Don't want to step into some kind of trap," Virgil said, as we descended the steps and started walking to the sheriff's office.

I glanced back. I could see Allie through the falling snow. She was looking out the door, watching us walking away.

"Who'd want to trap us?"

"Don't know," Virgil said, "but you can't always believe what you read."

"You don't think this has happened?"

"Not saying that," Virgil said. "Most likely it has. Just don't want to go riding in there because someone has asked for us to come. Not without knowing a few things we don't."

"Like what?"

"Driskill and his deputies should have been there by noon yesterday," Virgil said.

"Unless they ran into some trouble."

"Yep," Virgil said.

"The telegraph line being cut," I said, "makes sense why the butter-churning woman, Winifred, wasn't getting any response from the way station regarding the whereabouts of her husband, Lonnie."

"Does," Virgil said.

The snow was coming down pretty solid as we crossed the street and stepped onto the boardwalk.

"What do you want to do?" I said.

"Start with," Virgil said. "We send a wire back to the bridge way station."

"Rattle the cage?"

"Yep."

"See what is what?" I said. "Find out what we can."

"Yep."

Virgil and I walked to the sheriff's office and Book met us at the door.

"Skinny Jack's getting you ready," Book said.

"Seen Chastain yet?" I said.

"No, sir."

"Where can we find the Western Union operator that received this telegram this time of night?" I said.

"Right there at the office, that's Charlie Hill," Book said. "Should be there. He has a room there, just behind the office. Charlie and his little brother are both operators. They both live there."

Virgil and I walked up the street two blocks to the

Western Union office and I knocked on the door. The office was dark, but we could see light through the crack of a door at the rear of the office. I knocked again and then the door at the back of the office opened and a young man came out wearing his nightclothes and carrying a finger lantern. He set the lantern down and put on a pair of spectacles.

He looked out the door window and I showed him my badge.

"Oh," he said, opening the door. "Marshal Cole, Deputy Marshal Hitch. I figured I might be seeing you. Come in."

"You're Charlie?" I said.

He nodded.

"I am," he said. "Awful news."

"Anybody else know about this besides you?" Virgil said.

"No," Charlie said. "Well, my brother, and Deputies Book and Skinny Jack."

"Nobody else?" I said.

"No," Charlie said. "My brother and I are professional operators, not town gossips."

Virgil nodded.

"So the way station had been unresponsive, not communicative for a while?" I said.

"Yes, sir, it was, until the wire came in this evening about the bridge."

"The operator in now," Virgil said. "This time of night?"

"Should be," Charlie said. "They stay there."

"There more than one operator?" I said.

"Yes," Charlie said. "Like here and like most places. I know both the operators there. Well, I know them from all the correspondence. Husband and wife, Pedrick and Patty."

"I want to send a wire," Virgil said.

"Oh, well, sure," Charlie said.

Charlie was a small fella with thin hair and delicate features. He sat behind his desk and looked up to Virgil.

Virgil said, "Just write, 'Appaloosa law enforcement, wanting to know the . . .'"

Virgil looked to me.

"Status of workers and damage?" I said.

Virgil nodded to Charlie.

Charlie rubbed his hands together, pounded out the note on the key, then got to his feet.

"Be right back," Charlie said. "Kind of on the cold side. Get my robe."

Charlie ducked into the back room and came out a second later, tying the belt of the robe around his waist and carrying a pair of slippers. He dropped the slippers on the floor, slid his feet into them, then sat back at the telegraph desk and faced the key and sounder.

We all focused on the sounder and within a minute it went off and Charlie wrote the note.

"'Cleanup has been under way . . . Bridge completely gone.'"

Virgil looked at me.

"Respond, 'Has Sheriff Driskill been seen at the bridge camp?'" Virgil said.

I nodded.

Charlie keyed the note. Waited and then replied, when the sounder replied.

Charlie relayed the code.

"'No report of Sheriff Driskill of recent,'" Charlie said. "'Can check with camp and let you know right away.'"

Charlie looked up to Virgil and me.

"The way station is about thirty minutes from the bridge, so some of what will be in response may not be immediate."

Virgil nodded.

"How many dead, injured?" Virgil said.

Charlie keyed out the note and the sounder immediately sounded back.

"'Three dead,'" Charlie said. "'No injuries.'"

"Who were the raiders?" Virgil said.

Charlie tapped out Virgil's request and then spoke out the words as he wrote the sounder's reply.

"'It is uncertain who they were or how many . . . Dynamite placed on the bridge in the night . . . Bombers blew up bridge in the a.m. . . . Three men, early workers, were on the bridge . . . They were casualties of the explosion.'"

"Is G. W. Cox on location?"

Virgil looked at me.

"Curtis Whittlesey said Cox is the contractor," I said. "Was an attorney, been here for a while in Appaloosa and won the bid to build the bridge."

Virgil nodded.

Charlie keyed the note.

The sounder sounded back and Charlie shook his head.

"'As of an hour ago, last report, Mr. Cox was not at the bridge,'" Charlie said.

— 27 —

It was close to midnight by the time Virgil and I left the Western Union office.

"Why would somebody do this?" I said.

"Got to be some reason," Virgil said.

We stayed on the porch and watched it snow for a moment, thinking.

"Cox lives in the big house on the corner of Fourth Street," I said. "Maybe we let him know about this?"

Virgil nodded.

"Maybe he knows something," I said. "Something we need to know."

Virgil nodded.

"Maybe," he said, and we stepped off the porch.

We walked to Cox's place. It was a three-story structure toward the north end of town. We climbed the dark steps and I knocked on the door.

It took a while before a light appeared at the top

of the steps. Slowly a man descended and came to the door.

"Territorial marshals," I said. "Mr. Cox?"

We heard the door handle twist. It cracked open a little and a small black man peered out at us.

"No, sir," he said. "I'm Mr. Cox's butler, Jessup. Mr. Cox is asleep."

"We need to talk to him," Virgil said.

"Now?" Jessup said.

"Now," Virgil said.

"Let him know it's important," I said.

Jessup looked to me, then to Virgil, and opened the door.

"Come in," he said. "This way, please."

Jessup led us. We walked through a set of doors leading into a stately office with books from floor to ceiling. Jessup set the lamp down and lit two lamps that were sitting on the corners of a huge desk.

"I'll get Mr. Cox," Jessup said.

Cox's office was a shrine to his accomplishments. We walked around the room, looking at all the books.

"Goddamn library," I said.

"Is," Virgil said.

Behind the desk were gilded framed placards. I moved closer to read them.

"Graduate of Harvard University," I said. "Certificate of excellence from Philadelphia Law. He's no slouch."

"Look here," Virgil said.

I walked over to where Virgil was standing near the front window. Tacked on the wall were drawings of the

Rio Blanco Bridge and sitting on a table in front of the window was an impressive wooden model of the bridge.

"Damn," I said. "Something."

"Was," Virgil said.

"Yep."

"No more," Virgil said.

"Goddamn shame," I said.

"Lot of work," Virgil said.

We heard footsteps coming down the stairs, and in a moment G. W. Cox walked into the office, followed by Jessup.

Cox was very tall and thin, with broad shoulders. He was wearing a proper English robe with velvet lapels over a dark-colored silk sleeping gown. He looked to be in his mid-sixties. His hair was silver but his eyebrows, sideburns, and mustache were dark. His nose was long and pointed, with a high ridge in the middle. He had an instant, distinguished air of sophistication about him.

"Gentlemen?" Cox said in a deep southern baritone. "Jessup here said you men need to see me."

"We do," Virgil said.

Virgil stayed near the window next to the bridge model, and I moved toward Cox.

"We're territorial marshals out of Appaloosa," I said. "I'm Deputy Marshal Everett Hitch and this is Marshal Virgil Cole."

"G. W. Cox," he said.

I shook his hand.

"What is it? What's happened?"

I looked to Virgil.

"We got word," Virgil said. "A telegram from the Rio Blanco Bridge way station. Two days ago, the bridge was destroyed. Three men dead."

Cox didn't say anything right away. He just looked at us with a blank expression on his face.

"I'm sorry?" Cox said with his slow, long drawl. "Could you repeat that? Two days ago, *whhhuuut*?"

— 28 —

Virgil nodded to the model in front of the window.

"This bridge was blown up," Virgil said. "Three men died, they were killed."

Cox shook his head.

"This can't be," Cox said.

Virgil nodded.

"'Fraid so," Virgil said.

"Two days ago?" Cox said.

Virgil nodded.

"Any idea who would do this?" Virgil said.

Cox looked to the floor for a long moment. He shook his head slightly, then walked to the big desk and dropped into his chair.

"Leave us, Jessup," Cox said.

Jessup just looked at Cox for a moment.

"Now," Cox said. "I don't need you standing there looking like you are looking. Just leave."

"Certainly, Mr. Cox, sir," Jessup said, and closed the doors behind him.

"You know this to be a fact?" Cox said.

"Not seen it firsthand," Virgil said, "but that was the telegram."

Cox placed both of his hands squarely on the desk in front of him.

"Why am I just receiving this information?" Cox said.

"The lines were down," I said.

"Just recently fixed," Virgil said.

"When the communication connection was reestablished," I said, "we were contacted."

Cox stared at me blankly.

"To confirm, we made contact with the way station just a while ago," I said. "The bridge being blown up and deaths were confirmed."

"Got any idea why somebody'd do this?" Virgil said.

Cox looked away, then leveled a look at Virgil but didn't respond to Virgil's question.

"You got enemies?" Virgil said.

"I've spent most my life putting people in jail, Marshal," Cox said. "I have plenty of enemies."

Cox stood. He put his hands in the pockets of his Englishman's robe and walked slowly over to the bridge model. He looked at the model with a sad expression on his face as he shook his head slightly from side to side.

"Walton Wayne Swickey," Cox said.

"Who's Walton Wayne Swickey?" Virgil said.

Cox stared at the bridge model, not saying anything.

Virgil looked to me, then back to Cox.

"Who is Walton Wayne Swickey?" Virgil said again.

"A powerful, money-grubbing man," Cox said.

"Where would we find him?" Virgil said.

Cox shook his head.

"I don't know."

Virgil looked to the model, then to Cox.

"Why?" Virgil said. "Why would he do this?"

"Because I got the bid to build the bridge and he did not."

"Any other reason?" Virgil said.

"Like what?" Cox said.

"You tell me," Virgil said.

"I can't imagine any reasons," Cox said.

"No other bad blood between the two of you?" Virgil said.

"No," Cox said. "Nothing I'm aware of. I never knew the man until I bid against him, did not know him from Adam. I was warned, when I went up against him, though, that he was a ruthless, not-to-be-trusted son-ofabitch."

Cox looked back to the model and shook his head.

"But this?" Cox said. "Why anyone would do something so atrocious as this, Marshal, is beyond me. Even Swickey. Losing a goddamn contract? Well, hell, that offers no logical reason, or explanation for such awful nonsense as this, no matter how burned or scorned one might be. Just nonsense."

"He live here," I said. "In Appaloosa?"

Cox shook his head some.

"I don't know. He was here for the bidding," Cox said. "Not sure where he lives, though."

"You have no idea?" I said.

"No."

"And no idea of his whereabouts?"

"No, I don't know where he is," Cox said. "I've not seen him, but I'm not around here full time. In fact, I just returned to Appaloosa last week."

"From?" Virgil said.

"Philadelphia."

"When was the last time you saw Swickey?" I said.

"The day I was awarded the contract to build the bridge and he was not."

"What were your parting words?" I said.

"No words," Cox said. "He just smiled at me. A devil's smile, conjured up from the bowels of hell."

— 29 —

What now?" Cox said.

"Everett and me are riding over there," Virgil said. "Have a look at this firsthand."

"When?"

"Subsequently," Virgil said.

"I'll go with you," Cox said.

"Not necessary," Virgil said.

"Might not be," Cox said, "but I insist."

"Conditions are bad," I said.

"Yes," Cox said. "They are. No matter. I have a great deal invested in these men and this bridge."

Cox walked to the office doors and opened them.

"Jessup," Cox called.

"Yessir," Jessup replied.

"Get my horse ready to ride," he said.

Jessup showed up at the doors.

"Now?" Jessup said.

"Yes," Cox said. "Now."

Virgil looked to me and moved toward the door.

"We have readying to do," Virgil said. "We'll come back around here in a bit. If you're ready to ride, you can ride with us. We won't wait on you."

"I'll be ready," Cox said.

Virgil nodded and I followed him out of the office.

We left Cox's place and walked back in the direction of the sheriff's office.

"I think we need to try and locate this Swickey fella," I said.

"Yep."

"Not sure how best to go about that," I said. "Not this time of night, anyway."

"Same as before," Virgil said.

"Wallis?"

"Yep."

Virgil and I cut through the alley and crossed two blocks to Main Street. When we got to the Boston House, the saloon was locked up.

"Any idea where Wallis could be," Virgil asked.

"Don't," I said. "Not if he ain't at the saloon. Know where Tilda stays," I said.

"How do you know that?" Virgil said.

"She showed me."

Virgil looked at me, but I didn't look at him back as I walked on.

"She's just up the street here at Fletcher's old board-inghouse," I said.

When we got to Fletcher's we entered the small dark

lobby and climbed the steps to the second floor. The boardinghouse halls were lined with a few dimmed sconces. We walked down the cold hall, stopped at the last door and I knocked.

"Tilda," I said. "It's Everett and Virgil, sorry for the hour, but we need to ask you something."

We heard some bedsprings squeak and the sound of hushed voices. I knocked lightly again.

"Tilda?"

After a moment, Tilda cracked open the door.

"Hi," Tilda said shyly.

"Sorry to bother you this time of night, but we're looking for Wallis," I said. "Need to find out something from him. Know where we can find him?"

"Hold on a minute," Tilda said, and shut the door.

Virgil looked at me and frowned a bit.

After a moment, the door opened and Wallis stepped out with his breeches on over his unders. His hair was sticking out in every direction. He closed the door behind him.

"Bernice threw me out," Wallis said, like a kid with his hand in the cookies. "Tilda's just letting me stay with her for a while, till Bernice lets me back in or I have to relocate."

"It's okay, Wallis," Virgil said. "We ain't here to arrest you."

Wallis looked relieved.

"What ya need this time of night?" Wallis said.

"Swickey," Virgil said.

"What about him?"

"Know him?" I said.

"Walton Wayne," Wallis said. "Sure do."

"Where is he?" I said.

"Don't know that he's here," Wallis said. "He don't live here. He stays here some, though, always at the Boston House, but I've not seen him, not lately, anyway."

"Where's he live?"

"Across the Blanco," Wallis said. "He has a big spread over there, I hear. He owns damn near all the land on the other side."

Virgil looked at me and shook his head a little.

"What do you know about the Rio Blanco contract that was awarded to Cox and not Swickey?" Virgil said.

"Not much," Wallis said. "Cox and him I know were on opposite sides. Swickey is rich as hell and could buy damn near anything or anybody, but he didn't win the contract. Cox, I hear, had the construction experience. That's all I know."

Virgil nodded a little as he thought.

"Appreciate it, Wallis," Virgil said. "Sorry to interrupt."

"Oh," Wallis said, "no problem, you didn't interrupt nothin'."

"Don't think I'd call Tilda nothing," Virgil said.

— 30 —

Virgil and I collected G. W. Cox. We started for the Rio Blanco Bridge just past three in the morning. The snow was falling steady as we rode and it was beginning to stick.

Cox was dressed for the weather. He had on a fur-lined cap that covered his ears, thick mittens, and a buffalo-hide coat that draped down to the fenders of his saddle. He rode a big black sturdy-looking horse that had an oilcloth drape covering his neck and ass end.

We rode by the depot, crossed over the tracks, past the last few homesteads on the road, past the icehouse, the old stockyards, and the abandoned slaughterhouse, past the trash heap. Soon we were out of Appaloosa proper.

We kept our heads down and our collars up and didn't talk much on the journey. The ride was slow going, and by the time daybreak came upon us, the snow was near a half-foot deep.

"Could we stop for a moment's time," Cox said. "I'm not used to being in the saddle this long."

We stopped under a large cluster of oak trees to give our horses some rest. I got some kindling from the mule's panniers, gathered what dry branches I could, and got a fire going next to a large felled tree. Once the fire was burning steady I put on some coffee to boil.

Virgil removed the snow from the big tree and sat over the fire, warming his hands. Cox removed a rolled slicker from his cantle. He placed it on the ground on the opposite side of the fire and sat on it with his boots close to the flame.

When the coffee was brewed I poured Virgil and Cox a cup and handed it to them with a piece of hardtack.

I pulled my watch from my vest pocket and checked the time.

"Should be to the bridge camp by a little after noon, I figure."

Virgil nodded, holding his hands around the warm tin cup as he sipped his coffee. Cox just stared at the fire.

"Unless it's a damn sight clearer when we get there," I said, "it'll be hard to see much with this weather."

Virgil looked up.

"It will," Virgil said. "Weather's made itself more than comfortable."

"Damn sure has," I said. "Imagine it's just as bad at the bridge."

"There is no bridge," Cox said solemnly.

I looked to Cox. He was still staring at the fire.

"No," I said.

Virgil nodded and sipped his coffee. Cox remained staring at the fire.

"River's deep and wide," Virgil said.

"That it is," Cox said.

"Deep gorge," Virgil said.

"That, too," Cox said. "This was to be a major accomplishment. The bridge was over two hundred feet long."

Virgil nodded a little and sipped on his coffee.

"This Swickey fella," Virgil said. "You know anything about his spread? His operation on the other side of the river?"

Cox met Virgil's eye.

"I don't," Cox said.

"It was shared with us," Virgil said, "he owns damn near everything on the other side of the bridge."

"I heard he was a cattleman," Cox said. "At least I heard that is how he attained his wealth, but as I said, I know nothing of his life and how he leads it or where he leads it."

Virgil just looked at Cox and didn't say anything else.

It was real quiet out with the snow falling gently.

Our horses and the mule stood stock still with their heads down. Nothing was moving, no birds, no breeze.

The only sound was the quiet crackle of the fire burning under the grate the coffee pot was sitting on.

"How was it, Mr. Cox, you won the contract to build the bridge?" Virgil said.

"It's what I do," Cox said. "This is my business. I have the experience, the expertise."

"And Swickey?" I said. "He didn't?"

"That's right," Cox said. "Since I started in the contracting business I've built many projects, mostly bridges. I had the résumé and Swickey did not."

"How did you hear about this one?" Virgil said. "On the Rio Blanco?"

"I have connections in Washington, with Congress, I know where the appropriations are," Cox said. "I know when there are projects. I know where to go, and most importantly, I know how to bid. Most I don't have to bid because there are no other contractors bidding against me."

"Not a bad business," Virgil said.

"It's not," Cox said. "It is also a rewarding business. Build something and there it is. There it will be to help shape the future of this great country."

"And that's what got you to Appaloosa?" Virgil said. "The Rio Blanco Bridge?"

"It is," Cox said.

"You moved to Appaloosa?" Virgil said.

Cox nodded.

"Yes," Cox said. "I live where the projects are and then move on. The jobs I contract take a lot of time, so I've done my share of relocating, I can tell you."

"How long have you been in Appaloosa?" Virgil said.

"On and off for nearly two years," Cox said. "The bridge was in its final stages."

"How much?" Virgil said.

"How much what?" Cox said.

"How much was this contract for?"

"Roughly two hundred thousand dollars," Cox said.

"Lot of money," Virgil said.

"It is," Cox said.

We sat quiet for a bit, thinking about that.

"It was a big bridge," Cox said.

— 31 —

The snow kept falling and it was slow going for the rest of the journey to the bridge camp. When we arrived, it was two in the afternoon. The camp was a settlement of twenty-plus tents, small wooden shacks, and a few large beamed structures. Smoke and steam rose from the encampment and blended seamlessly with the falling snow.

When we entered the camp a large black dog ran out to meet us. He barked and spun and barked some more as we rode through the tents and sheds.

A large man emerged from one of the wooden structures. A sign above the door let us know the building was the bridge office. The man had long blond hair and a long beard. He was without a coat or hat and had only the top of his long johns covering his muscled torso.

"Come here, Gip," he hollered to the dog. "Now."

He put his arm around Gip's neck as we neared. He held on to the dog as he looked to us riding in.

"That you, Mr. Cox?" he said.

Virgil, Cox, and I were covered white with sticky snow.

"It is, Gains, it's me," Cox said.

"Get, Gip," Gains told the dog. "Go on, get."

Gip lowered his head like he wanted to play.

"Get," Gains said with a point. "Go."

Gip looked at us. He turned a few excited turns, then obeyed Gains and moved on as he was asked.

We angled our horses to a hitch in front of the office and stopped.

Gains helped Cox off his horse.

"Didn't expect to see you here, sir," Gains said.

"No," Cox said. "Neither did I, Gains."

Gains looked to Virgil and me.

"You must be the marshals?" Gains said.

"They are, Gains," Cox said. "This is Marshal Cole and Deputy Marshal Hitch. Gains is my foreman on the site."

Gains nodded.

"Come on in," Gains said. "Warm up. I'll get your animals looked after."

Gains whistled to a young fella walking through the encampment.

"Daniel," Gains said, "take these horses to the stock shed. Take care of them."

"Yes, sir," Daniel said.

Gip ran over to Daniel and lowered his head to play

as we ridded ourselves of as much snow as we could, then stepped into the office.

The office had a hard-packed dirt floor and a stove in the corner made from a huge round steel cylinder. Next to it was a stack of dried wood. The room was cluttered with books and papers. Scattered on the tables and tacked on the walls were construction drawings, like those on the walls of Cox's office in Appaloosa.

"Where is the wire office?" Virgil said.

"Just past us a piece," Gains said. "Up the road here a half mile on the way to Fletcher Flats. It's a long loop off the Santa Fe."

"We contacted them last night," Virgil said. "Asked about Sheriff Driskill and his deputies. Wire back said as of last report, there was no sign of them."

Gains shook his head.

"No, sir, we haven't seen them," he said. "They've not been here."

Virgil said, "They came up here looking for a fella named Lonnie . . ."

Virgil looked to me.

"Carman."

"Lonnie Carman?" Gains said.

"Yep," I said. "His wife expected him home days ago and was afraid for him, demanded the sheriff find him."

"He did his shift and left," Gains said.

Virgil looked at me.

"Any idea where he might be?"

"No," Gains said.

"Maybe Driskill found Lonnie and they're back in Appaloosa by now?" I said.

"Not sure how we'd miss them," Virgil said, then looked to Gains.

"Only one road between here and Appaloosa, ain't there?"

Gains nodded.

"Only one road," Gains said, "but if you know it, there is a shortcut, an alternate road that runs parallel. If you go that route, you're on that road for a good four hours but it takes off about forty minutes to an hour's travel time. That shortcut's a little rougher going."

"Where is that?" I said.

"Twenty-mile section toward the middle of the route," Gains said.

"How do you locate it?" Virgil said.

"It's not real clear, and kind of hard to find unless you have traveled the road a lot," Gains said. "And for sure it might, and most likely would, be hard to find in this weather."

"Not impossible, though," Virgil said.

"No," Gains said. "Not impossible."

Virgil and I just kept looking at Gains.

"You want to know?" Gains said.

"Do," Virgil said.

"You think maybe Driskill and his deputies might have . . ."

"Don't know," Virgil said.

"Well, coming from this way, there's an incline off to the right just after you get to a wide-open meadow,"

Gains said. "If you don't take the road through the middle of the meadow but instead go up that incline you'll pick up the shortcut. It comes out just past the creek, the only real creek you cross on the whole trail."

Virgil nodded, removed his hat, popped water from it with a slap on his knee, then set it on the back of a chair.

"Who found the broke wire?" Virgil said.

"Pedrick, the operator?" Gains said. "It was hard to find."

"The wire broke?" Virgil said. "Or was it cut?"

"It was cut," Gains said.

"Why was it hard to find?" I said.

"Where it was cut," Gains said, "was at the top of one of the poles on the insulator. It was cut but made to look like it was still tension-wrapped on the insulator."

Virgil nodded a bit.

"Who would do this?" Gains said. "Why?"

"Don't know," Virgil said. "But we aim to find out."

"Goddamn crazy," Gains said. "I never in my life heard or felt anything like that. The whole Earth shook."

"Who died here, Gains?" Cox said, as he took his coat off.

"Two new men," Gains said. "Brothers from Fletcher Flats, southern boys, and . . . the old man, Percy O'Malley."

"Their bodies found?" Virgil said.

"No, sir," Gains said. "We have looked, but there wasn't much left of anything found in one piece."

"Percy?" Cox said, shaking his head.

Gains nodded.

"How do you know they are dead?" Virgil said.

"Well," Gains said. "After the explosion we had roll call and they were missing."

"What time did this happen?" Virgil said.

"Just as the sun was coming up," Gains said. "Ten minutes later there'd have been at least thirty men killed. Everyone was getting ready to go out."

"These brothers, from Fletcher Flats, they have horses?" Virgil said.

"No, sir," Gains said.

"How'd they get here?"

"We provide transportation for a lot of the workers. We have a ten-seater," Gains said. "We transport workers to and from both Appaloosa and Fletcher Flats. That's where our crews are from and that's how the Cotter brothers got here."

"Cotter?" I said.

"That's right," Gains said.

I looked to Virgil and he looked at me.

"Hocus-goddamn-pocus," I said.

— 32 —

C otter?" I said. "You're certain that is their last name?"

"That's right," Gains said. "That's their names on the payroll, anyway. Dee and Dirk Cotter."

"So, Deputy Marshal," Cox said. "You suspect these two men were not killed but rather had a hand in this?"

"Don't know," I said.

"What do you know?" Cox said.

"Not enough," Virgil said.

"But you know this name?" Cox said. "Cotter?"

Virgil looked at Cox for an extended moment but said nothing. Then he looked to Gains.

"How long had they been on the job?" Virgil said, disregarding the question. "The Cotter boys?"

"Not long," Gains said. "A few weeks."

"You talk to them," Virgil said, "get to know them?"

"Some," Gains said. "I hired them."

"Thinking back," Virgil said. "Was there anything about them that was not right?"

"Not really," Gains said. "I suppose, if anything, they kept to themselves most the time. They seemed like good boys, though, quiet, hardworking."

"What'd they look like?" I said. "Describe them."

"They were young, twenty-five, twenty-six, maybe older," Gains said. "Big boys, strong and tough. Southern fellas, like I said. Pale complexion, both had beards, sort of reddish color, I'd say."

I looked to Virgil.

He met my eye.

Cox looked back and forth between us.

"What is it, Marshal?" he said. "What is this? What are you thinking?"

"Just thinking," Virgil said.

"What kind of 'just thinking'?" Cox said.

Virgil ignored Cox's question and looked to Gains.

"How far to the bridge site?" Virgil said.

"Just right here," Gains said. "Short walk."

"Like to have a look," Virgil said.

Gains nodded.

"First," Cox said. "What kind of thinking, Marshal? What is this about? What do you know?"

"We don't know, Mr. Cox," Virgil said, "but as soon as we can put something together that we feel we need to share, we'll let you know. Right now I'd like to have Gains show us the site and get to the business of figuring out the whereabouts of Sheriff Driskill and his deputies."

Cox was upset, but Virgil didn't feel the need to make him feel any less upset. Virgil always did well with questioning but never did well when it was the other way around and he was being asked questions.

Gains got himself ready with his coat and hat, and Virgil, Cox, and I followed him.

We walked through the encampment, down a snow-covered path, and up a short rise to the bridge site.

A one-hundred-foot hydraulic water crane, with its mast lying horizontal and parallel to the river's edge, sat idle on a high bluff. Its crown, beams, and crossbeams were covered in snow. We walked up the bluff to the base of the huge crane and looked out over the Rio Blanco River gorge.

Gains pointed.

"Across there," he said. "You can see what remains. Those posts, you see just there."

Then he pointed to the bottom of the river, some two hundred feet below.

"The explosion was in the span's middle," Gains said. "Over there, on the other side, you can see the collapse of the span lying in the water."

Everything was covered with snow, but we could make out where the bridge previously made landfall. Disconnected from the top section, the buckled bridge truss dropped and followed the hillside of the chasm down into the river.

"You can see what remains of the scaffolding below here, too," Gains said with a point. "And right there, those beams there, are this side's entrance."

"Good God Almighty," Cox said. "Good God."

"Took a lot of dynamite to blow this," Virgil said.

"Somebody damn sure knew what they were doing," I said.

"Did," Virgil said.

"You have dynamite on the location here?" Virgil said.

"No," Gains said. "We did when we first got started. We had some excavation that was needed but haven't had any dynamite here for a long time."

— 33 —

Gains got us some hot food; it was a venison chili the camp cook made up, and we ate at a long table in the office.

In the following hour Cox drifted off to sleep on a cot near the heater stove and Virgil and I sat on the opposite side of the room with Gains. We were drinking coffee with a tip of whiskey. Gip lay curled up at Gains's feet.

"Know anything about the man that bid against Cox for this project?" Virgil said.

"Swickey?"

Virgil nodded.

"Not really," Gains said. "I know he's a honcho cattleman."

"He been here?" Virgil said. "To the bridge?"

"Not that I know of," Gains said. "No."

"You know where his place is?" I said.

Gains shook his head.

"I don't."

Virgil nodded to Cox sleeping on the cot.

"You ever hear there was bad blood between Cox and Swickey?"

"Had to be some," Gains said quietly. "Mr. Cox getting the bid and all but I don't know . . . You think Swickey did this?"

"Somebody did it," Virgil said.

"They damn sure did," Gains said.

"Any ideas?" Virgil said.

Gains shook his head.

"All I know is I damn sure didn't do it," Gains said.

Gip growled.

"Quiet, Gip," Gains said.

Gip rolled over and Gains rubbed his belly with the heel of his boot.

"Not saying you did," Virgil said.

"No, I know," Gains said. "Just making it clear, I'm a bridge builder, proud to be one, that's all. I hope to hell whoever the hell did do this gets their due."

Virgil nodded to Cox.

"He make a good boss?" he said.

Gains tilted his head a little, followed by a slight nod.

"Late on paying bills and payroll these last two months," Gains said, "but I don't think it was any fault of his. I think it was just the territory with bureaucrats acting as bankers."

Virgil looked over to Cox sleeping on the cot.

"What will happen now?" Gains said.

"After I finish this coffee, Everett and me are gonna ride to the way station," Virgil said. "Maybe send us a wire or two."

We sat for a while longer, discussing the cleanup operations with Gains, then Virgil and I left him and Cox. We got our horses from the stable, mounted up, and rode off to the telegraph way station on the road to Fletcher Flats.

The snow was still falling and there was a good eight inches that had built up. We rode awhile without talking, then Virgil asked me the question I was expecting.

"Tell me about this fortune-teller woman?" Virgil said.

"What do you want to know?"

"Where she come from?"

"Not sure just where, but like I told you, she's part of the traveling show."

We rounded a mess of hillside spindly fir saplings that were sagging over the road from the weight of the snow.

"She come up with the name Cotter," Virgil said.

"She did," I said.

"Think she's got something to do with this?" Virgil said.

"Don't," I said.

"You sure?"

"Sure as I can be, Virgil."

"How then did she know?"

We rode for a bit before I answered.

"Well, Virgil, I don't know."

Virgil nodded a little.

"So you believe this," Virgil said. "She knows shit that she sees in her head?"

"I don't know what to believe right now. Damnedest thing. Before I didn't think much of her talk at all. Hell, I just enjoyed her female company and thought she was just full of her own musings and now this."

We rode for a bit.

"What do you think?" I said.

Virgil shook his head a little.

"What all she tell you again?" Virgil said.

"Said she saw men running. Someone or something called Codder or Cotter. And that my life was in danger."

"Goddamn," Virgil said. "Win. Place. Show."

I didn't say anything and we rode on for a while more before Virgil said anything else.

"That all the fortune-tellin' business she offered?"

"No."

"What else?"

"She said that my life being in danger was not the shoot-out with Bolger that she saw."

"What was it?"

"Said the life-in-danger business wasn't in Appaloosa."

Virgil turned in his saddle a little, looking at me.

"Not in Appaloosa?"

"Yep."

"Where?" Virgil said.

"Didn't say."

"So it's just a show-and-place ticket," Virgil said.

— 34 —

Virgil and I came upon the way station just as it was getting dark. It was a large low log cabin with a corral, a horse shed, and a number of small outbuildings behind it. Smoke drifted up lazily from the cabin's chimney and hung heavy around the old log structure like a dense, dark, ominous cloud.

A chubby man was relieving himself just outside the front door. He looked over, seeing us as we neared. He finished his business and stepped out, watching us as we got closer. He walked out to greet us and we moved our horses toward a covered lean-to hitch on the opposite side of the road.

"How do," he said.

"Evening," I said.

"You the operator?" I said.

"One of them," he said.

"I'm Deputy Marshal Hitch, this is Marshal Virgil Cole."

"Oh, I'm Pedrick," he said. "I take it you're here because of the bridge? Thank goodness."

"Need to send a wire," Virgil said.

"By all means," Pedrick said. "Please, come in. That we can most certainly do."

Virgil and I dismounted. We tied our horses to the hitch and followed Pedrick back across the road to the cabin.

Pedrick looked like a drunk. Probably was a drunk. He had a large red nose situated on a pink puffy face framed with thinning light-reddish-colored hair.

The way station was a small store, telegraph office, and saloon, all combined. We could smell the aroma of flavorful cooking happening somewhere.

Pedrick's wife walked out of the back room when we entered. She was wearing an apron and wiping fixings from her hands with a rag. She looked enough like Pedrick they could be brother and sister.

"These men are marshals from the bridge camp," Pedrick said. "This is my wife, Patty. She's the main operator. Patty, this is Marshal Cole and . . ."

"Deputy Marshal Hitch," I said.

"Yes," Pedrick said. "Hitch . . ."

Virgil removed his hat.

"Ma'am."

"Nice to meet you both and so glad you are here," she said. "This has been just so awful. Do you know who did this?"

"Not as of yet," I said.

"Well," Patty said, "I hope to God you find whoever is responsible."

"We do, too," I said.

"It is the saddest thing," Patty said angrily. "Just downright sad."

I nodded.

"They need to send a wire," Pedrick said.

"Absolutely," Patty said.

Patty continued to wipe her hands with the rag as she walked over to the telegraph desk situated in front of a west window.

"Honey," she said to Pedrick, "keep an eye on my stew, don't let it burn."

Pedrick nodded obediently.

"Will do," he said, as he scurried out of the room.

Patty sat in the chair in front of the telegraph desk and looked back to us.

Virgil looked to me some, then walked over to Patty.

"Were you here last night?" Virgil said.

"I was," she said.

"You received a number of wires from Appaloosa law," Virgil said.

She nodded.

"That was us," Virgil said.

"You got here quick," she said, wide-eyed.

Virgil nodded.

"Want to send a wire back to Appaloosa now," Virgil said. "Want to know if Sheriff Driskill and his deputies have returned or if they have been heard from."

"Want this sent from you, Marshal Cole?" Patty said.

Virgil nodded.

"Sure."

Patty nodded and tapped out the note on the key.

A quick response came back from the Western Union operator. Charlie Hill in Appaloosa said he'd check and for us to stand by.

Patty looked to Virgil and me.

"You fellas want a drink?"

"Sure," Virgil said.

Patty got up from the desk. She walked to the opposite side of the large room to a makeshift bar in the corner.

"Well, come on," she said, as she walked behind the counter.

Virgil and I moved over and sat on two stools opposite Patty.

She got a bottle and poured the three of us a drink.

Patty offered us a cigar from a box with *Florida's Finest* written across the top.

"Good ones," she said.

I shook my head.

Virgil nodded.

"Sure."

Patty clipped the cigar for Virgil and handed it to him. She struck a match and cupped it for him.

When Virgil got the cigar going good the sounder on the telegraph desk clicked. Patty tilted her head a little as she listened, then shook her head.

"Nope," Patty said. "No sign of Sheriff Driskill."

— 35 —

Virgil and I rode back to the bridge camp, and when we arrived we found Cox sitting at the end of a long table in the office and Gains sitting just next to him. Gip jumped up, excited to have more company, and started with his nonstop barking.

"Gip, stop," Gains said. "Stop it, boy."

Gip swayed his head a few times low to the ground. He wagged his tail rapidly like he didn't hear the command.

"*Gip.*"

Gip looked to Gains.

"No."

Gip wasn't happy, but he complied. He circled a few times and laid down where Gains was pointing.

"Any new news?" Cox said.

"No," Virgil said.

"I have a feeling if there were any news, you wouldn't let me know, so I'm not sure why I even ask."

"That's okay," Virgil said.

Cox just shook his head slightly.

"Keep in mind that this was my bridge and I'm accountable for all that transpires here, Marshal Cole."

"I will," Virgil said.

Cox just looked at Virgil for an extended moment.

"What now?" Cox said wearily.

"Everett and me are riding outta here before daylight," Virgil said. "You are most welcome to ride with us back to Appaloosa if you'd like."

"Well, I appreciate that, but I think it best I stay here for a while," Cox said, pouring on his long southern drawl, "for the morale of the men. This has been quite a trauma for them, Marshal Cole. Many of the men have been working here for two years. This place has served as home away from home for them. It's simply where I need to be."

"You won't stray away from here?" Virgil said.

"Stray?" Cox said with a frown.

"In case we need you," Virgil said.

"I'll be here, Marshal," Cox said. "And will return shortly, rest assured."

Virgil looked at Cox for an extended moment, then looked around the room. He walked over and looked at the bridge diagrams on the wall.

"One hell of a bridge," Virgil said.

"Yes," Cox said. "It was."

I poured myself some coffee and took a seat in a rocking chair next to a center lodge pole, which for some reason gave Gip the inclination to play.

Gip picked up a knotted cluster of old socks and dropped them in front of me.

"You feeling neglected?"

Gip whined a little and I threw the knotted socks. Gip fetched them and caught them almost before they hit the ground.

I kept throwing the socks as Virgil perused the plans on the wall. After a bit Virgil moved away from the wall and pulled out a chair at the opposite end of the long table from Cox.

"The Rio Blanco is a tough goddamn river through these parts," Virgil said.

"It damn sure is," Gains said.

"Deep gorge that the water runs through," Virgil said. "Rugged as hell for over fifty miles through here."

"Indeed it is, Marshal," Cox said.

Virgil looked back at the wall with the drawings on it for a moment, then looked to Cox.

"Let me ask you a question, Mr. Cox," Virgil said.

"What is it, Marshal?"

Virgil removed his hat and tossed it to the center of the long table.

"Let's say my hat there is the bridge and you are the land on one side of the bridge and I'm the land on the other."

"Yes?" Cox said.

"Let's say I'm the far side and you are this side."

"Your point?"

"I'm just trying to determine who benefits the most," Virgil said, "and who don't. So if I'm the far side, the side cattleman Swickey has land on, or your side, the Appaloosa and vicinity's side—"

"I certainly see where you are going with this," Cox said, interrupting Virgil. "I'm not unaware of the most obvious here. It is why the bridge was to be constructed in the first place, Marshal. The bridge would allow goods and services, including the transportation of cattle. There is no argument for one side benefitting more from having the bridge than the other."

"I'm not talking about benefitting from *having* the bridge," Virgil said. "I'm talking about who'd benefit the most from *not having* the bridge."

— 36 —

Virgil and I mounted up in the silvery cold morning and left the bridge camp slightly before daylight. The snow had let up, but there was a good foot packed on the ground and it was slow going as we rode.

There was not the slightest breeze. We traveled for eight solid hours in the silence of the snow-covered country. The woods were soundless and everything was still as we moved. We came to a wide-open section without trees and Virgil stopped.

"This must be the meadow Gains was talking about," Virgil said.

I looked around.

"And that there must be the incline he was talking about," I said.

Virgil nodded and we moved off the main road and started up the incline. It wasn't a steep rise, and when we topped the ridge it was clear we were on another road. We continued on riding for about two hours when Virgil stopped again. He turned in his saddle and waited until I was close before he spoke.

"Smell that?" he said quietly.

I looked around.

"Do," I said.

From somewhere in the woods in front of us we smelled smoke. We rode on for a bit more, then we caught a glimpse of smoke drifting through the trees off to our left. Virgil stopped and I sidled up next to him.

He pointed to the opposite side of the road to the right and we moved off the road and distanced ourselves from the origin of the fire. We stopped under some tall oaks, dismounted, and snugged our horses and the mule to a twisted old oak tree.

Virgil pulled his Winchester from his scabbard and I got my eight-gauge. We circled off the road so as to come upon the fire at a distance from the path.

We made it a step at a time, moving through the deep snow. It took us some time of slow moving before we were close enough to see the source of the smoke.

There was a small fire burning behind an outcropping of rocks next to a steamy creek.

We moved up ever so slowly, and when we were close Virgil signaled me to come in from one direction while he moved off to the other side so he'd come in from the opposite angle.

We kept each other in sight as we approached the camp.

I saw Virgil squat down and I did the same. After a moment Virgil brought the Winchester to his shoulder and pointed it in the direction of the fire.

"Don't move," Virgil called out. "I got you in my sights."

"I ain't armed," a voice called back.

"How many are you?" Virgil said.

"Just me," the voice said.

"Step out," Virgil said.

Just then I saw the backside of a figure rise up from the rocks. He held his left arm up facing Virgil's direction.

"I don't got no gun," the man said. "I'm friendly, by myself, and hungry. I don't want no harm to me or no one else."

"Who are you?" Virgil called.

"Name's Lonnie," the man said. "Lonnie Carman."

Virgil lowered his Winchester some and looked over to me.

"I'm just a worker from the bridge camp," Lonnie said, "and I need help."

"Lonnie," Virgil said. "If you are lying to me, you will die."

"Oh, hell," Lonnie said. "I ain't lying. I've been shot. I'm alone, cold, and real near dead like it is."

"Step out more," Virgil said. "Keep your hands away from yourself."

"Okay," he said. "I can barely move."

Lonnie stepped out slowly from the outcropping with one of his hands in the air.

"I can only lift my one arm," he said. "Barely."

Virgil nodded over to me and we moved slowly toward Lonnie.

When we got closer, I could see Lonnie clearly. He had his one hand on top of his head and he appeared to be in bad shape, facing Virgil as he approached.

"Lonnie," I said.

Lonnie turned, looking back to me. He squinted in my direction. He kept looking at me, as I got closer to him.

"Oh, sweet Jesus. Deputy Hitch?" Lonnie said with a tremble in his voice. "That you, Deputy Marshal Hitch?"

"It is."

Lonnie looked back to Virgil, as he got closer.

"And Marshal Cole?" Lonnie said.

"It is," Virgil said.

"Oh my Lord. My prayers have been answered. Oh, my. Thank you, Jesus. Thank you."

Lonnie looked back to me.

"Thank you, Jesus."

Lonnie started crying.

"It's okay, Lonnie," I said.

"Deputy Marshal Hitch," he said, then looked to Virgil. "And Marshal Cole. Oh, Jesus. Thank you, sweet Jesus. You fellas have no idea how goddamn glad I am to see the likes of you two. No idea."

— 37 —

When Virgil and I got close we could see Lonnie was not lying. He had been shot. He was alone, hungry, dirty, cold, and in bad shape. He had been under a cavelike outcropping where he'd been able to keep a small fire going.

Lonnie dropped when we got close. He'd obviously been living on sheer will, and the sight of us as reinforcement allowed him to give way to exhaustion.

"Hang on, Lonnie," I said. "Just hang on."

Virgil fetched our horses and I tended the best I could to Lonnie. I eased him under the dryness in the outcropping. I pulled back his coat and blood-soaked shirt and looked at his wound. He'd been shot in the back, just below his collarbone, and the bullet exited out the lower part of his chest. He had managed to somehow wrap the wound with part of his shirt he'd ripped up. He'd made a bandage with his belt. He'd wrapped it under one arm and over his neck and on the opposite side, holding the pieces of ripped shirt tight to his body.

When Virgil arrived with the animals I retrieved the medicine kit from the panniers the deputies packed. We got the fire going good, and I cleaned Lonnie's bullet wounds with hot water, doused them with carbolic acid, then wrapped his shoulder with bandages.

We cooked some venison strap we'd got from the cook at the bridge camp and heated up some beans.

Lonnie was hurt and weak, but he was hungry and had no trouble getting food down.

"Wanna tell us what happened here, Lonnie?" Virgil said.

Lonnie looked at us and shook his head a little.

"I run into some shit," Lonnie said.

"You seen Sheriff Driskill and his deputies, Karl and Chip?" Virgil said.

"No, I haven't," Lonnie said. "I sure wish I had, that've been a blessing."

"What kind of shit did you run into?" Virgil said.

"I was riding from the camp, on my way back to Appaloosa, and Ruth, my mare of twenty years, spooked. There was a goddamn rumble from the earth or some such, blackbirds shot out of a thicket and Ruth jerked up and sidestepped. Next thing I know she was walking funny. I got off her and there was bone sticking out of her leg. Poor Ruth. I hated it, but I had to put her down."

Lonnie paused. He looked down, thinking of his horse. He blinked a few times and looked back to us.

"I was on foot," he said. "Weather was getting bad. Started raining. I'd been walking for, hell, a good three hours when some soldiers come riding up behind me."

"How many?" I said.

"There was seven of them," Lonnie said. "And they had a buckboard."

Virgil looked at me.

"What happened?" Virgil said.

"Well, hell, I thought, *Thank God. Soldiers.* The soldier driving the buckboard looked kind of familiar to me. I asked them if I could get a lift back to Appaloosa. He said nothing but nodded to one of the other soldiers. That soldier got off his horse, friendly like, and asked me if I was heeled. I told him I was. He asked me to show him my gun. I did, I didn't think nothing of it. I didn't think nothing of it until he told me to take off running. He said he was gonna give me a ten count. I asked him what he was talking about and he started counting and, well, I took off running and he shot me in the back with my own gun."

"Then what?" Virgil said.

"They started laughing," Lonnie said. "I heard one of them say, 'Finish him off,' but I did not move. I laid facedown like I was dead."

"Then what happened?" Virgil said.

"I waited. I was just imagining he was gonna walk over and put a bullet in my head. I heard them talking, couldn't really make out what they had to say, and then, thank God in Heaven, the fuckers rode off."

"Then what'd you do?" I said.

"I laid there, afraid to move for 'bout an hour. But then I figured I better get up before I did die. It started raining harder and I found this place and took shelter. Thank God I had some jerky and matches or I'd be dead for sure. I started gathering wood and stashing it under here. I got a good bunch of it. I was able to find some fairly dry bark here and there and I finally got me a fire going. I gathered more and more wood and stayed hunkered down here outta the rain and tended to my wounds the best I could. I been here a long time, can't say how long, exactly, but a long time. I drank as much water as I could from this creek behind me here. I kept thinking the weather was gonna clear, but then it just got worse and worse and all I could think about was I'm gonna die. I'm gonna die in this goddamn pile of rocks. Then y'all came and thank God. Thank God."

— 38 —

Lonnie was too weak to be moved, so we kept him warm and let him rest up for the night. Through the evening the sky cleared a little and some stars came out.

Virgil and I drank coffee by the fire. The night was bright with the opening skylight reflecting off the snow. With the exception of the golden glow of the campfire, our snow-covered surroundings were a glistening steel blue.

"What the hell, Virgil?" It was a combination of a question, a query, and downright dismay.

Virgil stared at the fire for a moment before he answered.

"Them two men," Virgil said, "the Cotter boys. They didn't do this for shits and grins."

"No," I said.

"Somebody hired them," Virgil said.

I nodded.

"Paid them pretty good, too, I figure," I said.

"Yep," Virgil said. "They didn't spend two weeks working on the bridge because they were honest bridge builders."

"Who are they, I wonder?"

"Whoever they are," Virgil said, "they got hired by someone that wants the bridge gone."

"They hire on, get the lay of the land around the bridge," I said. "Plan the attack."

Virgil nodded.

"Those soldiers you saw riding into town," Virgil said. "They have mules?"

"No."

"Somehow they managed to get a shitload of dynamite," Virgil said. "We ain't talking about a little dynamite in saddlebags."

"No," I said. "That was a massive structure. Took a bunch."

"More than what a few horseman carried," Virgil said.

We thought about that for a moment.

"Then," Virgil said. "They cut the telegraph line at the way station so they give themselves as much distance as possible."

"It was damn sure thought out," I said.

"Was," Virgil said.

"Then they get picked up by the five other riders and hightail it," I said.

Virgil nodded.

"Get into Union uniforms," he said.

"They did."

"Like I said, gives them validation," Virgil said.

"Just like what happened here with Lonnie," I said. "He thought *Good* when he saw blue. *Bad* never crossed his mind."

"Yep," Virgil said, looking over to Lonnie, who was sleeping.

"Till they goddamn told him to run, and shot him in the back," I said.

"Yep," Virgil said. "And then they ride into Appaloosa for one night."

We thought about that for a bit.

"Why ride to Appaloosa?" I said.

Virgil looked at the fire for a long moment, then looked to me.

"Get paid," Virgil said.

"Paid by who is the question."

"Why is the question," Virgil said.

"We find out why, we find out who," I said.

Virgil nodded.

"You think this Swickey fella did this?" I said.

"Maybe," Virgil said.

"Cox?" I said.

"Don't think so," Virgil said.

"Something about him, though," I said.

"There is," Virgil said.

"Why would he blow up his own bridge?" I said.

Virgil shook his head.

"Like you said," Virgil said. "We look at the why and will find the who."

"'Spect we need to pay this Swickey a visit?" I said.

"We do."

"Just need to figure out where his place is," I said.

"Him running a big cattle outfit," Virgil said. "He shouldn't be too hard to find."

We watched the fire for a moment, then Virgil looked around as if he was looking for something. After a moment he looked back to the fire, staring.

"Should have come across something by now?" Virgil said.

He didn't say it, but I knew he was talking about Sheriff Sledge Driskill and his deputies Chip and Karl.

"Damn should have," I said.

"You think maybe they run into them Cotter brothers and company," I said.

"Don't know," Virgil said.

"Something," I said.

"Yep," Virgil said. "Goddamn something."

"One thing for sure," I said. "Somebody in the Cotter and company knew about this shortcut."

"They did," Virgil said.

"Maybe we'll run into something on down the road here," I said.

"Maybe," Virgil said, "maybe."

After a while Virgil and I got some blankets and prepared us a place to sleep. I let Virgil share the warm overhang where Lonnie was bedded, and I cleared a section of snow and lined it with wool.

When I laid down the night sky was brilliant, bright and clear.

I saw Orion's Belt and thought about Séraphine. I wondered what she was doing tonight. I wondered if maybe she was looking at the same stars I was looking at. I thought about her, remembering her . . . her smell, her skin, her hair . . .

— 39 —

By morning the clouds were back over us and a light snow was falling.

We got Lonnie situated as comfortably as we could on top of the mule between the panniers and traveled the shortcut the rest of the way back to the main road. We saw no sign of Driskill and his deputies on the route back to Appaloosa, but we arrived with Lonnie alive.

Lonnie insisted we let his wife, Winifred, know he was okay. We did, we stopped by their place, and Winifred scolded Lonnie regardless of his condition or what he had to say.

We left Lonnie and Winifred at Doc Crumley's, then Virgil and I made our way over to the sheriff's office.

It was five in the afternoon when we entered the office. Chastain was behind the desk and sitting in a cell next to Bolger was Beauregard Beauchamp. Beauregard looked up at us when we entered.

"There you are, gentlemen," Beauregard said in his big voice as he got to his feet. "I was trying to explain to your illustrious deputy here we are friends and that there was no need to lock me up. No need whatsoever."

Virgil looked to Chastain.

"He was drunk," Chastain said.

Beauregard laughed, shaking his head dramatically from side to side.

"No, no, no," Beauregard said.

"Goddamn were, too," Bolger said from the next cell.

"A simple misunderstanding," Beauregard said. "It was nothing more than a misunderstanding."

"Bullshit," Bolger said.

"One of the show people," Chastain said, "came over, said they heard Mr. Beauchamp yelling at Mrs. Beauchamp in their trailer. Was scared for her. Book and me went over there. We knocked on the door and Mr. Beauchamp here came out with his fists up like he was a boxer and started swinging at me. I had no choice but to lock him up."

"It was just a misunderstanding," Beauregard said. "My wife and I were rehearsing, you see, nothing more."

"You were drunk. Mrs. Beauchamp was frightened. And you, Mr. Beauchamp, were doing your best to hit me," Chastain said.

"Mrs. Beauchamp okay?" Virgil said.

"She is," Chastain said.

"He sober now?" Virgil said.

Chastain nodded.

"Should be."

Virgil got the keys and walked toward Beauregard's cell.

"See," Beauregard said to Chastain, "Marshal Cole and Deputy Marshal Hitch know all too well I am like them. I am a man of substance. A man of quick resolve."

Virgil unlocked the cell door.

Beauregard put on his fancy gambler's frock coat and meticulously placed his wide-brimmed hat on his head with a stylish sideways tilt to it.

Virgil pulled open the cell door.

"Why, thank you, Marshal," Beauregard said with a bow.

"I find you mistreating your wife or anybody else," Virgil said, "I will personally put a knot in your ass."

Beauregard gulped.

"Why, Marshal?"

"Get," Virgil said.

Beauregard was stymied for a brief moment.

Chastain stood up and opened the door to the street for him to leave.

Beauregard was unsure just how to regain some pride, some dignity. He pulled back his shoulders, pointed his nose in the air, and walked out the door with one shoulder leading the other like the seasoned thespian he was.

"Goddamn clown," Chastain said, closing the door behind him.

Chastain looked over us for a bit.

"Look like you been through it," Chastain said.

"Any word from Driskill?" Virgil said.

Chastain shook his head.

"Nothing," he said. "I was hoping he'd be with you or you'd know something."

Virgil shook his head.

"We don't," Virgil said.

"Not seen 'em," I said.

"Goddamn," Chastain said.

Chastain walked over and shut the door between the office and the cells.

"I was here, got your wire," Chastain said, "from the bridge camp way station."

Virgil nodded.

"What do we do?" Chastain said.

"Not much we can do with the weather like it is," Virgil said. "Rough and slow going out there with this snow. Be like birds looking for seeds. Soon as it gives way we need to mount a posse."

Chastain nodded.

"And the bridge?" Chastain said.

"Gone," I said.

Chastain shook his head slowly.

"My God," he said. "Who done it?"

"Know some of who done it," Virgil said. "Just don't know who had them do it."

"Who is the some of the who done it?" Chastain said.

"The soldier fellas that come through town," Virgil said.

"Soldiers?"

"They weren't soldiers," Virgil said.

I nodded.

"Who were they?" Chastain said, as he poured Virgil and me a cup of coffee.

"We don't know," I said. "Know two names, most likely aliases. Brothers, or claimed to be brothers, last name Cotter."

"Never heard of them," Chastain said, as he handed Virgil and me each a cup of coffee.

"You ever hear of Walton Wayne Swickey?" Virgil said.

Chastain squinted a little.

"Name's familiar," he said. "Who is he?"

"Big cattleman. Got a spread across Rio Blanco someplace," I said. "He was the one that bid against G. W. Cox for the bridge contract."

Chastain nodded a little.

"You think he's behind this?" Chastain said.

"Could be," Virgil said. "We need to find out his whereabouts and then find him."

"Being a cattleman, he can't be that hard to find," Chastain said. "I'll poke around."

"Do," Virgil said.

Virgil walked over to the window. He looked out for a moment as he sipped his coffee.

"Money," Virgil said.

Chastain looked at me.

Virgil continued staring out the window for a bit, then he said, "Swickey or not . . . It's all about the money."

"Ain't that always the case," Chastain said.

"Need to find out about this contract," Virgil said, looking back to Chastain and me. "The bridge foreman said Cox was late on paying. Them boys that had Bolger and his brother delivering goods said the pay chain was broke."

"What are you thinking?" Chastain said.

"Just need to figure out what's at stake here," Virgil said. "Maybe Cox was in trouble with money. Maybe he has been doing something else with the money. Need to know how and when he was paid. Maybe there's a policy he's collecting on or something. Maybe he's broke. Maybe Cox and Swickey are in on this together."

"Together?" Chastain said.

Virgil nodded a little.

"Gotta be something else. Everett, let's work up a letter, have Chastain send it, notifying the governor's office, let them know what happened and find out all we can."

— 40 —

O h my goodness," Allie said. "I can't believe Beauregard was arrested. Here in Appaloosa. How em-
barrassing."

"He didn't seem all that embarrassed," Virgil said.
"Did he, Everett?"

"Didn't," I said.

"I'm not talking about *him* being embarrassed," Allie said. "I'm talking about *me*, about *Appaloosa*."

"What are *you* embarrassed about?" Virgil said.

"This man, this renowned performer, has come here
to Appaloosa to give us some culture, some entertainment, and he gets arrested?" Allie said.

"He did," Virgil said.

"It's just awful," Allie said.

"Not sure I'd call scaring the daylights out of his wife
culture or entertainment," Virgil said.

"If he said he was practicing, he was practicing," Allie

said. "You don't understand entertainment. You know nothing about practicing theatrical performance, Virgil Cole."

"Sure I do," Virgil said. "It ain't practicing, it's got its own special name, don't it, Everett?"

"Rehearsing," I said.

"That's right," Virgil said. "Rehearsing."

"Well," Allie said. "I'm downright embarrassed over this, Virgil. Appaloosa is embarrassed."

"Pretty sure Appaloosa don't give a shit," Virgil said.

"They do," she said.

Allie turned sideways in her chair with her right elbow on the dining table and her shoulders slumped. She looked like she was gonna cry.

"Well, Allie," I said, as I got out of my chair and gathered plates off the table. "If it's any comfort to you, I really enjoyed this dinner you fixed tonight."

Allie wobbled her head a little and offered a slight smile.

"Why, thank you, Everett," Allie said. "At least one of you is grateful of me."

"Oh, goddamn, Allie," Virgil said. "I'm grateful of you, Allie."

"Are not," she said.

"I am, Allie," Virgil said. "I wasn't the one that arrested him. Hell, I was the one that let him out."

"He was, Allie," I said from the kitchen.

"Really?" Allie said.

"He was," I said, coming back from the kitchen to gather more plates.

Allie smiled a little. I think that made her feel better.

"Well," she said. "I know it has to be hard for them with this weather, the whole troupe cooped up in those trailers, going on days now."

Virgil nodded. He reached over and grabbed Allie's hand and gave it a squeeze.

"I love you, Allie," he said.

She smiled at Virgil.

"I love you, too, Virgil."

Virgil got up from the table. He walked to the mantel and got a cigar from his cigar box.

"You're not gonna smoke that in here, are you, Virgil?" Allie said.

"Wouldn't think of it," Virgil said.

Virgil put on his coat and stepped out the front door.

Allie got out of her chair and helped me finish cleaning off the table.

"I don't think Virgil really has a real bone to pick with Beauregard," I said.

"I'm not so sure," Allie said. "I think he's jealous."

"Virgil don't get jealous," I said. "You know that, Allie. Fact is, if there's one thing he personally don't know nothing about, it's jealousy."

"Oh," Allie said. "I suppose you're right, Everett. Maybe that's wishful thinking, what I miss."

"What you miss?"

"A woman likes to know her man is so interested in her he don't like to think about her having any other interest."

"You got other interest?" I said.

"Of course not," Allie said. "I'm speaking theoretically."

"Theoretically?"

"Yes," she said, then leaned her hip on the counter. "You know, a woman needs attention, Everett."

I poured some hot water that was heating on the stovetop in the dirty dishes into the washbasin.

"Virgil just don't like to see a woman, any woman, treated with disrespect. Whether she's practicing or rehearsing or what," I said.

Allie was just looking at me. Watching me.

"Most important, though," I said. "Right now, we got bad dealings. A no-good bunch of business we're dealing with, Allie, far more important business than Beauregard getting himself locked up and you needing attention. We got a two-hundred-foot bridge, no telling how many tons of iron that spanned the Rio Blanco River, blown up by somebody, somebody that is out there on the loose, and we got three Appaloosa law officials, good men, out there somewhere, missing."

— 41 —

I walked the streets of Appaloosa. The city was quiet. The evening was cold, and most every business, even the saloons, was shut down. The snow had stopped, but it was deep and I couldn't see where the boardwalks stopped and the streets began.

The newly installed streetlamps were not lit and there was no traffic moving about on the boardwalks or streets. It was cold, dead still, and silent out.

I stopped in at the sheriff's office and paid Chastain, Book, and Skinny Jack a visit.

The three men were sitting around the warmth of the potbellied stove, playing blackjack on a crate, when I opened the door.

"Howdy, boys," I said.

I kicked the doorjamb, freeing my trousers and boots of snow before I entered.

The three of them looked at me with somber expressions.

"You get some word?" I said.

They shook their heads.

"No," Chastain said. "We just keep thinking they'll walk through the door any minute."

I nodded.

"Just me," I said, and closed the door behind me.

I walked over to the men and looked down at the card game.

"Who's winning?" I said.

"I am, of course," Book said.

"Chubby shit's a card counter," Chastain said.

"I can't help it if I'm a good thinker," Book said.

"Shit," Skinny Jack said. "Just luck."

I put my eight-gauge in the gun rack behind the desk. And hung my shell belt next to it on a hook.

"Find out any news of Walton Wayne Swickey's whereabouts?" I said to Chastain.

Chastain sat back and shook his head.

"Not as of yet," Chastain said. "Got a number of wires out. The office said they'd let me know first response."

"Need to find him," I said.

"I will," Chastain said.

"Like Cole asked, I contacted the governor's office with his wire," Chastain said. "I let them know about the bridge. 'Spect they will know something shortly."

"'Spect they will," I said.

I walked back over near the desk. I could see Bolger

through the open door between the cells and the office. He was looking at me. I looked back at him.

I nodded to him and he looked to the floor. I continued to look at him sitting there on the bunk and then something occurred to me, something that I'd not thought about.

Could by God be . . . I thought, as I walked over to the door and looked in on him.

"Bolger?" I said.

He looked up.

"Hum?"

"Let me ask you a question," I said.

"You can ask," Bolger said. "Can't guarantee you any answers, though."

"Tell me about the buckboard," I said.

"What buckboard?" he said.

"The one you used to take the goods up to the bridge camp," I said. "That buckboard."

"What about it?"

"It yours?" I said.

Bolger just looked at me.

"Is it?"

"Is," he said. "Why?"

"Where is it?"

"Got stoled."

"Somebody took it?"

"Yep."

"Your brother?" I said.

Bolger looked away from my eyes.

"He the one who took it?"

"Now, why would my brother steal my buckboard?"

"You tell me?" I said.

"He didn't," Bolger said.

"You and him got into it?" I said.

"He's gonna find you," Bolger said.

"Didn't you?" I said.

"I don't know what you are talking about," Bolger said.

"You and your brother?" I said. "When you traveled back and forth to the bridge camp, did you use the shortcut?"

Bolger just looked at me.

"Not a trick question," I said.

"I don't know what you're talking about."

"Did you?"

"Shortcut?" Bolger said.

"Yes."

"What if we did?" he said.

"I'm just wondering," I said.

"We ain't stupid."

"So you did?"

"Like I said, ain't stupid," Bolger said. "Saved over an hour on the road. Why?"

"Just curious," I said.

"'Bout what?"

"You know some men that worked at the camp," I said. "Brothers, named Cotter?"

Bolger just looked at me with a blank expression on his face.

"Do you?"

Bolger shook his head, but I could tell he knew something of what I was talking about.

"Your brother? He know them?"

"I don't know what you're talking about."

"Your brother cut you out of the deal?" I said.

Bolger just looked at me.

"Did he?"

"What deal?"

"You know goddamn good and well what deal I'm talking about," I said.

"I don't," he said.

"You do," I said.

Bolger looked down and spit on the floor, then looked up to me.

"I don't," he said. "You done?"

"Almost."

"Good."

"It was just Ballard who hauled the dynamite," I said. "Wasn't it?"

"Dynamite?" Bolger said.

"Yep."

"I don't know nothing about no goddamn dynamite," he said.

"You got into a fight and he cut you out of the deal, didn't he?" I said.

"You're pissing in the wind," Bolger said.

"Am I?"

"You are."

"He don't give a shit about you, Bolger," I said. "Does he?"

Bolger didn't say anything.

"Tell you what," I said. "You think about it. If you come up with any information, you let me know. I will talk to the judge when he gets here and let him know how you are interested in not going to prison for attempting to kill a law officer."

Bolger just stared at me.

"Night, Bolger," I said.

I closed the door on him.

— 42 —

I walked back to my room. I thought about returning to Virgil's place and talking with him about Bolger and my summation about Ballard's involvement with the buckboard and the men at the bridge, but I figured it could wait until morning.

When I got back to my room I found a note lying on the pillow of my bed. *Hot bath? Windsor Hotel. Room 12. Séraphine.*

I was tired but only thought about the invitation for the amount of time that it took for me to hear the door of my room above the survey office close behind me.

Next to the Boston House, the Windsor Hotel was supposedly the nicest hotel in Appaloosa. An English couple that had made a successful go of it in the textile business back east operated the hotel. It was a classy establishment next to the depot that catered to stopover train travelers.

When I got to the hotel, a bell dinged above the door. The lobby was dark and empty. There was some light coming from a room behind the counter and a young man stepped out as I neared the front desk.

"Deputy Marshal Hitch, I presume," he said with a distinct British accent.

"I am."

He retrieved a key and held it out for me.

"Been expecting you," he said. "Top of the stairs. To your right, down the hall."

I walked up the steps, and when I got to the top and turned right, I saw her standing at the far end of the hall.

"I heard you," she said.

I removed my hat as I walked down the hall to meet her.

She was wearing a nightgown that hung to the floor, covering her feet. The light coming from the open door of her room lit one side of her body like an old-world painting. *Venus,* I thought, as I walked toward her.

Her long, dark hair was pulled up on top of her head with errant strands falling free, as if the whole of it were about to give way.

I moved close to her without saying anything. I could smell her intoxicating perfume. Her eyes were looking up at me. It was like before, like she was seeing into me, into my soul.

For a long moment we just stood looking at each other, then she said softly, *"Bonsoir."*

I leaned in and kissed her. She put her hand on the back of my neck and pulled me tight to her as she kissed me back. I leaned on her slightly and she moved back to the open door of her room. She slid her free hand up under the back of my coat and pulled my body to her. We kissed, hungry, like long-lost lovers. Then I pulled back and looked at her. Her eyes glistened with a haunting, otherworldly fire.

This felt like a dream to me. Everything felt as though I was on the outside looking in. The journey Virgil and I had been through, the hour of the evening, the coldness of the weather, the deep snow outside, and her, here in my arms. *Goddamn*.

"What's this about a hot bath?" I said.

"This is a fine establishment," she said. "Look."

I looked into the room. There was a fancy claw-foot tub in the corner.

"How about that?" I said. "And water?"

"It's all here," she said. "Let me show you."

She led me into the room and shut the door.

The room was small but elegant. There was an ornate cast-iron-and-brass stove in the corner opposite the tub. Two brass five-gallon buckets sat next to the stove full of water.

"I'll be damned," I said.

"No," she said, "never. This much I know."

She put one of the buckets on top of the stove, then looked back to me and nodded for me to . . .

"Undress," she said.

I just looked at her a moment.

She looked at me back; she smiled and nodded again, looking to my clothes.

"You won't get any argument from me," I said.

I took off my coat and vest and hung them on a coat-rack next to the door, then I sat in a chair in the corner and took off my boots.

"I'd ask you how you knew I was back, but I guess I don't have to," I said.

"No," she said, "you don't, but I will tell you."

"Friends, no doubt?"

She shook her head and smiled.

"I saw you and your partner come in, with the wounded man," she said. "I was walking the boardwalk and I saw you."

I stood up and undid my trousers and let them drop to the floor.

"Where were you walking to?" I said, as I unbuttoned my shirt. "Or from?"

"No place," she said.

— 43 —

I sat in the hot-water tub as Séraphine bathed me. She scrubbed my head with some special soap laced with rose, ginger, and rosemary. Then she lathered a wood-handled scrub brush with some other sweet-smelling soap and commenced to clean me. She scrubbed my arms and chest, then leaned me forward and scrubbed my shoulders and back. She moved to the other end, and starting with my feet, worked her way up my legs. I leaned back in the tub and closed my eyes.

"Best goddamn bath I've ever had in my life," I said.

She smiled and worked her way up my calves past my knees and scrubbed my thighs.

I looked at her.

She set the scrub brush aside, slid her hands under the water, and worked her hands up my thighs.

"I believe I'm pretty clean."

She smiled.

"I believe you are indeed."

She moved up and kissed me and I kissed her back.

She stood and got me a towel as I lifted myself from the water. I reached for the towel, but she held it back.

"I clean," she said, "and I dry."

She dried me some and I stepped from the tub. I took the towel from her and dropped it. I reached for her and pulled her to me. I kissed her, then turned her around and lifted her nightgown up. She raised her arms and I pulled the gown up and over her head. She turned and faced me.

"I will remember you," she said.

"Remember me?"

"*Oui,*" she said.

"Where are you going?" I said.

"No place."

"Then why do you say you will remember me," I said.

She moved, taking my hand and leading me to the bed. She pulled back the covers and slid her slender body between the folds. I moved in beside her.

"You see something else?" I said.

Her blue eyes were moist. She said nothing. She just stared at me.

"Oh," I said. "I'm the one that's going?"

"What I know is what I told you."

"Nothing else?" I said.

She shook her head.

"You're not a very good liar," I said.

"I'm not lying, Everett," she said. "I don't know how."

"Everybody knows how to lie," I said.

She shook her head.

"Not me," she said.

"Then tell me something," I said.

"What?"

"If you are going no place," I said, "and you haven't seen my inevitable demise, my earth's exit, why are you saying you will remember me?"

"I, too, live in uncertainty, Everett."

"So you are going?"

She just looked at me.

"Are you?"

"I don't know what will happen," she said. "It is just something I feel."

I laid back and put my hand behind my head and looked up to the ceiling.

"Some of what you told me the other night," I said. "Some of that came to be."

She didn't say anything.

"How did you know?" I said. "Can you tell me?"

"I told you," she said. "Your guides."

I smiled.

"How did you know the name Cotter?"

She sat up on one elbow, looking at me.

"You don't believe me, Everett," she said. "You don't believe in who I am and what I say."

"I just said what you told me. Cotter is the name or alias of someone we're after."

"Oui," she said, "but you think I know that because I know something, something I learned in the doing universe."

"In the doing universe?"

"Oui."

"What do you know about the whereabouts of Sheriff Sledge Driskill and his deputies Karl and Chip?"

She shook her head.

"Nothing," she said.

"What do you know about Walton Wayne Swickey and G. W. Cox?"

"I don't," Séraphine said.

"The soldiers?"

"Nothing."

"What else ain't you telling me?" I said.

She shook her head and lay back.

"I don't know anything," she said dejectedly.

We just rested there. A long silence settled between us.

As unusual and peculiar as this union was between us, I felt more alive and somehow more aware of my surroundings.

I reached for her and I turned her face to me. She was warm. And seemed vulnerable for the first time.

"I believe you," I said.

"You do?"

"Yes."

She smiled at me.

"I'm glad," she said.

"I do. I believe you when you tell me you will remember me, that you will do just that, remember me."

She smiled warmly and I kissed her. She kissed me back, tenderly at first, then hard and passionately.

Lord . . .

— 44 —

It did not surprise me to find Séraphine was gone when I woke up in the morning. *What else?* I thought.

My head was heavy and I felt far less alive and aware than I had felt in the evening. I felt as though I had been drunk, but the fact was I'd had nothing, nothing but Séraphine.

I looked around the room, and with the exception of her smell and the cooled water in the tub, there was no sign she had even been there.

I looked out the window and the landscape was just as it was the day before, a blanket of snow.

I could see the depot and smoke rising up from its chimney. The tracks were completely covered as far as I could see and there was no sign of sun.

I got dressed and made my way downstairs. The lobby was empty, but the young British fella was behind the counter. He smiled at me.

I started for the door and he said, "One moment, Mr. Hitch. I've got something here for you."

He retrieved a small envelope from the key box behind the desk and handed it to me. "Here you go."

I took the envelope.

"Appreciate it," I said.

Written across the envelope was one word. *Everett.*

I looked at it, and instead of opening it right away I put it in my pocket and left the hotel.

I walked by the depot and made my way back toward Virgil's place.

I knocked on the door and Allie answered.

"Everett," she said. "Why, good cold and snow-covered morning. Come on in."

I stomped the snow off my boots and stepped inside.

"Lands," Allie said. "That you?"

"Me what?"

She nuzzled her nose into my neck.

"It is," she said. "You sure do smell pretty."

"I took a bath," I said.

"Well, I should say so," Allie said.

She closed the door.

"You don't look so good, though. You look like you seen a ghost," she said.

"No ghost," I said. "Not this morning, anyway. Virgil in?"

"He'll be back in a minute," she said. "I sent him to the grocery to fetch me some baking soda. You feeling all right?"

"I feel fine, Allie," I said.

"Well, you smell fine."

"Could use a cup of coffee," I said.

"You bet," she said. "Sit yourself down right there and make yourself comfortable, Everett."

Allie walked to the kitchen and I took a seat at the table.

"Can you believe this weather?" Allie said.

"I can," I said.

"Think it will ever let up?" Allie said.

"It will."

Allie brought me a cup of coffee in a proper sipping cup with a saucer underneath.

"Fresh," she said.

I took a sip. It was thick and had a jolt to it, but I didn't do nothing but drink it.

Allie took a seat next to me.

"I thought about what you said last night, Everett," Allie said. "And you are right. I was being insensitive and self-centered."

I didn't say anything.

"What you and Virgil have been dealing with, Everett, is far more important and critical than my pettiness and blinded shame over what has happened with Virgil's inability to understand the arts and the man who brings them to us."

I almost spit my coffee. I didn't say anything. I didn't need to. I knew Allie well enough to know she was just getting started, so I just drank my coal-black coffee.

"This poor man, Beauregard, is misunderstood and good-hearted, but that is no reason to give his unfortunate circumstances more attention, more credence, than the serious circumstances that you and Virgil are facing. Not to mention my quarrel with Virgil is petty of me to even consider in times like these."

Allie put her hand on my hand.

"So. I want to thank you for setting me straight, Everett," Allie said.

I nodded.

"You know, Everett," Allie said. "I just have to stop thinking about myself. So I've decided I will do what I can do to give, instead of constantly needing to receive."

"What are you thinking about giving?" I said.

"Well," Allie said. "I'm glad you ask. For starters, I thought about poor Mrs. Beauchamp."

"What have you thought about her?" I said.

"Well, what with this weather like it is and with her being secluded," Allie said. "I feel it is my civic duty to see to it she doesn't get herself in the way of Beauregard and his creative needs, so I'm going to invite her over for tea."

Allie smiled, big.

I just looked at her.

"Who knows," Allie said. "Perhaps we will become good friends."

"Who knows?" I said.

"Yes," she said. "Who knows?"

"You think that is a good idea?" I said.

"I do," Allie said.

Virgil came through the front door and looked over, seeing me.

"Hey, Everett," Virgil said.

Virgil had a small box of groceries.

"I picked you up a few other things I thought you might need, Allie," Virgil said.

"Thank you, Virgil," she said.

Allie got up and took the box from Virgil.

"Oh, good, chocolate. Why, Virgil, you are so thoughtful."

Virgil looked at me. He sniffed the air a little.

"That you?" he said.

"Is," I said.

— 45 —

I unlocked Bolger's cell and brought him into the main office and sat him down in a chair next to the potbellied stove.

"There ya go, Bolger," I said. "Make yourself comfortable."

Virgil was sitting behind the desk, leaning back in the squeaky banker's chair. He had his boots crossed on top of the corner of the desk and a cup of coffee in his hand. Chastain was sitting in a chair that backed up to the front window of the office.

"How you feeing, Bolger?" Virgil said.

Bolger didn't say anything.

Virgil nodded.

"Want some coffee?"

Bolger nodded.

I poured him some coffee and handed it to him.

"Tell me about the dynamite," Virgil said.

Bolger snapped his chin to his chest and furrowed his brow as he shook his head.

"Dynamite?" he said.

"Yep," Virgil said.

"Don't know nothing about no dynamite."

"You don't?"

"No," Bolger said. "Don't."

"So, the judge will be here sometime soon," Virgil said. "The choice is yours."

"Well," Bolger said. "Don't know nothing about no dynamite."

"What do you want to tell us?" Virgil said.

Bolger looked at Virgil and shook his head a little.

"Nothing."

"Nothing?" Virgil said.

"I don't got nothing to say."

Virgil nodded a little, took a sip of his coffee, and set it on the desk.

"If I did have something to say," Bolger said. "I don't, but let's say I did. How is that gonna help me?"

"Like Everett offered," Virgil said. "We'll let the judge know you provided us with important information. The good judge will consider your good deed when you stand before him, facing him, on attempted robbery and murder charges."

"I didn't rob or murder no one," Bolger said.

Virgil nodded.

"Like I said," Virgil said. "*Attempted* robbery and murder."

"Need to be goddamn clear on that," Bolger said.

"We're real clear on that," I said. "And we're also clear on the fact you tried to kill me, a United States territorial deputy marshal, which you will serve a minimum of five years for, just for that. The attempted robbery and murder charges on the other two fellas, Grant and Elliott, will be separate."

"Shit," Bolger said with a point out to the street. "Them two silly fellers, it was all their fault."

"How's that?" Virgil said.

"I was working for them," Bolger said. "Hell, it was a job I was okay with. I like driving a rig."

"That right?" Virgil said.

Bolger nodded.

"But they didn't pay me like they said they was gonna do. Hell, I'm a good worker," Bolger said defensively.

Virgil knew who Bolger was. We'd seen men like Bolger a hundred times over the years. The west was full of them, men who came from a bad place, and as life carried on, things only got worse for them. Hardship and heartache were at the core of who they were. Bolger was a man of a simple way, with simple means, simple ambition, and simple instincts. A good enough worker until payday, then he'd drink and gamble and whore his money away. Guys like Bolger were always in and out of jail, drunks mostly, drunks who are just one bad shot away from Hell.

"I don't got time for your bullshit about you working, Bolger," Virgil said. "You boys hired on to sneak dynamite up there to the river bridge."

Bolger shook his head.

"Did not," he said.

"Bullshit," Virgil said.

Bolger shook his head.

"You did it," Virgil said.

"No," Bolger said with conviction. "I did not."

"Don't you lie to me."

"I'm not."

"You are."

Bolger was flustered. He shook his head hard.

"You did it," Virgil said.

"No, I didn't."

"Bullshit."

"I had nothing to do with that."

"Bullshit!"

"I didn't," he said. *"Ballard did!"*

— 46 —

Bolger sat up knowing he'd mouthed off. He wasn't too flustered about it because he knew, deep down, he was headed toward that decision, and so did Virgil.

"You both were in on this from the beginning," Virgil said. "Weren't you?"

Bolger shook his head.

Virgil, now, didn't believe Bolger was part of the plan, but he knew the more he included Bolger the more Bolger would defend himself and reveal the truth.

"Bullshit," Virgil said. "And if you keep on with your bullshit, we'll move on. Right now, though, we are offering you a way to get your ass outta this sling it's in."

"It was Ballard," Bolger said.

Virgil looked at Chastain, then at me, then at Bolger.

"Where is he?" Virgil said.

"That I do not know," Bolger said.

"Stop with the bullshit," Virgil said.

"I done told you he was the one that took up the dynamite," Bolger said. "I'd tell you where he was if I knew."

"Who was it that hired him to do this?" Virgil said.

"I don't know," Bolger said.

"What *do* you know?" Virgil said.

Bolger just looked at Virgil for a long moment.

"Tell me about the men he's involved with," Virgil said. "Tell me all you know. The more you tell me, the better your chances are. The more you lie, the better your chances are we will see to it your prison stay will be a good one."

Bolger looked at Virgil again for a long bit.

Virgil nodded for Bolger to talk.

"Well, shit," Bolger said. "I don't know who he's involved with. I don't. I been in Appaloosa for a while. Doing pretty okay. I had a few jobs here and there, but nothing really stuck. Then I got this here job with them boys. Like I told you, I was okay with it. Then my brother, he come to town."

"From where?" Virgil said.

"Wyoming."

"What was he doing in Wyoming?"

Bolger shrugged.

"He was up there chasing some pussy."

"What pussy?"

"Oh, some woman he got himself buggered up with," Bolger said. "I don't know."

"What kind of buggered up with?"

"He got his ass throwed in jail over her," Bolger said.

"For?" Virgil said.

"I guess she belong to someone else, some lawman," Bolger said. "Ballard and this lawman got into a fight, and I guess Ballard messed him up real good. Not a good idea to get into it with Ballard, lawman or no lawman. Ballard did, though, manage to get thrown in jail there. Spent sixty days, and when he got out he came here to see me."

"Go on," Virgil said.

Bolger looked to the floor, shaking his head.

"Tell us what went down," Virgil said.

"He started working with me," Bolger said. "I told him I was doing okay. Keeping outta trouble and that I didn't want no trouble. Things was going okay for a little while, but things don't go okay for too long when Ballard gets involved. He got put out, started doing other stuff."

"What other stuff?"

"Whores," Bolger said. "Said it paid better and smelled better."

"Pimpin'," I said.

"I guess you could call it that," Bolger said. "He made sure customers' payments were made in full."

"Where?"

"A place called the Back Door."

Virgil looked to me.

I nodded.

"Know it," I said. "That's the house we saw them redoing last summer."

"North of town?" Virgil said.

I nodded.

"A high-end whorin' establishment," Chastain said. "A good stock place. Caters to the big-money men in town."

"Who runs the place?" Virgil said.

"Owned by two mine owners," Chastain said. "Operated by some whore they brought in from Cincinnati named Belle."

Virgil looked back to Bolger.

"I never been over there," Bolger said. "Ballard was working there, though. He's got a way with women. Until they really know him, that is. Then they scare. Always some dealing with Ballard and women."

"He spell out the deal to you?"

"Some."

"What do you know?" Virgil said.

"A whore there introduced Ballard to one of her clients," Bolger said.

Bolger shook his head a little.

"The client had learned from the whore that Ballard had been making delivery runs up to the bridge camp before he did what he did at the whorehouse," Bolger said.

"What else?" Virgil said.

"All I know is this fella," Bolger said. "This client met with Ballard a few times and Ballard told me this guy hired him to make a special delivery for him."

"You know who this client is?" I said.

"I don't," Bolger said.

"Know the whore?" Virgil said.

"No," Bolger said. "Never met her."

"But Ballard told you this?" I said.

"He did," Bolger said. "He come to me, said he needed to use the team and the buckboard."

Virgil looked to me, then back to Bolger.

"How'd you know the special delivery was dynamite?" Virgil said.

"Ballard told me," Bolger said. "At first he was gonna cut me in on the deal."

"At first?" Virgil said.

"Then he changed his mind," Bolger said.

"Why?"

"That's Ballard," Bolger said.

"Tell us about that," Virgil said.

"I told him he'd have to pay me good, 'cause it was my buckboard and I haven't been even paid," Bolger said. "I was out of money."

"Then what?" Virgil said.

Bolger shook his head. "Ballard told me he wasn't paying me shit. Said he's taking the team and trailer, no matter."

"What happened?" Virgil said.

Bolger shook his head, thinking.

"We goddamn got into it, mixed it up right there in front of them boys' office," Bolger said with a crack in his voice. "But Ballard . . . Ballard and me, we been into it enough in the past I knew when to back down. Once he gets going he don't got no throttle."

"He took the team and buckboard?" I said.

"He did," Bolger said.

"What'd you do?" I said.

Bolger looked at me. His lip quivered a little.

"I stole some whiskey and got drunk," he said.

"What else he tell you about the deal?" Virgil said.

"Nothing," Bolger said, looking at the floor. "Nothing."

Bolger shook his head a little. He looked up to Virgil, then me, then looked back to the floor and started crying.

Virgil looked at me.

"You're doing good, Bolger," I said.

"Sure," Bolger said.

— 47 —

Book walked in the door just as we got Bolger back behind bars and closed the door between the office and the cells.

"Think he's telling the truth?" Chastain said.

"Do," Virgil said quietly. "He don't got the necessary resources to conjure up something like this."

"Poor bastard," Chastain said.

Virgil nodded a little.

"What now?" Chastain said.

"Me and Everett need to make a trip to the Back Door, pay this Belle a visit. Figure out what we can about Ballard, the whore, and who the fella was that hired him."

"You still think this Swickey is the man behind all this?" Chastain said.

"Could damn well be," I said.

"I haven't had any luck locating him yet," Chastain said.

"Keep looking," Virgil said.

"Maybe this Belle knows where he is," I said.

"Maybe," Virgil said. "If he does run cattle and has a big spread, he can't be that hard to find."

"We've contacted every census and court and scoured records but have come up empty, but we ain't done. We'll keep after it," Chastain said.

"Good," Virgil said.

Virgil and I left the office and walked up the street, headed for the north side of town.

The Back Door brothel was a newly reconstructed Victorian two-story house atop a tall foundation at the end of Reed Street.

Virgil and I climbed the long steps and knocked on the door. After a moment a distinguished-looking black man with a feather duster in his hand opened the door.

"I'm sorry," he said. "Won't be open for business until later this afternoon, gentlemen."

I showed him my badge.

"Not here for no business," I said. "Need to see Belle."

He leaned forward, looking at my badge, and nodded.

"I'll let her know you are here," he said, as he stepped back and let us in. "And you are?"

"Marshal Virgil Cole and Deputy Marshal Everett Hitch," I said.

"Sure," he said. "Please have a seat."

Virgil and I sat in the parlor as he walked off down the hall.

We sat there and waited, and after a moment longer than we needed to wait, Belle entered.

We stood.

She was short and round, with a wide smile. It looked like in her day she was a pretty lady, but like most women of her trade, the years had caught up with her.

"You need to see me?" she said in a husky voice seasoned from years of smoke and whiskey.

"We do," I said.

We introduced ourselves.

"I know you two," she said with a smile. "Well, at least I know who you are. Sit."

We sat.

"I'm sorry I'm not more put together," Belle said, "but you caught me before I went about the three-hour process of making myself up, so it goes without saying you must come back so you can experience the amazing transformation."

"Sure," I said, in an effort to be polite.

"Just need to ask you a few questions," Virgil said.

"I'll answer what I can," Belle said.

Virgil nodded.

"Swickey?" Virgil said.

"What about him?" Belle said.

"So you know him?" I said.

"I do," she said. "Not real well, however."

"When was he here last?"

"Oh, well, it's been a few months, I think," she said.

"He got a certain gal?" Virgil said.

"He did," Belle said. "Kim."

"Where can we find Kim?" I said.

"You can't," she said. "Not here, anyway. She moved on."

"Know where she moved on to?"

"Yep," Belle said. "She married one of her regulars and they moved back to Wichita Falls."

"Swickey been back since?" Virgil said.

"No," she said.

"What can you tell us about him?" I said.

"Well," she said. "He's a single man, he enjoys himself when he is here, and he spends a lot of money, but he's been here only a few times. Like I said, he liked Kim, but she's long gone."

"You know where Swickey lives?" Virgil said.

"No, I'm afraid I don't," she said.

"You hired a man here named Ballard?" Virgil said.

We could tell she didn't like the sound of the question.

"He's no longer working here," she said.

Virgil nodded.

"We know that," he said.

"I'm sorry," she said. "I'm not surprised he's someone you are looking for."

"Why?" I said.

"He's a . . . how should I put this," Belle said. "Ballard's rough company."

"Why'd you hire him?" I said.

"He had the credentials I was looking for," Belle said.

"Which are?" I said.

"He's intimidating," Belle said. "He was what I was looking for. He collected for me."

"You have any idea where he might be?" I said.

She shook her head.

"Not at all," she said.

"Fair enough," Virgil said.

"More importantly," I said, "we are looking for one of your girls who introduced Ballard to one of your clients, maybe Swickey."

Belle shook her head.

"I don't know anything about that," she said.

"This Kim," I said. "Was she friendly with Ballard?"

"No," Belle said. "Kim was intelligent and cautious, and she was not close to him that I know. Reason being she was close to me."

"Was Ballard friendly with one woman in particular here?" I said.

"Don't think so," she said. "The girls liked him. Well, they liked to look at him."

"What do you mean," I said.

"Good-looking, got that thing about him women want. Silent, strong, but he's a buck in the rut," Belle said. "Full on, with the horns and all."

"Describe him," Virgil said.

"Well," Belle said. "Like I say, he's strong. He's handsome as hell, a little over six foot, dark hair, full twist longhorn mustache. He sports a bowler with a white feather. He's kind of flashy, has a pretty flashy smile. But like I tell ya, don't be fooled, he's rough company."

"He just up and left here?" Virgil said.

"No, I told him to leave," she said.

"Why?" Virgil said.

"He went too far," she said.

"In what way?" Virgil said.

"He's one mean sadistic son-of-a-crazy-bitch," Belle said, nodding.

"What'd he do?" Virgil said.

"The last fella I had him collect for," Belle said, "he beat him up bad, tied him up, naked, and ransacked his place."

Virgil thought about that. He looked around the room at nothing and everything.

"How can we find out," I said, "who this woman is?"

"Be hard," she said.

"But not impossible," Virgil said.

"Not impossible, no," she said. "But you fellas know whores, and getting something outta them won't be like twisting water out of a wet rag. They like the men they fuck because they pay them well, and they like to keep it that way. Whores are whores because they are whores."

Virgil looked to me.

"So, like I say, not impossible," Belle said. "But my girls don't live here. But you can of course talk to each and every one of them . . ."

I slid my hand into the pocket of my coat as she was talking and I felt the envelope Séraphine had left for me at the hotel desk. I pulled it out and looked at it.

"Plus," Belle continued, "since Ballard, I've had turnover, too. Whoring ain't like it used to be. There is no loyalty . . ."

As Belle went on jabbering, I opened the envelope and read what Séraphine had written.

I looked up to Virgil and he was looking at me.

I looked back to the note. It had but one word written on it. *Slaughterhouse.*

— 48 —

I shared Séraphine's note with Virgil when we left Belle and the Back Door whoring establishment.

"By God," is all Virgil said.

"Yep," I said.

Virgil just shook his head a little as we walked.

I didn't say anything as we trudged through the snow-covered street, back down into town.

Virgil didn't say anything else, either, not for a while, anyway, as he thought about the single word Séraphine left me with.

Then he said, "Slaughterhouse."

I nodded.

"Beats hell," he said.

"Does," I said.

We walked for a bit more without saying anything.

"What do you figure?" I said.

We walked for a bit more.

"Well, given the fact this hocus-pocus fortune-teller lady friend of yours has provided us some pertinent information in regard to the goddamn bridge business we're dealing with," Virgil said. "Pertinent information that has come to light, regardless of how she got it, it might be a good idea we pay heed to this, Everett."

"That'd be my thinking, too," I said.

"As much as I don't like it," Virgil said.

"I know."

"Don't got much more," Virgil said.

"We don't," I said.

Virgil and I made our way back to the livery where we stabled our horses.

Salt was feeding the animals when we entered. He looked up at us when we walked in but said nothing as he went about his business.

By the time Virgil and I got our horses saddled Salt came over to us.

He watched us but said nothing.

"How much more of this shit are we going to see, Salt?" I said. "Got to give up sometime soon."

Salt looked out the open door of the barn and shook his head a little, then looked back to us.

"Pigs are still gathering sticks," Salt said.

Virgil looked at Salt.

Salt nodded a little, then turned and walked into the livery office.

Virgil and I mounted up and rode out of the livery and headed south.

It was cold. The temperature had dropped even more and it was foggy out.

It wasn't snowing, but the powder was deep as we moved slowly through the fog.

The road south of Appaloosa cut through solid forest of aspen, spruce, and fir.

In the spring the sides of the road were nothing but riparian, chaparrals, and prickly poppy, but now everything was a powerful and foreboding sea of white.

Just as we did when we made the journey to the bridge with Cox, we rode the same path by the depot, crossed over the covered tracks, past the last few Appaloosa homesteads on the road, past the icehouse and the stockyards.

The landscape seemed like it was from another place in time. The fog hung heavy some twenty feet above the ground, making the woods feel like there was something in the forest waiting, something lurking and unsatisfied.

The only sound was that of our horses, the chomp-clink of bit metal, the leather creak of our saddles, and the breathing of our animals under us, as they moved us forward into what felt like a prehistoric place, void of civilization.

From someplace secluded in the woods a phantom great gray owl hooted his ominous call.

We came to a stop on the road next to the old abandoned slaughterhouse.

The slaughterhouse was a long, low-built post-and-lintel building that was no longer in use since the bigger, newer version had been built to handle the growing cattle business.

The snow-covered slaughterhouse had loading docks on one end and dilapidated corrals and chutes on the other.

We dismounted and tied our horses to a pair of fir saplings near the road and walked through the deep snow toward the building.

The snow was piled high around the structure, and there had been no sign of tracks other than those of deer and rabbits.

When we got to the door of the slaughterhouse we cleared the snow back so we could open the door.

Virgil pulled his Colt and I did the same. Virgil stepped back to one side of the door and I got to the other. Virgil nodded and I opened the door. Instantly we were hit with the smell of death. We waited for a moment, then Virgil peeked inside. He leaned back and looked to me, shaking his head.

"Goddamn, Everett," he said.

— 49 —

Dim shafts of light shined sideways through missing pieces of siding on the backside of the slaughter-house.

The light revealed three hanging bodies.

They were clearly the bodies of Sheriff Sledge Driskill and his deputies Chip Childers and Karl Worley.

They were hanging side by side on meat hooks that had been gouged into the men, high on their backsides. Their shoulders and heads slumped forward and their hands were tied behind their backs.

"Oh, hell," I said slowly. ". . . Oh, hell, Virgil."

Virgil shook his head slowly.

Lying dead on the floor of the slaughterhouse were two mules and the lawman's three horses. The buck-board sat behind the hanging men and the dead animals at the opposite end of the structure.

The horses and mules had been killed, their throats slashed.

The whole scene was as gruesome as any aftermath of attacks I had witnessed in my days fighting in the Indian Wars.

I went to the opposite end of the building and tried to open the barn doors so to clear the air from the stench, but they wouldn't budge because of the snow.

I kicked out enough slats on the side so I could crawl through the opening. When I got out I used one of the slats as a shovel and went about clearing the snow from in front of the door. I worked at it awhile and eventually Virgil came out through the opening. He picked up a slat and we both worked at clearing the snow.

"Sonsabitches," I said.

Virgil didn't say anything for a moment as he moved snow with the board, then he said under his breath and almost to himself, "Bad hombres, Everett."

"One thing to blow up a goddamn bridge and get paid for it," I said. "But this is, this is, I don't know, it's . . ."

Virgil didn't say anything, he just dug and scraped snow.

We kept at it until we got the snow cleared and the doors could open freely.

When we opened the barn doors we could see clothing lying inside the bed of the buckboard.

"Their discarded stuff," I said.

Virgil nodded.

"Left when they donned the goddamn blues," Virgil said.

Virgil picked up one of the pieces of clothing. A vest. He shook his head a little and dropped it.

We wasted no time getting the men down from the meat hooks and into the bed of the buckboard.

I thought about the face of the man with the beard I saw riding through town. I remembered his eyes. I thought about the fact he looked at me sitting by the window of Hal's Café and gave me a slight wave as the men behind followed him, riding through the street.

I remembered talking with Hal about the look they had, and now, after seeing this brutal and evil dirty work, I knew why they looked the way they did. They had just done this deed. I added up the timing in my mind. When Driskill and his men left, and the timing when I witnessed the men ride by in front of Hal's.

"When I saw the bastards riding through, it was about noon," I said.

Virgil thought about that as we laid the body of young Chip in the bed of the buckboard.

"They stayed here through the night," Virgil said, "looking about the slaughterhouse."

"And took their damn time."

"They did," Virgil said.

Virgil and I covered the men with our slickers. We got our horses and hitched them to the buckboard. Then we drove the buckboard slowly back on the foggy road to Appaloosa.

When we arrived back in Appaloosa, we drove around

the outside of town so as not to draw attention. We cut through the alleys and stopped in behind the office of the undertaker.

I went through the back door and got the old undertaker, Joshua Ramos, and brought him out to the alley.

Ramos was a large, jovial man, always dressed in a tattered black suit and never without an unlit cigar wedged into the corner of his mouth.

"Hey, Virgil," Joshua said.

"Joshua," Virgil said.

When Joshua and I were close to the buckboard, Virgil pulled the slickers covering the dead men.

Joshua opened his mouth and his cigar dropped in the snow.

"Holy hell," Joshua said. "That's Sheriff Driskill?"

"It is," Virgil said.

"And his deputies," I said.

"Holy hell," Joshua said.

"Don't let no one know about this," Virgil said.

"I won't," Joshua said, shaking his head. "I most certainly won't."

"Want to notify the next of kin," Virgil said. "Post a town hall notice and let the mayor of Appaloosa make the proper announcement to the community."

— 50 —

Virgil and I got the clothes from the back of the buckboard and stuffed them into a gunnysack.

"Since it's freezing cold like it is," Joshua said, "it'd be best we put the bodies in here."

Joshua opened a shed connected to the back of his office.

Virgil and I put the bodies of the lawmen side by side on the floor.

"You want me to get them ready to be buried right away, I reckon?" Joshua said.

"I do," Virgil said.

"I got one box built for Old Bill Gibbons, but he ain't dead just yet, so I can use that one," Joshua said. "Just have to build two more."

"Get 'er done," Virgil said.

"Will do," Joshua said.

"With the weather like it is," Joshua said, "be hard as hell to dig a hole in this ground."

"Hard ground or not," Virgil said. "Need to get it started. Get some men to the cemetery with some pickaxes. Pay 'em, I'll cover it."

"You want me to put them side by side?" Joshua said.

Virgil looked at me.

I nodded.

We left Joshua and drove the buckboard to the open yard behind the Appaloosa Livery and unhitched our animals.

Salt came out to meet us. He took our horses and walked them into the barn.

Salt watched Virgil and me as we removed our saddles from the buckboard and walked to the barn. He could tell something was up, something different, but he didn't say anything and neither did we.

I took the gunnysack full of the clothes discarded by the killers with me as Virgil and I left the livery barn and started walking toward the sheriff's office.

We walked the three blocks without saying anything. The fact of the matter was we'd hardly talked at all, all the way back to Appaloosa from the slaughterhouse.

We crossed the street to the opposite boardwalk and as we neared the office we saw Book coming up the boardwalk from the opposite direction.

He saw us, waved to us, and hurried his pace toward us.

"Not real interested in this," I said. "Talking to them."

"No," Virgil said. "I know."

"These boys are gonna take this hard."

"They will."

"Driskill was like a father to them," I said.

"He was," Virgil said.

Book kept moving toward us.

"Boys to men, today," Virgil said.

"It is," I said.

"Hey," Book said, as he got closer to us. "Got some good news."

"What's that, Book?" I said.

We met directly in front of the sheriff's office door.

"Found the whereabouts of the cattleman you're searching for," Book said. "Chastain told me to find you. I have been looking all over for you. Wanted to let you know right away."

Chastain opened the door. Skinny Jack was right behind him.

Chastain had heard us.

"That's right," Chastain said. "You were right, Swickey runs a big spread across the Rio Blanco."

Virgil kicked his boots against the jamb a bit and walked into the office. I did the same and followed Virgil inside. Book followed me and I shut the door behind him.

The door between the office and the cells was closed.

"Got a direction on him?" Virgil said.

Chastain nodded.

"Know where to find him," Chastain said.

Virgil nodded.

"Good," Virgil said.

"Got a wire back from the Territorial Cattlemen's Association," Chastain said.

"Where is he?" Virgil said.

"Like you said, he's on the Blanco near Loblolly Mills," Chastain said.

"Loblolly," Virgil said. "That's just due east of here."

"It is, fifty, sixty miles. I didn't want to start inquiring any more than we done," Chastain said. "I didn't contact no one in Loblolly. I don't want to let him know we're looking for him."

Virgil nodded.

"What do you want to do?" Chastain said.

"Sit down," Virgil said.

"What?" Chastain said.

"The three of you sit down," Virgil said.

Chastain looked to Book and Skinny Jack and nodded to the chairs. Chastain sat behind the desk; Skinny Jack and Book sat opposite him.

Virgil walked the length of the room and when he got to the rear wall he turned to face the men.

They were looking at him, expectant.

Virgil walked slowly over to the desk. He put his hand in his pocket and one by one pulled out and placed the badges of Sheriff Driskill, Deputy Karl Worley, and Deputy Chip Childers on the desk in front of them.

— 51 —

When we entered Virgil and Allie's place, Allie and Nell Beauchamp were sitting side by side on the sofa near the fireplace. They were drinking tea. There was a bottle of Kentucky next to the tea tray that suggested the tea was most likely unsatisfying.

"Oh, good," Allie said, as she got to her feet. "Virgil, Everett, I believe you two have met Mrs. Beauchamp?"

"We have," Virgil said.

"Evening, Mrs. Beauchamp," I said.

She smiled. She remained seated on the feather sofa. Her legs were crossed under her expensive-looking dress and she leaned her body to one side, making her right hip slightly raised from the sofa. Her left elbow rested on the arm of the sofa with her forearm angled up, allowing her head to rest in the palm of her hand. Her right arm was outstretched over the curved back of the sofa. With the exception of having her clothes on, her position reminded me of a nudie pose from a backroom stereopticon show.

"Nell, please," she said. "No need for formality."

"Nell," I said. "Good to see you again."

"It is," Virgil said.

"Good to see you again, too," she said.

Nell didn't move a muscle from her pose on the sofa as Virgil and I hung our coats and hats next to the door.

"So glad you are back," Allie said. "I waited to start supper. I never know if and when they'll come home."

"We're here," Virgil said.

"They?" Nell said. "How fortunate for you."

"Well, Virgil," Allie said with a giggle. "I never know if and when Virgil will come home. Everett is . . ."

"I'm just here a lot," I said. "They can't get rid of me. I'm kind of like the town dog."

Nell laughed. She had a nice laugh.

"Well," Nell said. "You don't look much like a town dog."

"Am," I said.

"Do you bite?" Nell said.

"Do," I said.

"Well," Nell said. "I'll be sure and not get too close."

"Be a good idea," I said.

She laughed again, and again I thought she had a lovely laugh. I thought she was very pretty, but then almost from someplace deep inside, an undercurrent of my mind, flashed the horrific image of our men hanging in the slaughterhouse. It was such a private, brutal thought for this particular time.

I looked to the fire for a moment and thought secretly and intently about what we saw. I shook my head some. I realized that what we witnessed would haunt me for a very long time, perhaps for the rest of my life. *The godforsaken slaughterhouse . . .*

"I've invited Nell to stay the night," Allie said.

Virgil looked at me, then looked to the women.

"Mr. Beauchamp?"

"Resting," Nell said.

"Know where you are?" Virgil said.

Nell nodded.

"I let him know," she said.

"You did?"

"Yes," she said.

"And he heard you?" Virgil said.

"Virgil?" Allie said.

Virgil looked to Allie.

"You walked over there and got her and she told him she was staying the night?" Virgil said.

"It's okay, Virgil," Allie said.

"Just don't want him to come out of sleeping it off and find his wife missing."

"Virgil," Allie said, appalled.

"It's okay," Nell said. "Don't worry, Marshal. I assure you it's not an issue. He'll not see the chime of another hour until late tomorrow morning."

Virgil looked at her for a moment and nodded a little.

"Well," Virgil said. "Welcome."

"Thank you," Nell said. "Your home is beautiful."

"Appreciate it," Virgil said. "We put a lot into it."

Virgil looked to me.

"Everett helped," he said.

I smiled.

Nell looked to me and smiled. So far Nell had yet to budge even a smidgen from her pose on the sofa.

"Where's she gonna sleep?" Virgil said.

"With me," Allie said. "Just like sisters."

"Where am I gonna sleep?" Virgil said.

"Right there," Allie said, pointing to the sofa.

— 52 —

Virgil looked to the sofa.

"Kind of small, isn't it?" Virgil said.

"I can stay on the sofa," Nell said.

"No," Allie said. "Virgil will be perfectly fine sleeping right there. Won't you, Virgil."

I nodded a little.

"Beats sleeping in the barn," I said.

"Well," Allie said with a clap of her hands. "I'm sure you boys are hungry."

Virgil just looked to me, then back to the sofa.

Allie clasped her hands in front of her chest and looked to Nell.

"Well," Allie said. "Time to beat the daylights out of those pots and pans."

"I'm not much of a cook, I'm afraid," Nell said.

"Nonsense," Allie said, holding her hand out. "Come with me, it will be fun."

Nell took Allie's hand and rose up from her position on the sofa dramatically, like she was a queen. She looked to me and smiled as she walked off.

We watched the women walk to the kitchen.

Virgil shook his head a little.

"Timing has a way of being goddamn untimely, don't it?" Virgil said.

"Does," I said.

Virgil got a log from a pile of logs near the hearth and set it in the burning flames. He picked up the poker and poked around in the fire a bit, giving it some air.

"You gonna say anything?" I said.

"Not at the moment, I ain't," Virgil said.

Virgil set the poker aside. He walked over to the dining room breakfront. He got two glasses, came back to the table in front of the fireplace, and poured us each a decent nudge of Kentucky.

"She seems happy," Virgil said. "Want to let her stay that way. Talking about what happened today, about brutal murder, ain't light fare."

"No," I said. "It's not."

"People are gonna know soon enough about them," I said.

"If they don't already," Virgil said.

I nodded.

"Still, need to let the mayor know in the morning," I said. "Post notice, let him make the formal statement."

"Goddamn," Virgil said, shaking his head. "God-damn."

"I know," I said.

"Good boys," Virgil said.

"They were," I said.

Virgil and I sat across from each other. He looked at his whiskey for a moment, then threw it back.

I drank mine, too, and Virgil poured us two more.

"I been thinking about Ballard," Virgil said.

"'Bout?"

"He would have been hanging next to the others in the slaughterhouse if he wasn't interested in fucking them up, too," Virgil said.

I nodded.

"Belle said he was a buck in the rut," I said. "Horns and all."

"Ballard is older, too," Virgil said. "He most likely took over as the lead of this bunch."

"A gun to a knife fight," I said.

Virgil nodded.

"What we know about him is he's a hard-case bad-ass," Virgil said. "Snaps on women."

"And men," I said. "His brother included."

Virgil nodded.

"He beat up that fella Belle told us about, left him tied up, naked," Virgil said.

"A collector," I said. "An attractor and intimidator."

We drank a bit more as we looked to the fire.

"A killer," Virgil said.

"He's settled in," I said.

"He's by God right at home," Virgil said.

I sat back with the glass in my hand. I looked to the fire, watching it.

Virgil did the same.

We watched the fire for a long moment, then Virgil spoke without looking at me.

"Last thing we do, Everett," Virgil said, as he stayed looking into the fire. "Is bring them goddamn down like wolves on lamb."

— 53 —

Allie made a dinner of rabbit, carrots, and potatoes. The rabbit had been cooked too fast and was kind of tough to chew. We drank some wine with the food, which made the whole of it tolerable. I didn't really give a shit about the food or the wine. Fact was, it was hard to eat anything. All I could think about was seeing those men, our men, hanging like animals.

"So," Allie said, working her jaw muscle on the rabbit. "Please tell us, Nell. What's it like to have such an exciting life, such an exciting profession?"

Nell worked at the rabbit on her plate with her fork and knife for a moment before she spoke.

"I wish I had a home," Nell said. "Like this."

"Really?" Allie said.

"Really," Nell said.

"But you get to be in new and fascinating places all the time."

"Not sure how fascinating the places, the stopovers of the west, are, Allie," Nell said.

"But," Allie said, "you are onstage and people adore you and your husband. That has to be exciting."

"At first it was," Nell said. "But things change."

Virgil glanced to me.

"Nell's from San Francisco," Allie said.

"That right?" I said.

"Yes," Nell said. "Have you ever been?"

"I have," I said.

"And?" Nell said.

"Lot of people," I said. "A polyglot."

"True," Nell said.

"Do you miss it?" Allie said.

"Not so much," Nell said.

"I've never been," Allie said. "Virgil tells me he'll take me there, one day. I will believe it when I see it. You have family there?" Allie said.

"No," she said. "I don't."

"How did you become an actress?" Allie said.

"Allie," Virgil said. "Let her chew her food."

"Oh, it's okay," Nell said. "I was a dancer at first."

"How exciting," Allie said. "The ballet?"

Nell smiled.

"No," Nell said. "Dance hall."

"Oh," Allie said.

"Started when I was twelve," she said.

"Oh," Allie said.

"In the Barbary," Nell said, matter-of-fact.

"Oh," Allie said.

Virgil glanced to me.

It became clear to me the relationship between Beauregard and Nell. She was in the Barbary. He most likely pulled her out of the Barbary before she was completely devoured. The only women in the Barbary were whores. Nell and Allie had more in common, I thought, than what first met the eye. Both had a history of whoring, and given the fact they seemed to be two peas in a pod, it was becoming pretty clear just why.

"Let her eat," Virgil said.

Nell worked at cutting the rabbit on her plate into little pieces before she said anything else.

"He's not a bad man," Nell said, looking at Virgil. "If it were not for him . . . no telling where I'd be."

Virgil didn't say anything.

"Not a good man," Nell went on, as she continued to cut her rabbit.

She was sawing on the rabbit as if she were cutting up Beauregard.

"But not a bad man," she said, as she forked a piece of rabbit into her mouth and chewed.

After dinner, Nell insisted Allie and Virgil sit by the fire and enjoy each other's company while I helped her in the kitchen, cleaning the dishes.

We worked side by side, washing and drying the dishes for a long while without saying anything.

"He knows I like you," Nell said.

I just looked at her.

She looked at me.

"That's why he acted the way he did when I saw you

walk into the door of the hotel," she said. "He could see it in my eyes. He's beyond jealous. He watches me. Watches my every move. He knows I'm looking for a way out."

"I'm no savior," I said.

"I know," Nell said.

She continued to wash and I continued to dry.

"You could do one thing for me, though," Nell said.

"What's that?" I said.

"Before I have to leave Appaloosa," she said, "I'd like you to make love to me."

— 54 —

The night was dark and never without all the images of what Virgil and I had experienced this day and the last few that had preceded it.

The evening went on for certain without a roll with Nell or another strange encounter with Séraphine. Not sure I could have handled either. In fact, I knew I couldn't.

My room was cold. I got the Pettit and Smith heater going and the chill lessened. I kicked my boots off and got myself ready to sleep.

I laid down, but my mind was active and unsettled.

I thought back about Virgil and me sitting on his front porch, talking about the incoming weather, and Sheriff Driskill and his deputies Chip Childers and Karl Worley stopping by on their way to the bridge in search of Lonnie Carman. *An innocent enough mission,* I thought.

I looked to the ceiling, and thought about Virgil and me hearing the music and then seeing Beauregard and the troupe parade into town and how excited Allie had been.

I sat straight and picked up the bottle I had set on the floor. It had a little left in it and I drank it. I felt tired and in need of sleep, but my mind was restless.

I wondered what had happened that day, when Driskill and his deputies encountered those goddamn dressers. How did they get them, get the jump on them? *They were not even a quarter mile from town.* I kept playing out how it could have happened. It was hard for me to shake the image of the brutal torture the men had most surely endured.

Sledge Driskill's, Chip Childers's, and Karl Worley's smiling faces stayed in my head as I thought about them sitting on their horses in front of Virgil and Allie's porch.

Then I thought about today, about them lying lifeless in the back of the buckboard under our slickers as we rode back to town. I thought about us putting them in the cold shed behind Joshua's place and about the mayor making an announcement to the community of Appaloosa.

I tried to drift off to sleep in my shitty room above the survey office but continued to have a hard time.

I thought about Séraphine, and when she left me the note. I thought about her saying she would remember me.

I thought about Nell, too, and the rabbit dinner Allie made tonight. I thought about Nell's life with Beauregard, the older man, the actor with the black dyed hair, the jealous husband.

I thought about the Barbary Coast and what I remembered there. The rough men and women there and the rough life they led. I thought about Nell being there, and the life she had lived.

I thought about Virgil sleeping on his sofa and Allie and Nell sleeping in the same bed.

My mind would not quiet and I rolled and turned, trying to find some comfort, some peace, some slumber.

I thought about seeing the bridge blown up and the tons of wood and iron beams, draped down into the Rio Blanco River like a lifeless dead tree.

I thought of Bolger shooting at me, and of his brother, Ballard, and the buckboard and the clothes in the back.

Everything was revolving in my mind, including the cattleman Swickey. What could be his reason for blowing up the bridge? Or did he need one? *Maybe it was sheer hatred for Cox and for not getting the contract?*

I thought about us riding to Loblolly tomorrow and about finding him. I thought about who he was and what he looked like. I thought about confronting him and I wondered what to expect, if we would run into the men pretending to be soldiers there, too. *Would this be it; would it go down?*

I could not stop thinking about them, the pretend soldiers, *the goddamn no-good murderers*. The face of the bearded man who rode by Hal's Café and lifted his hand, giving me a slight wave as he passed. *Was that one of the Cotter brothers?* I kept seeing his face . . . and his eyes, his disturbing, killer eyes. I kept seeing those eyes looking right at me.

But the men hanging in the slaughterhouse was the vision that kept me awake, kept returning in my mind, and I could not shake it. I knew those boys, Chip and Karl and Driskill. I knew them real well, they were good men, good lawmen; they were friends to one another and they were my friends. *Goddamn . . . Goddamn . . . Goddamn . . .*

I n the morning I sat on my bed with a blanket wrapped around me and stared at the floor for a long time before I even considered getting out of bed and getting dressed. My Pettit and Smith heater had died out through the night and the room was cold. The wind was whistling a haunting melody through the cracks around the door.

Where is the damn light? I looked out the window; there was still no sign of sun, the weather remained cloudy and dark, and snow swirled in the bitter morning wind.

I dressed and stopped by Café Paris and drank some coffee. Café Paris was the first place Virgil and I ever ate and drank coffee when we came to Appaloosa. The same place where we met Allie for the first time. *Allison French*, she'd said her name was, and Virgil asked her, that very first time he laid eyes on her, if she was a whore.

— 55 —

As planned, I met Virgil at the livery. We got our horses saddled and ready to ride. Salt watched us as we mounted up and rode out of the barn. I looked back. Salt closed the barn doors when we left and did not look at us as we rode away.

Before we took off for Loblolly Mills in search of Swickey, we stopped in at the mayor's office to pay Ashley Epps a visit.

When we entered, Ashley was sitting behind his desk and a pretty young woman was sitting across from him as he dictated a note to her. He held up one finger for us to give him a moment.

We did.

When he finished with "God Bless, Yours Truly, Ashley Epps," he thanked the young woman.

She nodded.

"Will that be all?" she said.

"Yes, Silvia," Ashley said.

She curtsied a little to Ashley and offered us a smile on her way out.

Ashley stood up to greet us.

"Marshal Cole, Deputy Marshal Hitch, good to see you both. Please have a seat," he said.

We sat opposite his desk.

"How are you?" he said.

Virgil said nothing.

"Been better," I said.

Virgil nodded.

"I hope you are here to tell me you've apprehended the men responsible for the bridge?" Ashley said.

Virgil looked to me.

"What about the bridge?" I said.

Ashley looked back and forth between Virgil and me.

"Well," Ashley said. "Curtis Whittlesey told me."

"What'd he tell you?" I said.

"He told me about the bridge," Ashley said. "That it had been destroyed."

Virgil nodded a little.

"I wish you would have let me know," Ashley said.

"Sounds like we didn't need to let you know," Virgil said.

"Yes, well, I am the mayor," Ashley said, "as well as the minister, and it's my duty to serve and console those in need."

"Just had to keep this news from spreading the best we could," I said.

"That's hard to do with Curtis Whittlesey having knowledge," Ashley said.

"Seems to be," I said.

"Nevertheless," Ashley said. "I've prayed for all those involved for God's Peace to be with them."

"Be with them?" Virgil said.

"Yes?" Ashley said.

"Peace be with who?" Virgil said.

"Well," Ashley said. "Those involved, of course."

"Don't think God's got much to do with this one," Virgil said.

Ashley looked to me.

I didn't say anything.

After Ashley continued with his concerns about his authority, we gave him the news of our Appaloosa lawmen. We didn't provide any details, other than they had been killed in the line of duty and that a formal announcement needed to be made.

"Those fellas," Virgil said, "you can talk with God about."

We didn't waste any more time and bid Ashley good day, leaving him shaken and with tears in his eyes.

Virgil and I walked out of the Rains Civic Building and mounted up. We turned our horses and started to ride when we heard Skinny Jack.

"Hold up," he shouted.

We pulled up and looked back. Skinny Jack was coming up the boardwalk at a quick pace and Book was trying to keep up behind him.

"What is it?" I said.

"Goddamn glad we caught you," Skinny Jack said, out of breath.

"What is it?"

"Don't think you need to go looking for Swickey," Skinny Jack said.

"Why?" I said.

"The sonofabitch is here," Skinny Jack said.

"In Appaloosa?" I said.

"He is," Skinny Jack said, trying to catch his breath.

"Where?" Virgil said.

"Scared the shit outta us," Skinny Jack said. "Him and three men walked into the office just a while ago."

"And?" Virgil said.

Book caught up with Skinny Jack.

"Said he was looking for you," Skinny Jack said.

"Where you say we were?" I said.

"We didn't," Skinny Jack said. "We told them we didn't know."

Book nodded.

"We thought you'd be most likely gone already," Book said, as he worked to catch his breath.

"We thought you'd most likely already left to go find him," Skinny Jack said. "But we didn't say so."

"Glad to know you're here," Book said. "They're heeled, too."

"Where are they now?" Virgil said.

"Boston House," Skinny Jack said.

— 56 —

Boston House? More of the goddamn Boston House, I thought.

"He said for us to find you," Book said.

"What else he say?" Virgil said.

Skinny Jack looked to Book.

"That's it," Skinny Jack said. "Find you and let you know he'd be waiting on you."

Virgil looked at me.

"What do you make of that?" I said.

"Don't know," Virgil said.

"Saves us from riding to Loblolly Mills to hunt the sonofabitch down."

"Damn sure does," Virgil said.

"What the hell is he doing here?" I said.

"'Spect we'll find out," Virgil said.

"Not friendly," Book said.

Skinny Jack nodded.

"No," Skinny Jack said. "Not overly."

"Chastain at the jail?" Virgil said.

"No," Book said. "Just the two of us in this morning."

"He should be in directly," Skinny Jack said.

"Book," Virgil said. "Go back and keep house. Skinny Jack, you come with us."

"What should I do?" Book said.

"Just be there," Virgil said. "Let Chastain know when he comes in."

"Okay," Book said.

Virgil and I rode up the street in the swirling snow to the Boston House and Skinny Jack followed alongside.

When we got to the Boston House we saw the transportation belonging to Swickey and the three others. Two horses and an enclosed buggy, hitched to two sturdy horses, with their heads in muzzle feeders.

We stopped shy of the hotel and tied our horses to a hitch in front of the lumberyard.

"Skinny Jack," Virgil said, as he pulled his Winchester from its scabbard. "Don't really know what to expect. I don't think they got any intentions, but just in case, you just stay out on the porch over here. Everett and me will go inside and see what is what. If for some reason they do have intentions and things get lit up in there, and we don't come out for some reason, maybe one of them does, you hang back here with this Winchester and kill him."

Skinny Jack took the Winchester from Virgil. His Adam's apple went up, then down, as he nodded.

Virgil and I walked up the boardwalk to the hotel.

"You take the side entrance, Everett," Virgil said. "I'll come in from the lobby. Give me ten."

I nodded, and started counting ten seconds so to give Virgil time to come in through the front entrance. When I got to ten I pushed open the side door just as Virgil came through the pocket doors leading into the lobby.

Wallis wasn't in. His second barkeep, a young Irishman named O'Malley, was behind the bar and the saloon was empty except for the four men sitting near the bar at the big round eight-player table, drinking coffee.

They looked first to me standing with my eight-gauge and then to Virgil with his frock pulled behind his bone-handle.

A big man leaned back in his chair, looking back and forth between Virgil and me.

"Which one of you is Virgil Cole?" he said in a huge, commanding voice.

"Who's asking?" Virgil said.

The man took his hat off and stood.

"I'm guessing that'd be you," he said to Virgil.

Virgil didn't say anything.

"I'm Walton Wayne Swickey," he said.

Swickey was well over six feet tall. He was clean shaven and powerful-looking. His hair was cut tight to the sides of his head but the top was a thick crop of dark gray. His face was weathered but strong. He had high cheekbones and deep-set pale blue eyes. He wore a dark pin-striped wool suit with a vest and a string tie. Like Book said, he was heeled. He had a butt-forward pearl-handled Colt in a black leather holster.

The three men with him scooted back from the table a bit. The three were younger than Swickey, but all were tough-looking, and they, too, were heeled. One of them looked familiar. I was thinking back, curious if maybe this was one of the dressers I saw ride by Hal's Café.

"You Cole?" Swickey said to Virgil.

"I am," Virgil said.

"I understand you've been looking for me," Swickey said.

"Deputies said it's you who has come here to Appaloosa, looking for me," Virgil said.

"I damn sure did," Swickey said. "Fifty miles in the cold."

"'Bout?" Virgil said.

"'Bout the bridge," Swickey said.

— 57 —

Virgil took a few steps toward Swickey.

"What about it?" Virgil said.

"You think I had a hand in it," Swickey said.

Virgil didn't say anything.

Swickey moved a little closer to Virgil with his shoulders squared and relaxed.

"Don't you?" Swickey said.

Virgil remained quiet, letting Swickey show as many cards as he was willing to turn over.

"You think I did it," Swickey said. "You think I blew the sonofabitch up?"

"Who said it was blown up?" Virgil said.

Swickey looked at Virgil for a moment, then nodded slowly.

"I know it was, for certain," Swickey said.

"You do it?" Virgil said.

"No," Swickey said.

"Then what makes you certain?" Virgil said.

Swickey looked to one of the men at the table.

"Me," the man said.

"Who are you?" Virgil said.

"David Daniels," he said.

David slid back in his chair a bit more. He was a slender, strong-looking man. He wore a flat-crown wide-brim hat with rawhide straps hanging from its sides that funneled through a .45 casing just below his chin.

"Go on?"

"I saw it," David said.

"You were there?"

He shook his head.

"Rode up on it," David said. "We was gathering cattle and come up on it, I seen it."

Virgil didn't say anything.

"I heard you were looking for me," Swickey said. "Inquiring about me, so I figured I'd save you the looking and pay you a visit."

"You didn't come all the way over here," Virgil said. "'Cause you wanted to pay me a visit."

"Not really," Swickey said.

"Then why?" Virgil said.

"For a few reasons," Swickey said.

"Which are?" Virgil said.

"You think I had a hand in this?" Swickey said. "Because of Cox?"

"What about him?" Virgil said.

"I don't like the sonofabitch," Swickey said. "Everybody knows that."

Virgil didn't say anything.

"But I damn sure didn't blow up his bridge because I don't like him," Swickey said.

"Who did?" Virgil said.

"Hell," Swickey said. "I don't know."

"What do you know?" Virgil said.

"That bridge was going to bring me prosperity," Swickey said.

"What kind of prosperity?" Virgil said.

"I'm no goddamn bridge builder," Swickey said. "But I wanted that bridge, that's why I even put in a bid on it in the first place. I wanted to see it built."

"That the prosperity you're talking about?" Virgil said.

Swickey shook his head.

"No," he said. "I damn sure could have made money on the contract. Good goddamn money. But that bridge was a goddamn gateway for me."

"How so?" Virgil said.

"The money I would save on moving my cattle alone is one hell of a reason I wanted more than anyone to see that bridge built. The bridge would have connected the Southern Pacific to my back door, allowing me to move my cattle by rail. It would double my operation."

"You said a few reasons," Virgil said. "What's the other reason?"

"Got my suspicions about who did this," Swickey said.

"Who?" Virgil said.

Swickey looked to his chair behind him.

"Mind if we sit?" Swickey said, extending his hand to the open chairs at the table. "Goddamn trip, riding in that damn buggy wore my ass out."

Virgil glanced to me, then the chair, then nodded slightly to Swickey.

Swickey nodded and smiled some. "Knees and back aren't as friendly as they used to be. Hell, nothing is," he said, as he sat slowly back in the chair.

Virgil and I moved to the table. Virgil pulled a chair back away from the table a few feet and sat with an empty chair on each side of him. I sat in a chair at a table just next to them.

Swickey looked back to O'Malley behind the bar. He'd been standing the whole time, watching Virgil and Swickey talk as he wiped down a rack of beer mugs.

"Young fella," Swickey said, as he picked up the coffeepot off the table. "Could we get some more coffee here, please?"

"Certainly," O'Malley said.

O'Malley came around the corner of the bar. Swickey handed off the pot to him, then turned and faced Virgil with one elbow on the table and one on the back of his chair.

"There's a good number of cow-calf operations over here on this side of the bridge that goddamn sure didn't want to see that bridge built."

"There one in particular?" Virgil said.

"There are a few, I'd suspect. But considering another aspect of all this, Eddie Winslow here," Swickey said, looking to the man sitting just to the right of him, "has other information I feel is something you will want to hear."

"What's that?" Virgil said.

"Eddie had some bad dealings with someone he thinks had a hand in this," Swickey said.

"Who?" Virgil said.

"Cotters," Eddie said. "Two fellas, name Cotter."

Virgil looked at me and shook his head a little.

— 58 —

What sort of bad dealings?" Virgil said.

Eddie Winslow wasn't a big fella, but he looked to be as tough as they come. He was an angular, raw-boned cowboy with a dark complexion and steely eyes.

"Tell him, Eddie," Swickey said.

Eddie swiveled in his chair a little, facing Virgil, and placed his strong hands on the table in front of him.

"Me and my partner, Jim Lee, we was working for an outfit up on the north fork of the Red," Eddie said. "Things petered out for us, and we come down this way. Jim was from this part of the country. We hired on with an outfit between Yaqui and here, pretty good-size outfit."

"What outfit?" Virgil said.

"Rancher's name is Westmorland," Eddie said.

Swickey shook his head.

"Don't think Westmorland is any part of this,"

Swickey said. "I don't know him, but I know of him. He's a second-generation rancher and he's a family man, always had a good reputation. I'd be surprised if he had any part in this, but of course you never know."

Eddie nodded.

"He was fair; seemed so, anyway," Eddie said. "He was good to us, fed us good, paid us regular and treated us good. He had some good hands, too, but then these two fellas hired on, them Cotters. They seemed nice enough to me, but I'm a dumbass. Jim was the one that said they was up to no good, and sure enough he was right."

Eddie stopped talking for a moment. He looked down at his hands clasped on the table in front of him, then looked back up to Virgil and continued.

"Jim come back one night and told me them two asked him if he'd consider throwing in with them, doing a job with them."

"What kind of job?" Virgil said.

Eddie glanced to Swickey, then looked back to Virgil.

"Jim didn't spell it all out, exactly," Eddie said. "Had to do with shutting down the bridge that was being built over the Rio Blanco, though. Said there'd be good money involved."

Eddie stopped talking when O'Malley came to the table with a pot of coffee and two extra cups.

"Here ya go," O'Malley said.

Eddie watched O'Malley walk away, then started talking again.

"See, my friend Jim was a rough sonofabitch and all

the hands knew he spent time in Brigham's Hole in Salt Lake for holding up a bank and killing a teller. These two Cotter hands figured Jim was a good pick for doing something dirty. But Jim had given up his wicked ways. He told them to fuck off, that he didn't want no part of nothing that would put him back behind bars."

"Where is Jim?"

Eddie looked to his hands again, then looked back up to Virgil, shaking his head.

"Dead," Eddie said. "That following day was Jim's last day on God's green earth."

Virgil looked to me.

"What happened?" I said.

Eddie took his time before saying anything.

"Them two killed him is what happened," Eddie said, looking intently at Virgil. "He didn't go along with their shit and they for sure killed him. They did their lying best to pin it on Mexican rustlers. Mexican rustlers, shit . . . They had Jim's horse when they come back, too. I knew damn good what happened."

"What'd you do?"

"While they were spinning their bullshit yarn," Eddie said, "telling the day boss what went down, I got on my horse and got the hell outta there."

"You never saw them again?" Virgil said.

"No," Eddie said. "I got out of there and didn't look back. I was owed money, too, but I just got out of there while the getting was good. They knew Jim and me was good friends and I figured it'd be just a matter of time 'fore they did the same thing to me they done to Jim. I just run off."

Eddie looked to me, then back to Virgil.

"I knew where they'd been working that day," Eddie said. "I rode out and found Jim's body."

"Where?" Virgil said.

"He was hanging from a goddamn scrub oak," Eddie said. "They strung him up."

Eddie stopped talking for a moment. He looked away, then back at Virgil with a fierce expression on his face.

"They tortured Jim," Eddie said, shaking his head slowly from side to side. "It was like they enjoyed it or something. His face was all swollen and . . . his trousers was down . . . it was . . ."

Cotters done it?" Virgil said. "You're certain?"

Eddie nodded.

"Hell, yes, they did," Eddie said. "Jim saw something in them the first day. He told me to stay away from them. He told me they was no good and he was right."

"Tell me everything else you know about them," Virgil said.

"Don't know nothing, really," Eddie said.

"What'd they look like?" I said.

"They kind of looked alike," Eddie said. "Twenty-eight, thirty maybe, one was a little older, bigger, they both are good-size fellas, beards . . . I don't know."

"Any idea where they are, or where they could be?" Virgil said.

Eddie shook his head.

"I don't," Eddie said. "But Jim's handle for them was 'them boys from the brakes.'"

"The brakes?" I said.

Eddie nodded.

"Yaqui Brakes?" I said.

"I don't know," Eddie said. "Jim knew this country. I guess he was talking about the Yaqui Brakes, I don't know. Jim said they bragged they had their own whorehouse or some shit, and that they'd supply him with all the ax he could handle."

"Whorehouse?" I said.

Eddie nodded.

"You sure about that?"

"That's what Jim said," Eddie said.

"We been through there, Virgil," I said.

"We have," he said.

"Where is this," Swickey said. "The Yaqui Brakes?"

"Brush country," I said. "Off the tracks in bottomland between here and Yaqui."

Virgil nodded.

"Rough holdout place," Virgil said.

"It is," I said. "Scrawny creek through there. Summer was sixty, seventy transient tenters, campers, when we was through there. Winter now, won't be as many down there, I'd say. Southern no-good holdouts, mostly."

Eddie nodded.

"Those boys were southerners," Eddie said. "That's for damn sure."

"Whorehouse down there seems like the type of place they'd be," I said.

"Least till they felt like they were in the clear," Virgil said.

"Not that far," I said. "Worth a try."

"You going there?" Eddie said.

Virgil looked at me.

"If so," Eddie said. "And if it's okay with you, Mr. Swickey, I want to go with them."

"Let these men do their job, Eddie," Swickey said.

"Jim was my only family," Eddie said.

"No matter," Swickey said.

"Does matter," Eddie said.

"These men are lawmen, Eddie," Swickey said.

"There ain't been a day gone by since I saw him hanging there that I've not thought about him, Mr. Swickey," Eddie said. "He was good to me. We'd been together for a good long while. He taught me a lot. When I rode away that day, I felt like a coward for not going back and standing up for what was in my heart, and I've felt like a coward every day since . . . If it's okay, I'd like to go."

Swickey started to speak, but Eddie continued.

"But if you don't want me to," Eddie said, "I understand, but if so I quit."

"Quit?" Swickey said.

"Just as soon quit you, Mr. Swickey," Eddie said, "than to let Jim go like this, like I done."

Eddie looked to Virgil and me.

"I'm no gun hand," Eddie said. "Not really good with one, but I can be helpful. Just as soon die as live another day thinking about them and what they done to Jim."

Swickey looked at Eddie for a long moment, then looked to Virgil.

"What about the ranchers?" Swickey said.

"What about them?" Virgil said.

"What is your order of priority?" Swickey said.

"As in looking for them?" Virgil said.

"Yes," Swickey said. "I don't know the new upstarts over here, but I do know some names of some of the older groups that could, not saying they are, but could, be behind this."

"Better to snuff out the wick before pouring out the oil," Virgil said.

"Is," I said. "At least since we know the Yaqui Brakes might well prove to be their whereabouts."

"No guarantee," Swickey said.

"Never is," Virgil said.

"You gonna go?" Eddie said.

"We are," Virgil said.

"Okay I go?" Eddie said.

Virgil looked to me.

I nodded.

Virgil looked to Swickey.

Swickey looked to Eddie, then Virgil, and nodded.

"What would you like for me to do, Marshal Cole?" Swickey said.

"The best we can hope for," Virgil said, "is we capture one of these mutts and get to the bottom of who paid them to do what they did. If for some reason that don't play out for us in that fashion, you could let me know the names of outfits that you feel might be behind this."

"Already have," Swickey said.

Swickey pulled out a piece of paper from his vest pocket and handed it to Virgil.

Virgil looked at the paper. He read it and handed it to me.

"Good enough," Virgil said.

"When will you go to the brakes?" Swickey said.

"Now," Virgil said.

"And Eddie?" Swickey said.

Virgil looked to Eddie.

"You think you got the stomach for this?" Virgil said.

"I don't got the stomach not to," Eddie said.

Virgil nodded and stood up. He walked to the side door and looked out. He stepped outside.

"Skinny Jack," Virgil called out. "Come here."

Virgil walked back into the room and looked at everyone looking at him.

"Here we go," Virgil said.

— 60 —

We left Swickey and his other hands at the Boston House and made our way back to the front of the sheriff's office, where we met with Chastain and readied ourselves to ride.

"What if they ain't there?" Chastain said.

"Then they ain't there," Virgil said.

"If they are there," Chastain said, "you think they will *all* be there? Still be together?"

Virgil looked to me.

"Good chance," I said.

"Is," Virgil said.

"Like a pack of dogs," I said.

"Think Ballard will still be among 'em?" Chastain said.

"We do," I said.

"He's come this far with them," Virgil said. "And

going by what we know of him he could very well be the goddamn stallion of the herd by now."

"Don't figure they'll still be dressed in no blues," Chastain said. "Do you think?"

Virgil looked to me.

"Don't think so," I said.

"Wouldn't be very fitting to wear a Union uniform in a holdout camp," Virgil said.

"Never know, though," I said.

Virgil nodded.

"They might," he said.

"Might all think it a goddamn funny novelty," I said.

"Well, let's say they don't," Chastain said. "And like you, I doubt they'd still be tramping around in uniforms, so how the hell will we know these men?"

Virgil pointed to Eddie.

"Eddie knows the faces of the two of them," Virgil said. "The Cotters."

Eddie nodded.

"I damn sure do," he said.

"I know one of them," I said. "When I saw them ride by Hal's on their way into town. I won't forget that face. Not ever. I suspect he was one of the Cotters."

"And Ballard's a cock hound," Virgil said. "Tall, handsome man, longhorn mustache. Got a good idea we'll know him."

I nodded.

"They all had Union saddles," I said. "McClellans. They didn't bother to take our men's saddles when they killed their horses, so unless they had some other saddles someplace or bought some saddles, we'll have that to look for."

"That leaves four more," Chastain said. "How will we know them?"

"Don't suppose we'll know," Virgil said. "Maybe we'll get lucky and find that Ballard and the Cotters strung them up like the others they've left in their wake."

We left Skinny Jack and Book to keep the peace in Appaloosa and the four of us, Virgil, Chastain, Eddie, and me, rode out of the city just before eleven o'clock, and headed for the Yaqui Brakes.

The snow had stopped falling and the clouds looked to be separating some, but the roads were snow covered and the ride was slow going.

The brakes were a good five miles of high, thick brush with passages through them that led to a central camp where the tents were pitched next to the creek.

There were other holdout camps like the Yaqui Brakes, and this one was not unlike the others we'd seen. Holdout camps consisted of mostly nonconforming southern miscreants and rabble-rousers who thought the war was still going on, or at least thought it should be going on. They were uncomfortable being around anyone who wasn't as crossways as they were or thought the way they thought.

The bad news about the Yaqui Brakes was there were at least ten ways in and ten ways out.

As we neared the brakes the snow was not as deep as it was back in the Appaloosa direction, and the riding became increasingly easier.

Late in the afternoon, when we came upon a low section of land where the rail and the road next to the rail turned to the west, I stopped and looked back to the others trailing behind me.

"This is it," I said, pointing to the lowland to our left.

Virgil nodded and looked around.

"It is," Virgil said.

"How far, in there?" Chastain said.

"Five miles, maybe," I said.

"How do you want to go about this?" Chastain said.

"Want to wait till dark," Virgil said.

— 61 —

It's damn near dark now," I said.

"It is," Virgil said.

"We go in the dark and see them," Chastain said, "in their camp light and they don't see us?"

"That'd be the idea," Virgil said.

"It's a long walk in there," I said, "but that's the only way, I'd say. Don't you think, Virgil?"

"I do," Virgil said.

"So we go in on foot?" Chastain said.

"We do," Virgil said. "Taking horses in there would be like wearing cowbells."

We rode down into the low section and followed the rail for a while until we came to a truss bridge where the rails crossed over a wash.

It was damn near dark when we dismounted under the bridge and got our horses secured and readied our weapons.

"How we gonna go about taking out hornets and not disrupting the whole nest?" Chastain said.

"Holdouts for the most part are blowhards," Virgil said.

"They are," I said.

"Yep," Virgil said. "That's why they bunch together like they do."

"You don't think they'll have bigger balls the more they are?" Chastain said.

"There is no way of knowing for sure just how this will go down," Virgil said. "But they will not know how many we are."

Chastain nodded and pulled his carbine from its scabbard.

"If the situation calls for it," Virgil said, "we'll let them all know they are surrounded."

"What situation would that be?" Chastain said.

"Don't know all the particulars," Virgil said. "I suspect we'll know if and when that sort of declaration needs to be made."

"Weather's in our favor," I said.

"It is," Virgil said.

Chastain nodded.

"Not exactly the kind of weather for lying on a blanket and watching the stars," Chastain said.

"Not," Virgil said. "The lot will be hunkered inside where it's warm."

Chastain cocked his carbine.

"We go?" Chastain said.

"We do," Virgil said.

"What do you want me to do?" Eddie said to Virgil.

"Keep that Winchester at ready," Virgil said. "We'll all move together, slowly, quietly. When we get close we'll see what we can see and we'll go from there."

We made certain before it was too dark that we found an entrance into the brakes. We followed the path down toward the creek and in no time it was so dark we couldn't see a foot in front of our face. We relied on the brush on either side of the path to guide us as we moved through the darkness.

We walked and walked for more than an hour and it seemed we were moving in circles, but then we heard some distant laughter and we knew we were near.

After walking a little while longer and as we got closer we smelled smoke and heard more sounds of the hold-outs in front of us.

Virgil pulled us close together and whispered, "Let's keep moving toward them. The very first sign of light we see, we stop."

We moved on, doing as Virgil said, until we saw through the thickets some light ahead of us and we stopped.

"Everett, you and Chastain stay put," Virgil said. "Eddie, you come with me. We'll get a little closer and have a look-see, maybe you can spot one of them?"

Virgil and Eddie moved off and we waited.

After a while we saw the vague outlines of Virgil and Eddie as they made their way back to us.

"What'd ya see?" I said.

"I didn't see them," Eddie said.

"We're on the end of the camp here. Everything is spread out that direction," Virgil said with a point to his right.

"What do you figure?" Chastain said.

"Let's move off this way," Virgil said, pointing to his left. "We'll cross the creek and move down the bank on the other side. Have a better view."

We did as Virgil said. We walked to our left until we were in complete darkness again, then we crossed the creek and moved down the bank on the opposite side.

We stayed out of the camp's spilling light as we moved slowly and cautiously.

We could hear voices, muffled conversations coming from inside tents, but like we figured, as cold as it was, there were only a few people moving about.

We passed by one man chopping wood beside a tent and two others drinking beer as they watched him.

A little farther down the way from them, two men sat next to a spit, turning what looked to be a goat.

Virgil led the way; Chastain was behind him, then Eddie, and then me. Eddie stopped, grabbed my arm.

He was looking at the two men over the spit.

"That's him," Eddie said.

— 62 —

Virgil," I said softly.

Virgil stopped and looked back. He moved closer to Eddie. He followed Eddie's look to the two men and the goat.

"The one on the right," Eddie said. "I think that's him."

"You think?" Virgil said.

"I'm pretty sure that's the younger one," Eddie said. "Hard to tell from here, what with him all bundled up and all, but I think that's him. Could tell for sure if we got closer."

"The good news is," I said, "there aren't many others moving about."

Virgil leaned forward, looking to his left, then looked to his right. Then he looked to the two men at the spit.

"That big tent across the way from them with the

wood sides, Everett?" Virgil said. "That the chicken hole?"

"Think so," I said. "Got some ladies' stuff on top of that tent rope there."

"That other fella at the spit there," Virgil said. "You maybe recognize him as one of them you saw that day when they come riding by Hal's?"

"Don't," I said.

Virgil watched for a moment.

"What do we do, Virgil?" Chastain said.

"Everett?" Virgil said.

"Might as well waltz in there, sort of quiet like," I said. "Sit by the spit, see what comes up."

"Got to start somewhere," Virgil said.

"Good a place as any," I said.

"It is," Virgil said.

"Two stay back," I said. "Keep cover."

Virgil nodded.

"Two of us go in," I said.

"Chastain," Virgil said. "You and Eddie move up on either side of that tent there."

The two of them nodded.

"Everett and me will do like Everett's saying," Virgil said. "We'll walk in there and sort out what we can. See who's interested in going to jail or who's interested in dying."

"Okay," Chastain said.

"Eddie," Virgil said. "You walk with me across the creek and come up on this side of the tent. You'll have a better view of that fella over the spit."

Eddie nodded.

"Everett," Virgil said. "You and Chastain come up on that other side. Once I get the nod from Eddie, you walk in from that side of the tent and I'll walk in from the other."

"What if Eddie don't identify him as one of the Cotters?" Chastain said.

"That's a good point, Chastain," Virgil said. "But like Everett said, we gotta start someplace."

"What happens if all hell breaks loose and shooting starts?" Chastain said.

"Shoot straight," Virgil said.

"But we're after the seven," Chastain said. "Not everybody."

"I figure anybody with a gun that is using it is most likely going to be one of them."

"And if they are not?" Chastain said.

"Then they got no goddamn reason to be raising arms on lawmen," Virgil said. "So shoot and shoot straight."

Virgil looked to each of us in turn, and we moved out.

We crossed the creek and when we did I thought about what Séraphine had said to me. About the warning she left me with, about my life in danger. About men running and that she saw me away, elsewhere from Appaloosa, and there would be water. *Holy by God, water,* I thought, as I crossed the shallow creek.

Chastain and I did as Virgil instructed. We posted at the back of the tent on the right side.

We could see Virgil and Eddie. They were at the rear of the tent on the left side.

Chastain and I watched Virgil. We waited on a signal, and after a moment, Eddie nodded. Virgil looked to me and nodded.

Here we go, I thought.

Virgil and I walked deliberately past the tent and directly over to the two men and the goat they were turning on the spit.

"Evening, fellas," Virgil said.

They looked up.

"Who are you?" the man with the beard said.

"My name is Virgil Cole. The fella here next to me with the eight-gauge is Everett Hitch."

I nodded politely.

"Everett and me are lawmen," Virgil said.

I looked around to see if we were drawing any attention from anyone yet, and so far there was no one looking or coming in our direction.

"I'm a territorial marshal," Virgil said. "And Everett here is my deputy marshal."

The man with the beard shifted his eyes back and forth.

In an instant, his body shot up and across the campfire in an attempt to run, but I swung my heavy eight-gauge the way the baseball fellas go after the ball and caught him just under his chin. His feet flipped out from under him and he hit the ground so hard on his back it knocked the wind right out of him.

He grasped his throat, trying to get a breath.

The second man was much slower, and Virgil just put his Colt between his eyes.

"Just stay seated," Virgil said.

I got the bearded man by his hair and propped him up near the fire. I put my boot to his chest with the eight-gauge barrels pointed at his head and pushed him back toward the flames lapping up from the spit.

"I think the combination of my eight-gauge hitting your throat and you hitting the ground hard like you did is making it difficult for you to breathe," I said. "Regardless, I know some shit about you."

I dug my boot hard into him, pushing him toward the fire.

"I'm gonna ask you a few simple questions. If you don't answer, or if you lie to me, I'm gonna burn your face off in this fire. You try to move for some stupid reason, I'll blow your head off with both barrels of this eight-gauge."

The bearded man just looked at me as he tried to get his breath.

"First question is," I said, "what is your name, but before you answer, just know, I know what your name is, so if for some reason it comes out wrong, I start burning your face."

— 63 —

Fuck you," he said.

I crammed my boot fast and hard under his neck and pushed him back to the fire. His hair started to burn.

"Ahha," he rasped as he squirmed trying to worm out of the fire, "Ohhh . . . stop! Stop . . . Dee! Fuck. Dee. Name is Dee."

"You murdered the sheriff and his deputies of Appaloosa?" I said. "Yes or no?"

"I don't know what you are talking about," Dee said.

I shoved him back into the fire and he fought me, but I held him to it.

"Ahhh," he cried.

I wanted to pull both triggers on my side-by-side and watch his face explode, but I took another tactic and let up on him.

"Oh, fuck," Dee said, as I let him out of the fire.

"Oh, fuck . . ." he continued. "Oh, fuck . . ."

"This fella here with you and this goat?" I said. "He part of your rotten gang?"

Dee's eyes were just wide with pain and madness.

"What's your name, your real name?" I said to the man Virgil had his Colt leveled at. "You lie to me and I will burn you, too."

"Dmitry," he said.

Dee squirmed and I dug my boot into his neck.

"I ain't done nothing," Dmitry blurted out. "I didn't kill nobody. Honest."

Dmitry was a little man with a wool head cap. He had thin lips and slits for eyes.

"There's gonna be a few options for you, Dmitry," Virgil said. "One is you will die, the other is you will go to jail."

"I didn't do nothing to no one," Dmitry said.

"How many are you, Dmitry?" I said.

"Fuck him," Dee said.

Virgil looked around. I glanced around, too, and for the moment there was no one moving about except for the men fifty yards down the way in the darkness. The men were still chopping wood and they were unaware we were even in camp.

"How many are you, Dmitry?" I said.

Dmitry's eyes worked back and forth.

"Talk," Virgil said, as he pressed his Colt on Dmitry's forehead.

"Seven," Dmitry said, "There's seven of us . . ."

Dee squirmed some more. He was clearly not liking the idea that Dmitry was forthcoming.

A hefty man wearing long johns walked out of the tent that was flanked by Chastain and Eddie. He saw Virgil and me, and Dee on the ground, and guns out. This sight was obviously a confusing and unexpected one.

"Wha . . . what's going on out here?" he said.

"We're just having a visit," Virgil said.

"What?" the hefty fella said.

In an instant, Chastain was at his side with his rifle crammed into his ear.

"Down," Chastain said quietly.

The man just looked to Chastain, and Chastain slapped him hard on the side of the head with the barrel of the rifle.

"Now," Chastain said with a harsh hush.

The hefty guy did as he was told and got down on his knees. Chastain peeked quick into the tent, then looked to Virgil and me and shook his head, letting us know there was no one else inside. He put his boot in the middle of the hefty man's back and shoved him hard face-first into the dirt.

"Don't move a muscle," Chastain said.

"Fat fella one of your clan?" Virgil said to Dmitry.

Dmitry glanced to Dee, then nodded.

"Eddie," Virgil said.

Eddie was standing in the dark beside the tent and looked out a little.

Virgil nodded for him to step out.

"Here," Virgil said.

Eddie moved out into the open road area, looking both to his left and to his right as he made his way over to us.

Dee cocked his head, looking at Eddie. He recognized him.

"I'll be goddamned," Dee snarled. "You fuck."

Without saying a word, Eddie took one bounding step and kicked Dee so hard between the legs his head jerked forward and he busted his mouth on the barrels of my eight-gauge.

"Goddamn," Dee cried, as he crunched his legs up and spit out pieces of his bloody teeth. "Goddamn . . ."

— 64 —

Eddie," Virgil said, tossing Eddie his knife, "cut some lines off that tent. Tie up that big boy under Chastain's boot first. Tie him up good."

Eddie nodded and did as he was told. He cut the tent ropes, then moved to the man under Chastain's boot.

"Hands behind your back," Chastain said.

The man did as he was ordered.

"Snug 'em tight to his feet, Eddie," Chastain said.

Eddie did just that. He tied the fella's hands behind his back, then looped the rope around his feet, and with a half-hitch jerk he pulled the man into an uncomfortable backward arch.

"Gag him," Chastain said.

Eddied nodded and crammed his handkerchief into the man's gaping mouth.

From a ways down the dirt path of shacks and tents that lined the creek we heard some music start up, a fiddle and a guitar. They were working on some dancing tune.

"Dmitry," Virgil said. "The more you tell me, the better off things will be for you when we take you in, that is *if* we take you in. If things go a way we might not appreciate, there's a good chance you will burn and die here tonight."

"Don't listen to him," Dee said, struggling to speak.

"The less you tell me of what you know, Dmitry," Virgil said, "the worse things will be for you."

"Wha . . . what do you want to know?" Dmitry said.

"First thing I want to know is where are your horses?"

"Corral down at the end here," Dmitry said.

"All seven of you here?"

Dmitry nodded.

"Where are the other four?"

Dmitry nodded up the path.

"Whore shack," he said.

Out of the darkness came the three men we saw chopping wood. The woodchopper was a big man and he had the ax in his hand. The two men following him were kind of pint-sized. They both were holding beer mugs.

"What the hell?" the woodchopper said.

Chastain and Eddie trained their guns on the men.

"Don't move," Chastain said. "Stay right where you are."

The men raised their hands up away from their bodies.

"They with you?" Virgil said to Dmitry.

"They are not," he said.

"We're law," Virgil said. "Just stay where you are."

They did as they were told.

"You damn sure," Virgil said to Dmitry, "they're not part of your kettle?"

"They're not," he said.

"You lie to me," Virgil said, "and if shit goes down, you will be the first to die."

"They're not," Dmitry said.

Virgil looked to Dmitry for a bit, then looked to the men.

"You fellas," Virgil said. "Like I say, we're law. We've located these critters here and we're sorting them out for the lawbreaking they've done. You can be part of this or you can go back down on the other end and keep out of this. The choice is yours."

The three of them started backing up.

"We got no dealing with nothing that the law needs to be part of, mister," the woodchopper said, "No dealing."

"Okay," Virgil said. "I see you or anyone else come down the road this way, they will become part of something they'd be better off not being part of, *comprende*?"

The men nodded and started backing away.

"One thing," Virgil said to the men.

"Yes, sir," the woodchopper said.

"How many people are here?" Virgil said. "In this camp?"

"There's us down here," the woodchopper said. "Six of us, we're all from Missouri. Be on our way to California when the weather clears. And down there, on the other end, there's them fellas there, them seven, and there's five other fellas, regulars that are here all the time."

"Whores?" Virgil said.

"Three," the woodchopper said. "Indians."

Virgil nodded.

"Go on back," Virgil said to the men. "Go on back or get yourself into some shit you don't want no part of. Go on."

The three backed on down the road and disappeared into the darkness they came from.

"Who's behind all this?" Virgil said to Dmitry.

"Goddamn you," Dee said.

I pressed my eight-gauge on Dee's bloody mouth.

"Behind what?"

"Don't fuck with me," Virgil said.

"I'm not," Dmitry said.

— 65 —

"Who paid you to blow up the bridge, Dmitry?" Virgil said.

"I don't know," Dmitry said nervously, looking between Dee and Virgil.

"Bullshit," Virgil said. "You got paid, you killed the Appaloosa lawmen, and you came to town to get paid. By who?"

"I don't know. Honest, I don't, I'm just a hand. That was all his big brother's plan," Dmitry said. "It was Dirk and that Ballard who was in charge. I didn't kill nobody."

"You boys came into Appaloosa," Virgil said. "To get paid, by who?"

"I swear to you, mister, I don't know," Dmitry said, then looked to Dee. "It was all his brother's plan."

"Shut up," Dee said.

"It was just his brother," Dmitry continued hurriedly.

"His brother, Dirk, that got the money, him and Ballard. I don't know from who or where. They did it. I just did what they told me to do."

"Shut the fuck up," Dee said. "Shut . . ."

I pushed my eight-gauge under Dee's nose, shoving his head back.

"I was just promised money," Dmitry said, shaking with fear. "His brother, Dirk, he got me to help 'cause me and Big Billy know about dynamite. I ain't lying."

Dmitry pointed to the heavy fella on the ground.

"Me and Big Billy there," Dmitry said. "We worked in the mines. Ask Billy. He was the one who knowed Dirk and Dee, not me. I swear to you."

"You're lying," Virgil said.

Dmitry shook his head hard.

"I'm not. Billy and me don't know who paid and we didn't kill nobody," Dmitry said, looking at Billy tied up on the ground. "Ask Big Billy."

"Who killed the lawmen?" Virgil said.

Dmitry just looked to Dee.

Virgil pressed his Colt hard into Dmitry's head.

"Talk or die now," Virgil said.

"Them three," Dmitry said. "They done it. They, they scared the hell outta Big Billy and me, they made us watch and, and . . ."

"Ballard, Dee, and Dirk killed the lawmen?" Virgil said.

Dmitry nodded.

"They did," Dmitry said. "I never seen no men like them."

"Fuck you," Dee said. "You lying piece of shit."

"Dirk, Ballard, the others are in the whore shack," Virgil said. "Which tent?"

"Big tent just there with the wood sides," Dmitry said.

"Besides Dirk and Ballard," Virgil said. "How many others in there?"

"Just Leonard," Dmitry said, "and Ray."

"Goddamn you," Dee said to Dmitry.

I pressed Dee hard in the throat with my boot again and stuck the eight-gauge even harder under his nose, shutting him up.

"Ray, Leonard," Dmitry said quickly, "Dirk, and Ballard, I swear."

Virgil wasted no more time with dumbass Dmitry. He grabbed Dmitry and jerked him to his feet.

"Eddie, Chastain," Virgil said, as he shoved Dmitry toward the tent near Chastain, "do the same with this one, tie him up."

Eddie nodded and commenced to cut more rope from the tent.

I reached down and grabbed Dee hard by the collar and yanked him to his feet.

Like we'd been told, Dee was a strong, good-sized fella, but at the moment he felt like a limp rag doll to me as I hoisted him upright.

Eddie and Chastain quickly got Dmitry tied up in the same fashion as the heavy fella.

"Drag them inside that tent," Virgil said.

Eddie and Chastain dragged the hefty man and Dmitry into the tent.

"Him, too?" Eddie said, looking at Dee.

"No," Virgil said. "Dee has a few things he'd like to talk about first. Don't you, Dee?"

Dee didn't say anything.

Virgil looked back to Eddie.

"Cut the rest of the tent ropes," Virgil said. "Drop that tent on them."

Eddie cut the remaining ropes and the tent collapsed on the two men that were bound and gagged under the weight of the canvas.

"Good," Virgil said, then turned to Dee.

I had Dee by the back of his singed hair and had my eight-gauge tucked tightly under his bloody chin.

"Dee," Virgil said. "Let's walk over to this tent where your brother and the others are and see what might be their evenin' interests."

— 66 —

Chastain, Eddie, Virgil, and I left the two men tied up under the dilapidated tent and walked down the trash-cluttered road toward the wood-sided tent with hurting and hunched-over Dee in tow.

"Who's behind this, Dee?" Virgil said, as we walked.

Dee's mouth was bleeding heavily from being smashed into the eight-gauge. He just shook his head.

"Talk, Dee," Virgil said.

Dee didn't respond.

In the short walk, we were at the tent on the opposite side of the creek with women's garments hanging on the stake ropes. We passed a few small tents and shacks as we got closer but didn't see any other of the holdouts milling about.

Like we'd figured, with it being winter, the Yaqui Brakes weren't at their full capacity.

When we stopped in front of the big wall-sided tent, a new guitar and fiddle tune started up from inside.

"This it, Dee?" Virgil said.

Dee didn't answer, but we could tell this was where we needed to be. In fact, looking down the pathway of the camp road, there were no lights and no fires burning.

"Good, Dee, appreciate it," Virgil said, as he looked around. "Do me a favor and have a sit right here."

Virgil pointed to a crude chair made from green branches. The chair was sitting in front of an expired fire pit on the opposite side of the narrow road just across from the wood-sided tent.

Dee dropped in the chair and looked to the ground.

"Eddie," Virgil said, without looking at Dee. "You stay out here with your Winchester at the back of his head."

Virgil nodded to Chastain and me.

"The three of us are going inside here and pay these other fellas a proper visit," Virgil said. "If this one here has any intentions of doing anything other than staying in this chair, kill him."

Eddie nodded.

Dee remained looking at the ground, watching the blood drip from his mouth.

Virgil looked off down the path toward the men at the far end, but they were gone. Then Virgil looked to the big tent, then to Chastain and me. He nodded.

"Let's go," Virgil said.

We started toward the tent, but just before we got to

the opening, Dee sprang out of the chair, shouting and running toward the tent, *"Dirk! Fucking law, Dirk! Law! LAW . . . DIRK!"*

The report of Eddie's Winchester echoed loudly through the brakes. The bullet hit Dee in the back of the head and he fell face-first in the dirt. Without a moment of hesitation I was through the entrance of the tent, with Virgil and Chastain right behind me.

Inside was chaos. The guitar player and the fiddler, two older fellas, cowered and dropped to the ground. Two half-naked women screamed loudly. A man next to them raised his arms above his head, but the man next to him came up quickly with a sawed-off.

I let go with one barrel of the side-by-side. The sound was deafening, as the eight-gauge double-ought buck blasted out of the barrel. The man's head exploded and splattered over the wall behind him.

Another naked man came out of the back of the tent with a pistol in each hand and my second shot detonated with a blast of fire that knocked him back the way he came.

We heard two shots fired outside the tent, followed by Eddie shouting, "Two, out here."

I followed Virgil and Chastain as they backed out quickly from the smoke-filled tent.

"Got one," Eddie said, pointing to a man on the ground next to the tent, writhing in pain. "They came out the back. The other is running off that way, in the creek."

"Stay right here," Virgil said to Chastain. "Shoot anybody else who needs it."

I'd already reloaded as I moved toward the creek.

"I'll take the creek, Virgil," I said. "You take the road."

Virgil was moving.

I pointed my eight-gauge at the man on the ground next to the tent. I could tell right away this was the bearded man I saw riding into town. This was Dirk, Dirk the cold-blooded murderer Cotter. He looked up at me.

Those were the eyes, the eyes I remembered: the murdering eyes. He was fully dressed. He'd been shot in the back and he was clutching his gut where the bullet exited. There was a rifle just out of his reach he'd obviously dropped when Eddie shot him. I grabbed it and slung it back toward Eddie. I thought as I moved off down into the creek bottom, *How fitting. How fitting that both Dee and Dirk were shot by Eddie.*

Just as I heard the water splashing under my feet, I heard a shot and saw ahead of me the flash of a muzzle as the bullet hit me.

I felt my legs give out. I fell back and dropped into the icy creek. Then all I could hear was the cold water rushing past my ears. I could see the stars above me.

I thought about Séraphine, beautiful, mysterious Séraphine. I thought about being in her arms. I thought about her long, slender legs and her dark, silky hair. I thought about touching her, touching her soft porcelain skin. I thought about her eyes, her beautiful blue eyes looking at me.

I remembered her intoxicating smell. I remembered. I remembered. I remembered. I smiled thinking, *Cotter, men running, and water, water, water*. I remembered. I remembered . . .

There's Orion's Belt just there, I thought. *It is, that's Orion's Belt.*

— 67 —

Thunder rumbled. Dark clouds turned and twisted. Currents of stiff wind pushed and challenged strong trees to stay rooted, and jagged lightning cracked across the sullen sky.

Embers skittered violently from a waning fire and the horses whinnied loudly. They were restless, anxious, and frightened. Was it just the weather that had them spooked or was it something else out there in the dark that was causing them agony?

Then from inside the dark and ominous rolling clouds I saw a shimmering light, a dim shimmering spot of light on the horizon. It was coming closer and closer. The spot flickered as it got bigger. Then it came like a tornado, clearing the darkness, and suddenly it was bright.

It was a lantern, a ceiling lantern. I stared at it for a long moment, then looked slowly to my right.

Sun streamed through the thin lace curtains. There was an opening in the curtains and I could see glistening water dripping from the eaves.

I looked around the white spartan-styled room.

It was stark and sanitary, but it was warm. Above my head on the wall behind the bed was a small wooden cross. To my right, just beyond the window, was a framed printed painting of Jesus. He wasn't looking at me. He was looking to his right toward the window, toward the light. On the stand just left of the iron-framed bed I was lying on was an ivory-colored water pitcher and a single glass. I looked back out the window, watching the water dripping and the steam that was rising from it. I looked back to Jesus. *Least I made it to a hospital.*

"*Bonjour,*" she said.

I looked to my left toward the foot of the bed. There she was, Séraphine, standing in the doorway.

"Look who's here," I said.

She smiled.

"*Bonjour* back," I said.

"Feeling better, I see," she said.

"*Oui,*" I said.

She smiled and moved a little closer into the room.

"For some damn reason, I'm drifting in and out of sleep," I said.

"Need your rest," she said.

"Damn doc's keeping me drifting," I said. "Opiates."

"Morpheus," she said.

"The dreams and here," I said, "mix."

"I'm here," she said.

"Yes, you are," I said. "I can see that."

She looked radiant in her long, pale blue dress. She slowly moved toward me.

"Matches your eyes," I said.

She stepped close to the bed. She reached out and gently with her fingers touched the bandage around my chest.

"It's good your heart is not on this side," she said.

"What heart?" I said with a grin.

"A beautiful heart," she said.

She leaned in and kissed me softly on the lips.

"Yes," I said. "I'm awake."

She smiled.

"I'm not dreaming," I said.

"I'm right here," she said.

"Yes," I said.

She moved a lock of hair that was hanging down in front of my eye.

"Time for a haircut," I said.

She just looked at me and smiled warmly.

"I'll be up soon," I said. "Think I'm close to being ready."

She smiled but didn't say anything.

I looked to the window.

"Warming," I said.

She followed my look to the window.

"*Oui,*" she said softly.

"That weather came on harsh," I said.

"*Oui,*" she said.

"Thought March was the lion," I said.

"Roared early," she said.

"Damn sure did," I said.

"It will make for a better spring," she said.

"It will," I said.

She took my hand and just looked at me.

"Are they setting up now," I said, "readying the show?"

"Preparations are under way," she said.

I laid back and looked to the ceiling. The lantern looked foggy and dim.

"Futures told," I said.

"Oui," she said. "Legendary adventures revealed."

— 68 —

It was Ballard who'd shot me, and it was Virgil who'd shot Ballard. His bullet hit Ballard in the temple and killed him instantly. By the time Virgil and Chastain got me out of the icy water, Dirk had died, too. The two men I'd shot with my eight-gauge inside the tent, Leonard and Ray, were both members of the gang, so there was no one left to provide any details other than Dmitry and Big Billy. They were the only two of the outlaws to survive the shoot-out at Yaqui Brakes.

"We've interrogated the goddamn living hell out of them," Chastain said.

Virgil nodded. He was standing with his back to me as he looked out the window next to the painting of Jesus.

Chastain was sitting in a chair next to the door.

"They don't know anything else?" I said.

"Other than Dmitry and Big Billy providing details

about Ray and Leonard being the fellas that did the work," Chastain said, "they don't know shit."

Virgil turned from the window.

"They don't," he said.

"Couple of dumbasses," Chastain said.

"They signed on," Virgil said, "thought they'd make some good money."

"Little did they know," Chastain said.

"Don't think they knew what they were getting into until it was too late," Virgil said.

"Yep," Chastain said. "They was scared as hell of both Dirk and Ballard."

"Dee, too," Virgil said.

Chastain nodded.

"Said they wanted to back out," Chastain said. "But they were scared they'd kill them."

"Most likely right," Virgil said.

"How about the telegram we sent to the governor's office?" I said. "Any word back regarding the financials and whatnot?"

Virgil shook his head a little.

"Only that someone would report from the office as soon as the weather permitted," Virgil said.

Doc Crumley came into the room with a dark bottle and a spoon.

"Oh," Doc said. "Didn't know you fellas was up here."

"'Lo Doc," Chastain said.

"Doc," Virgil said with a nod.

"No more, Doc," I said.

"Too soon not to," he said.

"No more," I said.

"You sure?" he said.

"More than sure," I said. "I've had enough of that, don't know if I'm coming or going."

"You're gonna be in pain," he said.

"I know," I said. "No more. If I go ahead and die, at least I will be alert enough to know it."

"Okay," he said. "Let me know if you change your mind."

"Will do," I said. "But I won't. And I will be walking outta here shortly."

Doc put his fists on his hips.

"Don't want to push it, Everett," he said.

"I'm good," I said.

Doc shook his head.

"You're tore up inside," he said, "and that needs time to heal, Everett."

"I know," I said. "I'll take it easy."

The doc looked to Virgil and Chastain and shook his head a little, then looked back to me.

"Don't get on any horses," he said.

"I won't, Doc," I said.

Doc Crumley left the room, shaking his head.

"So what now?" I said.

Virgil folded his arms and looked to the floor for a moment.

"Chastain and me rode out and talked to each of the ranchers from that list Swickey provided us," Virgil said, shaking his head.

Chastain nodded.

"We don't think none of them had a hand in this," he said.

"No," Virgil said. "We don't."

"We talked to the rancher Eddie worked with, too," Chastain said.

"Westmorland," Virgil said. "The one that Dee and Dirk had worked for."

"And?" I said.

Virgil shook his head.

"He'd be the last to muster something like this," Virgil said. "Good man."

"Leaves us with the whores," I said.

Virgil nodded.

"We talked to a few," Chastain said.

"And we'll talk to them all, but it's like Belle was saying. Whores are whores because they are whores."

— 69 —

I'm done with being looked after, Allie," I said. "Really."

"Nonsense," Allie called from the kitchen.

"Not nonsense," Virgil said. "If Everett wants to be left alone, leave him alone."

After I left the resting room above Doc Crumley's, Allie had insisted I stay with her and Virgil. The bullet I received from Ballard was a .45 that Crumley took out of me. Crumley said if it'd been an inch to the left it would have been *the last train*.

I was weak from the loss of blood, and got around a little slow due to the pain, but was on the mend.

Allie had a special down-filled cot she borrowed from one of her gal friends with the ladies' social. She placed it near the fireplace and demanded I stay with them until the snow was all melted and it was no longer muddy.

Allie came out of the kitchen carrying a tray with a bowl of soup and a chunk of bread.

"Everett needs continued rest," Allie said. "And my special nourishment."

"Hell, Allie," I said. "That's pretty much all I have been doing, is eating and sleeping."

"Well, that's just the way it is," Allie said. "It's not every day I get to take care of somebody."

"By God, not true, Allie," Virgil said. "You take care of me every day."

"Oh, pooh," Allie said, swinging her tail like a cat as she walked back to the kitchen. "Nobody takes care of Virgil Cole . . . 'Sides, Everett likes to be looked after by me."

She poked her head back out the kitchen door.

"Don't you, Everett?"

I picked up my spoon and smiled.

"I appreciate what you do for me, Allie," I said. "I certainly do."

"See, Virgil," Allie said. "Everett knows the meaning of appreciation."

Allie tucked back into the kitchen.

"Only so much appreciation a man needs," Virgil said. "Since Everett left that halfway room above Doc Crumley's office all you been doing is looking after him. I think Everett might have just had his fill of appreciation."

"And thank that Jesus on the wall of that halfway room above Doc Crumley's office," Allie said, as she came back into the living room with a glass of milk, "that Everett's come back this halfway of that room and not the other half so I can take proper care of his recovery. Here you go, Everett."

"I will say, Allie," I said, "I've had enough milk to last me a lifetime."

Allie pinched my cheek.

"Oh, moo," she said with a giggle. "Drink it. It's good for you, help you get your strength back."

"Quite frankly," I said, "I'm looking forward to having a nudge or two of that Kentucky."

"Oh, Everett," Allie said.

We heard footsteps on the porch followed by a musical rat-a-tat-tat rap on the door.

Allie leaned over me and looked out the window.

"It's some little fellow in a checkered suit wearing a hatbox derby," Allie said.

Virgil got up and answered the door.

"Might you be Marshal Virgil Cole?" the man said with a crisp British inflection.

"I might," Virgil said. "And you?"

I leaned forward in my chair to have a look at the little man in the brown-checkered suit.

"Sebastian Winthrop," he said.

"What can I do for you, Mr. Winthrop?"

"I was wondering if I might have a few words with you," Sebastian said.

"Words about what?" Virgil said.

Sebastian leaned forward on his toes, looking past Virgil to Allie and me.

"Well," he said, glancing at Allie and me through the door, "it is, perhaps, a rather delicate matter."

"What sort of delicate matter?" Virgil said.

"Um, well," he said. "It's a matter regarding the Rio Blanco Bridge project."

Virgil looked back to me, then opened the door for him to enter.

"Come on in," Virgil said.

"Why, thank you," he said.

He entered and removed his derby. Virgil closed the door behind him.

Sebastian nodded to Allie and me and smiled.

"This here is Allison French," Virgil said. "And my deputy marshal, Everett Hitch."

"Sebastian Winthrop," he said with a click of his heels.

— 70 —

Sebastian carried a small leather satchel. He was completely bald, without even a hair on the sides of his head, though he had full eyebrows. He sported a small mustache that was curled up with a twist at each of its ends, firmly fixed with a touch of wax.

For a little man, there was something about him that made him seem somehow larger than his size. He was strong-looking, and his eyes were curious and perceptive.

"What matter regarding the bridge?" Virgil said.

"Well," Sebastian said. "Thanks to you, Marshal Cole, for reaching out to the governor. You've uncovered something that has alarmed him and his staff, and I'm here on the governor's behalf. I would have been here sooner, but the trains were slowed by the weather, of course, and it wasn't only until the last few days the rails were even operable to Appaloosa and this area. But, nonetheless, I'm here now."

He looked to a chair.

"May I?"

Virgil glanced at me, then nodded to Sebastian.

"Thank you," Sebastian said, as he sat. "I've been traveling for days, mind you . . . I've yet to even have a proper glass of water."

"Oh, well," Allie said. "We do have water."

"Why, thank you, Miss French," he said.

Allie started for the kitchen.

"Tea, I presume, is out of the question," he said, with the tips of his fingers together just in front of his silk tie.

Allie looked to Virgil and nodded some. Then she looked back to Sebastian and smiled.

"We do have tea," Allie said with an added refined inflection to her voice.

"Well, tea would be lovely," Sebastian said. "If it's not too much trouble."

"Not at all," Allie said.

"That would be superb," Sebastian said.

"Well, then," she said. "Superb tea it is."

"Delightful," he said.

Allie removed my soup bowl, bread, and milk, and set them on the table in front of me, then sashayed off to the kitchen with the tray. Sebastian watched her until she disappeared into the kitchen.

"One can never be too careful," Sebastian said, after Allie left the room, "when one does not know who is who and what is what."

"What's this about the bridge?" Virgil said.

"Are you familiar with Lloyd's of London?" he said.

Virgil nodded a little and looked to me.

"Insurance?" I said.

"Yes," Sebastian said. "I'm an investigator for Lloyd's. I'm relatively new to the U.S. . . ."

"What brings you here?" Virgil said. "What do you know about the bridge?"

"To put it simply, there was a policy on the Rio Blanco Bridge project," Sebastian said. "A rather hefty policy, I might add."

Virgil looked at me and shook his head a little.

"Go on," Virgil said.

"When there is a substantial payout such as this," he said. "We investigate to make sure there is no fraud involved."

"How much of a payout?" Virgil said.

"Two hundred and fifty thousand dollars," Sebastian said. "Quite substantial."

"I take it by the fact you are here," I said. "You believe there is fraud?"

"Perhaps."

"This have to do with Cox?" I said. "The contractor?"

"Perhaps."

"What's not perhaps?" Virgil said.

"Were you aware the Rio Blanco Bridge was to be a toll bridge?" Sebastian said.

Virgil looked at me and shook his head.

"No," I said. "We weren't aware of that."

Sebastian opened his satchel and pulled out a folder.

"This is a copy of the policy," Sebastian said. "It's not a Lloyd's policy, per se, but it is a policy that includes some of Lloyd's underwriters. According to this policy, there's more than one party with insurable interest."

"Someone besides Cox?" I said.

"Actually, I'm not sure where Mr. Cox fits in here at all. The policy itself, the first name insured on the policy is the Territory Bridge Authority, the governor himself. That's normal."

"What's not normal?" I said.

"There is a business-interruption endorsement on this policy," Sebastian said.

"You mean, future tolls?" I said.

"Precisely," he said. "The Rio Blanco was designed for both rail and standard commerce; a licensing fee for the rail carriers and individual tolls for market fare, cattle, goods and services, individuals, et cetera. We're talking a substantial amount of future revenues, mind you."

"And the payout for this business interruption is two hundred and fifty thousand dollars?"

"Yes," Sebastian said.

"Take a lot of years of toll to earn that," I said.

"It would indeed," Sebastian said. "But I need to be perfectly clear, so let me reiterate. I'm looking into *possible fraud* here. I need to understand the business behind the endorsement."

"What business?" I said.

"Well," Sebastian said. "The right of way, the property ownership, comes into engagement here."

"So the beneficiary of this business interruption on this contract is not Cox?" I said.

"It's not," Sebastian said. "He could perhaps have

some participation in this endorsement, I don't know. That is why I'm here."

"But you know who's on the contract there with the endorsement?" I said, pointing to the contract. "Who's the beneficiary?"

"Yes," Sebastian said. "But how all this came about I'm still unclear on."

"Well," I said. "If it's not Cox, then who is it?"

"The First Baptist Church of Appaloosa," he said.

"Tea time," Allie said, as she came out from the kitchen carrying the tray with the tea.

— 71 —

Allie poured the tea for Sebastian.

"There you go," she said.

Sebastian nodded.

"Oh," he said. "I thank you so very much."

"Well, you are so very welcome," Allie said. "It's not every day I get to prepare a splendid cup of tea for an English gentleman."

"We got some business to finish up here with Mr. Winthrop, Allie," Virgil said.

"You go right ahead," Allie said, as she took her shawl from the coat rack by the door and wrapped it around her shoulders. "I'm late meeting Nell in town as it is. I'm helping her to distribute flyers for the opening of the show."

Virgil nodded.

Allie looked to Sebastian.

"I'm sorry I'm not available to share some proper tea with you, Mr. Winthrop, but duty calls."

"Perfectly understandable," Sebastian said, as he got to his feet. "Perfectly understandable. Perhaps some other time."

"Perhaps," Allie said. "That'd be wonderful."

"Until then, Miss French," Sebastian said with a bow.

"Until," Allie said.

She gave Virgil a kiss on the cheek and walked out the door.

"Lovely," Sebastian said, as he sat back in his chair. "Simply lovely."

"The First Baptist Church of Appaloosa?" Virgil said.

Sebastian nodded as he picked up the teacup. He took a sip and grimaced a little.

"Yes," he said with a slight clearing of his throat. "The church. It seems there was a transaction between the landowner and the church."

Sebastian picked up the folder and thumbed through the pages.

"The land the bridge was built on," Virgil said. "Deeded the land over to the church?"

"Yes," he said.

"Who's the executor?" I said.

"The First Baptist Church's pastor," Sebastian said. "A Mr. Ashley Epps."

Virgil looked to me.

"Ashley got his hand in the till?" Virgil said.

"Again," Sebastian said. "This might all prove to be perfectly legitimate."

"Or perfectly planned," Virgil said.

"That, too," Sebastian said.

"The trustee as recipient of the deed would have to file this, right?" I said.

"Yes," Sebastian said. "The deed is filed with the county clerk at the county courthouse."

"That'd be Curtis Whittlesey," I said. "I was shooting pool with him the night I received word about the bridge. He never said anything about this. Fact, he was the one who first mentioned Cox's name to me. Telling me he was the contractor that was building the bridge."

"And Cox?" Virgil said. "Where's he fit in to all this?"

"He would have had to know about the business-interrupting endorsement on the policy, wouldn't he?" I said.

"Not necessarily," Sebastian said. "The policy belongs to the Territory Bridge Authority and the church's business-interruption endorsement is attached to that policy, you see."

"We asked Cox if he knew of any motives and he damn sure didn't mention this," Virgil said. "He could be in on it."

"Yes," Sebastian said.

"Sounds like a bunch could be in on this," Virgil said.

"Yes," Sebastian said. "Precisely, and precisely why I'm here. The whole payout will go through and nothing will ever be done about it unless there is a way to link the business-interruption endorsement to the actual blowing up of the bridge. It's that simple."

Sebastian opened the file and put it before us on the coffee table.

"Here we go," he said. "It's all in here. The property the bridge was built on was owned by a man named Thaddeus Cotter."

Virgil looked at me and shook his head a little.

"You said *was* owned by Thaddeus Cotter?" I said. "*Was?*"

"According to the paperwork I have here," Sebastian said. "He's deceased."

"When did Thaddeus die?" I said.

"Approximately one year prior to the beginning of the bridge's construction," he said. "When Thaddeus died, his will provided for the creation of the church to own the land."

Virgil walked around the room for a moment, thinking. He stopped in front of the fireplace and turned to face us.

"Cotter is the name of two of the men we caught that did the dynamiting of the bridge. No doubt they are related to this Thaddeus."

Sebastian nodded.

"I see where you might be going with this," Sebastian said. "And correct me if I'm wrong, but this sort of business comes up quite a bit in my line of work. The matriarch or patriarch leaves an asset to an organization such as a charity and or church and those next in line are disgruntled and retaliate."

"No," Virgil said. "They instigate."

I nodded.

"The land belongs to the church," I said. "The church collects, the preacher collects, the brothers collect, maybe Cox and maybe even Whittlesey."

"Yep," Virgil said. "Them Cotter boys could have made a deal with Ashley Epps."

"Could have threatened him," I said.

"That, too," Virgil said.

"Hard to know how deep this goes," I said. "The goddamn whole of Appaloosa could be in on it."

Virgil nodded.

"Only one way to find out," Virgil said. "Can you go ahead and pay this out?"

"Certainly," Sebastian said. "In fact, we'll have to. Unless I can prove fraud, the company will have no choice."

"Turn on the lamp," Virgil said. "And let's see what kind of night-flying bugs we get."

I nodded.

"Wire the money," I said. "See who shows to collect."

"Yep," Virgil said, looking at Sebastian. "Bug knows where it's going by the light of the moon, but once he comes close to a bright flame he don't know if he's coming or going."

Sebastian looked at me and smiled a little.

— 72 —

After discussing the situation at length, the best plan we could come up with was to set the trap and see what happens. We didn't know what degree of corruption there was associated with the blowing up of the bridge. What we did know was the First Baptist Church of Appaloosa would be receiving a sum of two hundred and fifty thousand dollars.

Who the money would ultimately end up with, however, was uncertain.

The request for the money to be wired to the First Territorial Bank of Appaloosa went out the very afternoon Sebastian paid us a visit. The following day, and prior to the money's arrival, we had set up a strategy.

We knew Ashley would be the recipient of the funds, and he did in fact make a trip to the bank the very afternoon of the transaction. He carried a large satchel.

We didn't alert the bank because we didn't want to

draw attention to any wrongdoing on either side. Who knew who could be involved in the scheme?

We watched our suspects from a distance.

Chastain kept an eye on the court clerk, Curtis Whittlesey; Virgil watched G. W. Cox; and Sebastian and I followed Appaloosa's mayor and preacher, Ashley Epps.

I was tender in my chest and my whole upper body was sore, but my movement was improved and I had been getting around pretty fair for the last few days.

It was Wednesday evening, and Sebastian and I were positioned outside in the dark alley behind the First Baptist Church of Appaloosa, listening as Ashley Epps wrapped up an impassioned midweek sermon to a full congregation.

"He sounds mad," Sebastian said.

"I take it you've not spent much time in these parts?" I said.

"No," he said.

"Well, it's just what the preachers do here," I said.

"Fascinating," he said.

"Particularly preachers with Baptist outfits," I said. "They get after you like a cete of badgers. Want to scare the hell out of you."

"And for what purpose?" Sebastian said.

"It has to do with going to Heaven or Hell and what have you," I said.

"No, no, I understand," Sebastian said. "I've heard something about this. It's a bit different in my country."

"How so?" I said.

"Oh," he said. "Well, it's nothing like this, I assure you. It's much more reserved."

I didn't say anything, and we just listened to Ashley as his sermon became more and more impassioned.

"In my country, one just listens, and then one makes up one's own mind about the Lord and Savior," Sebastian said.

"You don't accept Jesus into your pumper here in this program, you're going south," I said.

"Yes, yes," Sebastian said.

"One-way-ticket kind of deal," I said. "No leeway for nobody else, you are either part of the regiment or not. Jews, Pygmies, Indians, everybody else is on the short end of the stick."

"Interesting," Sebastian said.

"They even got their own schools," I said. "Preachers go to school to learn how to put the fear of God in others."

"Why?" Sebastian said.

"Good question," I said. "They got some fear in them, I guess, and they're not satisfied until everybody else gets on board."

"Surely there is more to it than that?" Sebastian said.

"You'd think," I said.

After the sermon was over Ashley hollered to the crowd to come down to the front, get on their knees, and ask for forgiveness.

"My word," Sebastian said.

"Yep," I said.

We waited until the service was over. We stayed in the dark near the rear of the church but were positioned where we could see everyone leaving.

Ashley Epps stood out front on the church steps next to his wife and children until the last person was gone.

Sebastian and I moved closer but were completely unseen. Ashley told his wife and children to go on home and that he had some praying to do and would be home shortly.

We watched as his family walked away, and after a moment Ashley locked the doors of the church and moved off in the opposite direction carrying the satchel.

"Like we did today, let's have you keep him in sight and I'll follow you," I said. "Light the cigarette."

Sebastian nodded.

"Take this," I said, handing my dingus to him.

"I have no need for a gun," he said.

"Just take it," I said.

Sebastian looked at the derringer I was holding out to him. He took a deep breath, took it, and put it in his pocket.

We let Ashley get ahead of us, then Sebastian moved out following him. I followed Sebastian. I remained a good two hundred yards back as I trailed him.

Sebastian walked north a few blocks, making a few turns, and I kept him in sight. He walked east another two blocks, then turned north up Fourth Street and stopped.

— 73 —

I waited in the dark under an awning, watching Sebastian. He turned, faced me, and lit a cigarette. The cigarette was the sign we'd set when Ashley stopped at his destination. I stayed put under the awning as planned.

The idea was to let some time pass and see who and how many were to meet up with him and Cox.

After about ten minutes Sebastian lit another cigarette.

Black Jack, I thought.

The second smoke indicated another participant.

I waited a little longer, then started walking up the boardwalk toward Sebastian. He moved to meet me under the overhang of a drilling office.

"He's just there," Sebastian said.

"What we figured," I said. "That's Cox's place."

We stood there, staying back in the dark and waited.

After some minutes passed, Chastain came out of the alley across the street from us and waited under an overhang as well. We just watched and waited some more.

"Marshal Cole," Sebastian said.

Virgil was on the same side of the street as Chastain and was walking in Chastain's direction.

Chastain saw Virgil and moved out a little to meet him.

After a minute or two Virgil and Chastain crossed the street to where Sebastian and I were waiting.

"Here we go," I said.

"How you want to go about this?" Chastain said to Virgil.

Virgil thought for a moment.

"Don't think we're dealing with any gun hands here," Chastain said.

"No," Virgil said. "But we go at this like they are loaded to the hilt. Last thing we want to do is be on our heels. Best swimmers are the ones that drown."

Chastain nodded.

"Everett and I will go in quick through the front door," Virgil said. "We'll first figure out what room they're in, and we'll push on through fast, no knocking."

"Providing the door is locked," I said. "And most likely it is. You'll have to be the one busting the door, Virgil."

Virgil knew I was referring to the fact I was weak in my upper body, and nodded.

"That door is gonna take some force, too," I said. "It's a solid sonofabitch."

"I'll get through it," Virgil said.

"Most likely they'll be in the office," I said.

Virgil nodded a little, then looked to Chastain and Sebastian.

"That office is on the front, northwest corner of the house," Virgil said. "Chastain, Everett and me will give you and Sebastian enough time to get around to the back. Just watch the back door, and if anyone comes out the back, interested in hightailing, you can sort them out."

"Sounds right," Chastain said.

"Sebastian has my dingus," I said.

Virgil nodded, looking at Sebastian.

"You good with everything that I'm saying here, Mr. Winthrop?" Virgil said.

Sebastian nodded.

"I don't carry a weapon as a matter of practice," he said. "But I spent ten years with Scotland Yard, so let's not be concerned or tarry here on my accord."

Virgil looked to Chastain.

"Chastain, you and Sebastian go on through the alley and come up on the house from the back side," Virgil said. "Everett and me will give you enough time to get set."

Chastain and Sebastian nodded. They did as Virgil instructed and moved off down the alley.

Virgil and I didn't walk the street as we approached the house. We moved cautiously, staying in the shadows of the boardwalk, and when we got close, we edged our way to the side window of the office.

I peeked in and could see through the curtains the three men and I could hear the talking. I looked back to Virgil and nodded.

Virgil and I readied our Colts and moved slowly, staying in the dark the best we could, and moved up the steps quietly.

I tried the knob just in case, but the door was locked. I shook my head, looking at Virgil.

Virgil took a few steps back and charged the door with his shoulder, and he was right about getting through it. The thick door crashed open, taking splintering pieces of the doorjamb with it, and Virgil and I moved quickly inside.

— 74 —

We rushed past the startled butler, Jessup, who stumbled back onto the staircase as Virgil and I burst into the office where the three men, G. W. Cox, Ashley Epps, and Curtis Whittlesey, sat completely dumbfounded and looking at us with our Colts pointing at them.

Cox was sitting in his big chair behind his desk and Curtis and Ashley sat across from him.

On Cox's desk were three stacks of cash.

"What?" Ashley said, wide-eyed. "What is happening?"

"You don't really need to ask, do you?" Virgil said.

"I think there must be some kind of misunderstanding," Ashley said nervously.

"Misunderstanding?" Virgil said.

"Yes," Ashley said. "Of course."

"No misunderstanding here," Virgil said.

"But—" Ashley said.

"Ashley," Cox interrupted, shaking his head a little as he leaned back in his chair with his hands on the arms of the chair. "Let these men do what they came here to do."

"You three are under arrest," Virgil said.

"Marshal," Ashley said. "I can explain this . . ."

"Sheriff Sledge Driskill," Virgil said, "and his deputies Chip Childers and Karl Worley are dead because of you. Chip and Karl were both just past twenty years of age."

"I'm innocent," Curtis blurted out as he got to his feet.

"No, Curtis, you're not," I said. "You even sicced me onto Cox at the pool hall, thinking maybe he'd get sorted out and you and the preacher here would have a bigger payday."

"No . . ." Curtis said. "I . . ."

"Sit down, Curtis," I said. "And shut your ass up."

Curtis sat slowly back in his chair.

"You men have fucked up," Virgil said.

"God knows," Ashley said, shaking his head from side to side, "you are mistaken here."

"Pretty sure God don't got a goddamn thing to do with this murder and robbery you put together here," Virgil said.

"I don't know what you mean," Ashley said.

"No?" Virgil said.

"What would you like us to do?" Cox said calmly.

"Don't buy into this," Ashley said. "They have nothing here that was not part of God's plan."

"You might not have intended to do what you did," Virgil said. "But you did it, and three lawmen lost their lives over what the three of you have done here. You fucked up."

Curtis started crying.

"No, no, no," Curtis said hysterically. "This can't be, it can't be, it can't be . . ."

We heard two clicks behind us.

"Don't turn around," Jessup said.

I glanced back to see Jessup holding a side-by-side twelve-gauge shotgun pointed at our backs.

"Looks like it was you who fucked up," Cox said, as he pulled a pistol.

"You don't want to do this," Virgil said over his shoulder.

"Oh, but I do," Jessup said.

I saw out of the corner of my eye as Jessup moved the shotgun off us and onto Cox.

"No!" Cox shouted as he raised his pistol at Jessup, but Jessup let Cox have it with both barrels and Cox's head exploded, drenching his diplomas and the placards of his achievements with his blood and the last thinking portion of his brain.

"Dear God," Ashley cried.

"Virgil. Everett," Chastain called from someplace toward the rear of the house.

Virgil turned to Jessup, who was holding the gun in the same position he'd shot Cox.

Jessup stood frozen, looking at the blood on the wall. He had a single tear running down his cheek.

"We're here," I called to Chastain. *"Office."*

Sebastian and Chastain hurried from the back hall and into the office.

Virgil reached for Jessup's shotgun.

"It's over," Virgil said to Jessup.

Jessup's teary eyes slowly looked to Virgil.

"Over," Virgil said.

Virgil pried the shotgun from Jessup's hands and sat him down in a chair.

Jessup just stared at the floor.

". . . it comin'," Jessup said very quietly. ". . . He had it comin'."

Virgil just looked at Jessup for a long moment. Then he looked to Curtis and Ashley, then looked slowly around the room, resting his eyes on the model of the bridge.

It was over.

— 75 —

I was sitting in a comfortable chair on the porch of Virgil and Allie's place with the morning sunshine warming my face. The early snow was all gone now and the temperature was pleasant. The streets were still muddy, but the crops and fields in the area were thankful for the early winter soaking.

Business was back to normal in Appaloosa. The streets were busy with activity. I thought about what Wallis had said, about how many people were in the town now. Appaloosa had changed damn near before our eyes from a little town to a city, a full-grown city. *Hocus-goddamn-pocus.*

Nell came walking up the boardwalk, spinning her parasol on her shoulder. Her chin was high and her posture was erect. She had a degree of purpose and pride to her step. She waited for a buggy to pass, then crossed the street. She was smiling when she approached the porch.

"Hello," she said.

"Morning," I said.

"A nice one," she said.

"It is," I said. "And I suspect the warmer conditions we got now, and the fact the tent-show outfit is finally going to get rigged up, that you're feeling somewhat chipper."

"How did you know?" she said, as she walked up the steps.

"Well, hell, I could tell it," I said. "Saw it right off. Watching you coming a block away."

"Why," she said with a smile and a spin of the parasol, "are you some kind of officer?"

"I am, as a matter of fact," I said back with a smile. "Have a seat."

"Why, thank you," she said. "You the only one home?"

"I am," I said. "Virgil's at the office and Allie's with her ladies' social. She's drumming up ticket sales for your show."

"She's something else," Nell said.

"Yes, she is," I said.

Nell sat in the center of the hanging bench swing just to the left of me. She was wearing a yellow gingham dress under a long, thin dark green topcoat with brown velvet cuffs and lapels.

"You're looking better, Everett," she said.

"Than what?" I said.

"Than before," she said.

"Before what?" I said.

"When you were at Doc's."

"You came?"

She tilted her head and smiled.

"You're a devil," she said.

"Am I?"

"Did I come?" Nell said with a slight pull of her chin to her collarbone. "I most certainly did."

"Doc Crumley had me on double doses of the devil himself there for a while," I said. "So there was a lot of chasing butterflies, running through fields of flowers, and kissing beautiful women and that sort of thing."

"Imagine that?" she said with a smile. "And that sort of thing."

"Only so much time for flowers, butterflies, and beautiful women," I said.

"Yes, a shame, really," Nell said. "We all need more of that sort of beauty in our lives, don't you think?"

"As long as it's not in a bottle," I said.

She nodded. Smiled.

"Well," she said. "I'm very glad to see you're looking well."

"Thank you," I said.

She reached out and grabbed my hand and squeezed it a little as she looked directly at me.

"Scary?" she said.

"Not at the time," I said.

She just looked at me for an extended moment, then looked to the street. She smiled a little.

"My husband was right," she said, looking back to me.

"About?" I said.

"Me," she said.

"What about you?"

"That I have a good eye," she said.

I had a good idea what she was getting at, but I was in the mood, so I asked anyway.

"What do you mean?"

"When I first saw you," Nell said. "He was right."

"About?" I said.

"You, of course," she said.

"Me?"

"Yes, you," she said. "Being a man of substance. A man of quick resolve."

We sat together in silence. She looked off down the street for some time, then looked back to me.

"About what I said," Nell said. "When we were washing dishes together."

"It's okay," I said. "You don't have to say anything." She smiled.

"Not that I've not thought about it," I said. "I have."

"Thought of it?" Nell said.

"Yes," I said, "but another man's wife is another man's wife."

She looked at me, nodding slightly, and a slow smile came to her face.

"Thought about it?" she said.

I nodded.

Nell nodded . . . "Can I ask you a question?" she said.

"Of course," I said.

"Do you think I'm beautiful?" Nell said.

"I do."

"Good," she said. "I needed to make sure."

"Make sure?" I said.

"Yes," she said. "I just needed to know it was beautiful me with the flowers and the butterflies."

"Now that you mention it," I said. "I'm pretty sure it was you."

She laughed and looked away.

"What's funny?"

She looked back to me, that certain look in her eye.

"There's no 'pretty sure' to it," Nell said.

— 76 —

Nudge?" Virgil said.

"Sure," I said.

"Isn't this exciting," Allie said, walking up the hall to the parlor.

Allie's face was covered with a white cream. She was barefoot, wearing just her corset, bloomers, and chemise, when she entered the living room, vigorously rubbing in the cream with her fingertips.

Virgil looked at me and shook his head a little as he got out of his chair and walked to the breakfront.

"It is," I said.

"Finally get to see them perform," Allie continued on, as she entered the kitchen. "Lord knows there's been some awful business recently, for all of us."

Virgil got two glasses and the Kentucky and closed the breakfront door.

"Especially you, Everett," Allie said, as she came back

from the kitchen, wiping the goo from her face with a rag. "You getting shot there at the Yaqui Brakes being the absolute worst of all for me, the worst for me."

She stood, continuing to wipe her face as she talked to us.

"I know it has been absolutely dreadful, all that has happened recently, but tonight will be uplifting and inspiring for Appaloosa and us," she said. "This will be special, and I know you won't be disappointed, Virgil."

"Okay," Virgil said. "You gonna put some clothes on, or are you planning on going like that?"

"I'm wearing the new dress I ordered and you paid for," she said with a chirp. "What time is it, Everett?"

I looked to the clock on the wall behind me.

"Quarter past," I said.

"Oh," she said. "I got to get myself moving."

"Well, do," Virgil said. "Get going, get yourself ready."

"I won't be long," she said, as she turned for the hall. "But I do need this time to make myself pretty."

"You don't need no time for that, Allie," Virgil said. "You're pretty as a peach just as you are."

Allie stopped and turned back to Virgil.

"Why, Virgil Cole," she said. "Aren't you adorable?"

"Don't think that's the right word, Allie," Virgil said. "But I appreciate it all the same."

She walked up to him and kissed him on the lips, leaving a circle of white cream around his mouth.

"You are," she said, as she rubbed the cream off his face with the rag. "Adorable. Don't you think, Everett?"

"I do," I said.

"Go on," Virgil said, pointing to the hall behind her.

Allie turned and scampered off down the hall.

"I won't be long," she said. "I do not want to be late."

Virgil watched her, then turned to me, holding up the bottle and glasses.

"We'll be on the porch waiting on you, Allie," Virgil called to her.

Virgil opened the door and I followed him out to the porch.

We sat in the side-by-side chairs that backed up to the house. Virgil poured us each a nudge of whiskey.

"She's excited," I said.

"She is," Virgil said.

We sat for quite a bit watching the sun dropping as we sipped on the Kentucky.

"Maybe she's right," Virgil said.

"'Bout what?"

"Maybe this Extravaganza will be uplifting and inspiring," Virgil said.

"Has been some bad business for Appaloosa," I said.

Virgil looked at me out of the corner of his eye.

"Look forward to seeing this fortune-teller," Virgil said. "This sage."

I nodded a little but didn't say anything.

"Hard to figure," Virgil said. "That business?"

"Is," I said.

We sat quiet for a bit, drinking our whiskey. I thought about her. Séraphine the fortune-teller. Wondered about her and where the hell she came from and where she'd be going. I imagined what it might be like if she stayed and what it'd be like to be with her on a day in, day out basis. On many levels we were certainly goddamn good together. Maybe it was possible. *Hocus-by-God-pocus,* I thought . . . anything is possible.

"Hear that?" Virgil said.

I listened a moment and nodded.

"Music."

"Sounds as if they're getting things going over there," Virgil said.

I nodded.

We just listened for a while to the faint sound of the music being played by the tent-show band from where they pitched camp north of town. It carried an eerie echo through the streets.

Virgil, Allie, and I walked the streets to the vacant lot where the big tent was set up. With each block we walked we could hear the band getting louder and louder.

Other Appaloosa townsfolk were moving through the streets, too, and we soon found ourselves in a stream of traffic headed for the festivities.

When we rounded the corner we could see the band sitting out in front of the tent playing a lively tune, as two jugglers kept numerous colorfully painted balls in the air.

Beauregard stood next to the tent's entrance, greeting the crowd with big how-do-you-dos.

He was in costume. His face was painted with makeup. His eyebrows were dark, his face was powdery white, and his cheeks and lips were bright red. He was dressed like Porthos the Musketeer, with a huge feathered hat that flipped up in the front, a velvet frockcoat and waistcoat, knee-high boots, a sword attached to his hip, and a handkerchief protruding from under his coat sleeve.

"Oh, goodness," Allie said with the enthusiasm of a child. "Oh my goodness."

"Looks like a good turnout, Allie," I said.

"Oh, it does, Everett," she said. "It certainly does."

"I suspect your promotional efforts paid off," I said.

"There's Nell," Allie said.

Nell exited the tent in an elaborate Marie Antoinette–like pannier-hooped dress with a low-cut bodice that exposed a good part of her bosom.

"Oh my word," Allie said.

"Guess it's almost showtime," I said.

Allie excitedly scurried her way through the crowd and over to Nell.

"Guess so," Virgil said.

"Big to-do," I said.

"It is," Virgil said, looking around.

Beauregard saw Virgil and me as we moved closer toward the entrance with the rest of the townsfolk.

"Hello, gentlemen," he said, over the top of the others in front of us.

Beauregard stepped away from the crowd and got in step with Virgil and me as we moved toward the entrance.

"Marshal Cole," he said. "And Deputy Marshal

Hitch. Welcome. I am certainly glad you came out to-night. We have an exciting show in store for you this evening."

"Looking forward to it," I said.

"And you, Marshal?"

"Me, too," Virgil said.

"Fantastic," he said, then stopped walking.

We stopped as well, because he was leaning in as if he needed to say something.

"Look," Beauregard said. "I know we got off on the wrong foot and I know you don't much care for me. But I just want you to know, as much as you may despise me, I hold no one more accountable for those despicable feelings toward me other than me."

"Despicable feelings?" Virgil said, looking around at the crowd. "We're here like everyone else, to see your show. Ain't that right, Everett?"

"Just like everyone else," I said.

"Fine and dandy," Beauregard said. "But I don't imagine there's a day that goes by that either of you are even remotely close to being like everyone else."

The insides of the tent's walls were painted to look like a European landscape with various villages on the horizon.

Virgil, Allie, and I took our seats and the show began, starting with Beauregard stepping onstage.

"Appaloosa," he said. "Let's start by giving yourselves a big round of applause for being here tonight."

He clapped and most everyone in the two-hundred-plus crowd did the same.

"Let your friends and family know," he said. "We will be here each and every evening with a variety of new and exciting entertainment, so keep coming and we'll keep you feeling glad that you did."

Beauregard went through the list of the evening's events to be presented. He let everyone know there would be a three-act play, with intermissions, along with singing, dancing, and fortune-telling by Madame Leroux.

Beauregard ended his intro by saying, "Following the play, we have the most magnificent of magic from Dr. Longfellow, so sit back and enjoy . . . the show."

The show got under way and for the most part it was very entertaining. The play was funny. Beauregard and Nell were good performers, and Beauregard actually made Virgil laugh.

The first intermission had a rousing singing and dancing number that included Nell showing off her legs as well as her vocal skills. The bit was enjoyable, but I was curious to see what the next intermission brought with Madame Séraphine Leroux.

The second act of the play seemed to go on forever. It was engaging, but I was anxious to see her when the act ended and Beauregard stepped out onto center stage.

"Now, this is something really special," he said. "Something I know you all have been waiting for. Allow me to introduce to you the one, the only, the mystic, the clairvoyant, the beautiful . . . Madame Leroux."

Beauregard held out his hand toward the side wing and Madame Leroux walked onstage.

Virgil leaned forward and looked to me.

I could not take my eyes off of her.

Madame Leroux was a beautiful woman wearing a turban, but she was someone else, someone other than Séraphine. She was an exotic-looking woman, but she was weathered, with a dark complexion, and looked to be maybe sixty-five or seventy years old.

Virgil leaned Allie forward a bit and edged himself over behind her, cupping his mouth as he spoke in my ear. Allie looked back and forth between Virgil and me.

"Nice-enough-looking lady, Everett," he said. "A little long in the tooth for you, though, don't ya think?"

He leaned back in his seat but remained looking at me.

I looked at him.

He nodded, offering a slight encouraging smile with his eyebrows raised.

— 78 —

Before Madame Leroux wrapped up her show of holding cards to her head and guessing the numbers and suits, or picking people from the audience and telling them where they came from and letting them know someone just died or someone was just born, I got up from my seat and walked out of the tent.

From inside the big tent I heard whistles and clapping as I made my way through the pavilions and found Madame Leroux's trailer.

I knocked on the door, but there was no answer. I opened the door and had a look inside.

"Hey," a gruff voice said. "Whatcha doing there, mister?"

The voice was from a little fella in a high-top silk gent's hat. He was wearing suspenders holding up baggy trousers over his long johns.

"Looking for Séraphine," I said.

"This is Madame Leroux's trailer," he said.

Just then Madame Leroux came walking up.

"This fella was looking through your trailer," the man said.

"Not looking through your trailer," I said.

"Said he's looking for . . . ?"

"Séraphine," I said.

"This is my trailer, young man," she said.

"Why are you looking through her trailer?" the fella said.

"I'm not," I said.

"Looked like it to me," the fella said.

"Séraphine. I'm looking for Séraphine."

"I know," he said. "You said that."

Madame Leroux shook her head.

"This is my trailer," she said.

"Do you know where I can find her?" I said.

"No," she said. "I don't know any Séraphine."

The little man shook his head.

"No Séraphine on this show, bub," he said.

"I saw her," I said. "In this very trailer when you rode into this town. I saw her in the window of this trailer."

"I know Deputy Chastain," Madame Leroux said. "He's made an arrest here before and he will do it again. If I find anything missing, you could find yourself in trouble."

I was listening to her, but I wasn't really listening to her. I looked around, thinking, but wasn't even sure what the hell I was even thinking about. My mind was racing as I tried to come to some understanding about everything that had led up to this very moment.

Without even thinking, I showed Madame Leroux and the fella with the top hat my badge.

"You don't have to worry about me stealing anything from you, Madame Leroux," I said. "I'm a territorial deputy marshal. My name is Hitch, Everett Hitch."

"Oh," she said, "Well, okay, I'm sorry . . ."

"No, no," I said. "It's okay."

"Do you have a young lady on the show," I said, "lovely, intense, beautiful, with very long dark hair, pale complexion, blue eyes. She's slender, a little on the tall side?"

The little man shook his head.

"Sorry, young man," Madame Leroux said. "Sounds to me you've been duped."

The little fella nodded.

"No woman like that on this show," he said. "I can tell you that for certain."

Wallis, I thought. *Wallis.*

"Appreciate it," I said. "Thank you . . ."

I walked off, leaving Madame Leroux and the little fella in the top hat, and headed for the Boston House.

I walked briskly through the streets as my mind raced. *What the hell? What was this? Who is she? Where is she? Why did she lead me to believe she was with this damn show? She was here, by God. She was most certainly here.*

The Boston House was busy when I entered, and Wallis looked up at me when I walked in and made my way through the crowd and up to the bar.

"Everett," he said with a big smile. "What can I get you?"

"Need to talk to you," I said.

"You want something?" he said.

"Not at the moment," I said.

"What's up?" he said.

"You remember when I was here," I said, "a while back? I came in when you were closing up?"

"Sure," he said.

"You remember the woman that walked in?" I said. "We sat right there?"

"What woman?" he said with a blank look on his face.

I pointed to the table where we sat.

"Right there," I said. "You served her a brandy."

Wallis looked at me, maintaining the blank look on his face, then smiled.

"Well, hell, Everett, I've drunk my share and have dropped a few marbles in my day, but I damn sure do remember her, of course I do," Wallis said.

"You do," I said.

"Sure," he said.

"Have you seen her?" I said. "Have you laid eyes on her since?"

He shook his head.

"Nope," he said. "She sift through?"

I just looked at Wallis, then looked around the room. Everybody in the place seemed to be talking louder than they needed to be talking. I looked back to Wallis.

"I suspect," I said.

Wallis looked at me a moment, then grabbed a bottle and poured us both a healthy swallow. He scooted the whiskey across to me and held up his glass.

I looked at the whiskey, staring at it for a moment, then picked up the glass and looked to Wallis.

"To the moon," he said.

— 79 —

N ice evening," I said.

"Damn sure is," Virgil said.

We sat silent for a bit, sipping on the Kentucky.

"That weather came on good," I said.

"Damn sure did," Virgil said. "Didn't it?"

"Next few months might prove to be mild," I said.

"You think?" Virgil said.

"For some reason," I said, "I do."

"Warm now," Virgil said.

"Unseasonably so," I said.

"Is," Virgil said. "Ain't it?"

"Might be a good time to paint," I said, looking up at the underside of the porch.

"Thought you said you'd help build but weren't interested in painting?" Virgil said.

"I did say that."

"Change your mind?" Virgil said.

"Often do," I said.

"A man does that once and a while," Virgil said.

"They do."

Virgil looked up at the underside a bit.

"I'll get the paint," he said.

"Do," I said. "Before I change my mind."

"By God," Virgil said.

I nodded.

Virgil looked back out to the horizon and we sat quiet for a long spell without talking, as we watched the evening sun.

"She rubbed off on you," Virgil said, without looking at me.

I looked to Virgil.

"Obvious?"

"Is," he said.

I shook my head a little.

"Some," I said.

"Where you figure she went?" Virgil said.

"Don't know."

"Maybe she ain't gone."

"She is."

"How do you know?"

"Just do."

Virgil looked at me.

I saw Allie up the street. She was walking our way, carrying a box of groceries.

"Allie," I said softly.

Virgil looked to her. We just watched her. The setting sun was shining on her. Her hair was a bit untidy and moving with the breeze as she walked. She looked almost angelic the way the golden sunlight was shining on her. She greeted a few folks on the boardwalk as she neared. She looked as happy as I'd ever seen her.

"Allie," I said quietly again.

Virgil nodded.

She saw us as she crossed the street.

"Hey, boys," Allie said with a smile. "It's so nice out, isn't it?"

"It is," Virgil said.

"You need some help?" I said.

"No, no," she said. "I got it."

She walked up the steps, carrying the box.

"Just wait and see what I'm fixing for supper," she said.

"Okay," Virgil said.

I got up and opened the door for her.

"It will be scrumptious," she said. "Oh . . . got you something, Virgil."

Allie balanced the box a little on her knee. She retrieved a cigar from the box and handed it to Virgil.

"Don't say I never got you nothing," she said. "Mr. Sadler said it came all the way from Cuba."

"Why, thank you, Allie," Virgil said.

"You're very welcome," she said, as she continued on inside. "You know I'd have got you one as well, but thankfully you don't have the habit . . . Just leave the door open for the breeze, Everett."

Virgil looked back to me and smiled a little.

I picked up the bottle of Kentucky, refreshed our drinks, then sat back down.

Virgil looked at the band on his cigar and nodded a little. He bit the tip and spit it over the rail. He fished a match out of his pocket and dragged the head of it on the leg of his chair. He cupped his hand, keeping the flame from the breeze, and lit the cigar. He worked on it some till he got it going good, then flicked the match away and leaned back and looked at the cigar for a moment.

We heard the familiar clamor of pans from inside.

"You okay in there?" Virgil called.

"Oh, yes. Fine," Allie said. "I'm fine, just, it's fine . . ."

"You sure?" he said.

"I'm fine," she said.

Virgil smiled a little. He sat back in his chair and puffed on his cigar for a bit.

We sat quiet for a bit, watching the very last piece of sun until it was gone.

"What is it?" Virgil said, tilting his head a little. "Where are we?"

"December," I said. "Second day of."

"Is it?"

"It is."

Virgil shook his head.

"What happened to November?"

"It came and went, Virgil," I said.

ACKNOWLEDGMENTS

Much obliged to my crew of enduring construction workers for helping me get this bridge across the divide. First and foremost, Jan Griesenbeck, for allowing me to set up camp and bunker down in her Spicewood retreat—thank you so much, Jan! Outrider Rob Wood of Rancho Roberto, for keeping the bullethead blueprints in order, and Jamie "Whatnot" Whitcomb, for his continued supply of ammo. My ex–oil field pard Lowell Reed, for his knowledge in all things engineering, mountain guide Rex "Hook-em" Linn, for his steady tracking, and Kevin "PG" Meyer, for his expertise across the deep and wide. Also, a big thanks to ex-con Billy Ray Snipes for his policy smarts, and Vanessa Rose and Genevieve Negrete, for sorting out the rivets. Robert Woodfin Griesenbeck, for keeping it between the ditches, and most certainly and always, Ed Harris, for bringing Virgil Cole to life on the big screen, and talking in my ear as a sounding and unwavering foreman.

My deepest sympathy to all of those who carried the dynamite: Alison Binder, Steve Fisher, Josh Kesselman, Jayne Amelia Larson, Nat Toppino, Alice DiGregorio, Gabriel Marantz, my sisters—the Clogging Castanets—Sandra Hakman and Karen Austin, and as always, Julie, for everything . . .

And for Bob and Joan, for without them looking over this construction, Appaloosa would be but a memory.

LOOK FOR IT IN HARDCOVER

Itinerant lawmen Virgil Cole and Everett Hitch return in the gritty new installment of the *New York Times* bestselling series. And there's a new menace in town: a wealthy, handsome easterner—and the owner of Appaloosa's new casino—Boston Bill Black.

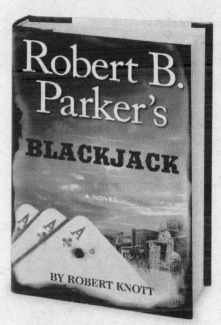

RobertBParker.net
 RobertBParkerAuthor

PUTNAM | Penguin Random House

M1700JV0715

LOOK FOR IT IN HARDCOVER

A nor'easter blows into Paradise and churns up the past—in the stunning new addition to Robert B. Parker's *New York Times* bestselling series featuring Police Chief Jesse Stone.

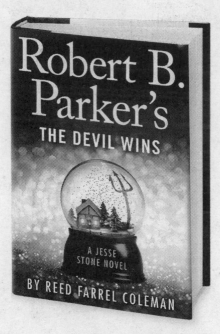

RobertBParker.net
RobertBParkerAuthor

M1680JV0515

LOOK FOR IT IN HARDCOVER

Police Chief Jesse Stone is back in the remarkable new installment of the *New York Times* bestselling series.

RobertBParker.net
facebook.com/RobertBParkerAuthor

M1569JV0914